Miss Mary Investigates
Book Four

Death

in

Sensible

Circumstances

A Sense and Sensibility Mystery

RIANA EVERLY

MISS MARY INVESTIGATES BOOK 4

DEATH IN SENSIBLE CIRCUMSTANCES:
A SENSE AND SENSIBILITY MYSTERY

Cover design by Mae Phillips at coverfreshdesigns.com

ISBN-13: 978-1-7781297-3-5

Dedication

To all those, past and present, who have worked to create order out of
the chaos.
Lawyers often have a bad name, but they help shape our world into
something sane and sensible.

Contents

RIANA EVERLY

Acknowledgements

How can I write these novels without thinking about Jane Austen, who created Mary Bennet and left her for us to expand upon and learn to love. This last summer I had the great fortune to visit Winchester, England, and stand at her burial site in the beautiful cathedral there, and I whispered a "thank you" from all of us who love the worlds she created.

As always, a book like this owes its existence to a great many people. My cheering squad is indefatigable, and my family get my hurrahs and high-fives for putting up with me and encouraging me as I ignored them in favour of Mary and Alexander.

I owe more gratitude than words can say to Mikael Swayze, who not only edited and proofread too many times to mention, but also spent countless hours helping me wade through old English case law in search of the details on which this story is based.

I also wish to thank my wonderful beta readers whose comments and advice have been invaluable. Particular thanks to Kirstin Odegaard, Barry Richman, and a huge batch of chocolate brownies to the amazing Liz Martinson, a fabulous author in her own right.

Thanks also to Hadassah Swayze for her work on the silhouettes, and, as always, to Mae Phillips for her beautiful cover art. They say not to judge a book by its cover, but having something eye-catching and beautiful on the front never hurts, does it?

The photograph on the cover is of Hyde Park in the springtime, right about when Mary and Alexander would be strolling through.

Cover design by Mae Phillips at coverfreshdesigns.com

RIANA EVERLY

Prologue

March 16, 1814

The two brothers stared at each other across the expanse of an overly hot and too elaborate parlour. The fire blazed in the hearth despite the sunshine on this March day, and the windows, for some unknown reason, were closed, permitting in no breeze to alleviate the stifling heat. It would be a matter of moments to ask a maid to open the French doors leading out to the terrace, or for Edward to rise and do it himself, but such was the ponderous weight of the atmosphere in the room that the action seemed all but impossible. The close air was far more suited to the feeling of oppression than would be the cool and fresh breeze from outside.

"She cannot be all that ill," Robert said at last. His voice sounded as world-weary as Edward felt. Every syllable was laden with lead weights, the act of enunciating the words requiring an effort almost too great to be borne. "She was perfectly well when we all left London three days ago."

Edward blinked. How could blinking require so much energy? He met his brother's eyes once more. "These things can come on all at once. Or so I have heard." He stopped speaking, but when Robert said nothing in reply, he added, "I was surprised to be summoned here. I never thought to see Mother again; or that she would wish to see me. She was quite vehement when last we spoke on the seventh that I was no longer considered her son."

"She was very angry. Will you not reconsider?"

Edward laughed. It was not a mirthful sound. "It would not be honourable. I made a commitment, and I shall stand by it. If I agreed with Mother and went back on my word, I could not live with myself."

"You are giving up a great deal."

Edward allowed his head to fall back onto the heavily upholstered chair. It was unlike his brother to think of anything past his own wants and needs. Robert, certainly, would have gone back on his word in an instant, knowing what was at stake. No, even before that. He would have reneged as soon as the commitment became inconvenient. But Edward was a different sort of a man. "I know that. Can you imagine that this does not weigh on me at every moment?"

"Is it indeed what you want?"

This was the question Edward had not even dared to ask himself. But he was committed. He must make the best of it. "Of course!" His voice sounded false, even to himself. "It is exactly what we wanted."

Suddenly, the heat of the room grew too much to tolerate. Edward pushed himself up from the armchair and strode to the doors, throwing them open. In contrast to the stifling interior, the March air was cool on his skin, despite the warm sun, but he stepped out onto the terrace, regardless. He was seized with a desperate need to be doing something, and shivering in the bright sunlight would do for now. To his surprise, Robert stepped out after him.

"What of you?" Edward asked as they stood at the balustrade, surveying the expansive lawn and ornamental pond before them. Further in the distance, the lawn faded into a growth of trees, past which, Edward knew, lay the fields and open countryside that would soon host this year's crops and be dotted with flocks and herds. If one looked carefully, one could see the river that flowed on the far side of the stand of oaks as it made its determined way to the sea. All of this... All of this had been his.

"And now it is yours." He did not need to supply the first part of his thought. Robert knew what he meant.

His brother looked smug, but perchance there was some humanity in him. He was only twenty-two, after all. There was still time for him to develop a character worth having. "Yes. It is mine. But talk to her, Edward. When the doctor is gone, talk to her. Change your mind, and perhaps she will change hers."

"You know it goes against everything I believe to break my promises. And really, I am not made for this. I want a quiet life. I have no need to be something great, as Mother and Fanny insist I should be. I would be most happy in a small country parish. As long as I have enough to keep a roof whole and my family fed, that will be enough for me." He laughed that bitter laugh again. "Besides which, Mother is stubborn. She has made the arrangements and signed the papers, and will never change her mind now."

He turned back to Robert, who smirked. "So be it."

Edward had no doubts that this was exactly the conversation his brother wished to have. He knew that Edward would never change his mind, and that their mother would never change hers. He could now revel in his good fortune with the balm to his conscience of having made an attempt to restore to Edward what ought to be his. Not that Robert had much of a conscience to assuage.

"Why, then, do you think Mother asked me to come here? I am certain it was not to make amends. The ink on her new will is hardly dry. And why come here at all? Mother hates the place. There is a reason she lives exclusively in London."

The smirk grew wider. "Who can say? Mother is devious. I ought to know, for I have that from her. Perhaps she wished for you to see what you have lost. For you, dear brother, are as stubborn as she." Robert paused and gazed out for a long time across the lawn that was just beginning to go green. "Or perhaps it was not her idea at all." He said nothing more, but turned and ambled back into the stultifying parlour.

Edward did not follow, but stayed where he stood, letting the light breeze play with his hair and tease the folds of his cravat. No perfect starched linen for him! He had never been one for display and had no use for a valet. Now, especially, when all he had was the two thousand pounds from his inheritance. The interest from that would not go very far. He must become quite inured to tying his own cravats.

But perhaps he had been too firm in his steadfastness... Perhaps his commitment was a wrong thing. He had so many inducements to beg off. There was no legal obligation, after all, merely the word of a gentleman, and that could hardly be pressed in court. Gentlemen went back on their promises all the time.

If he were to beg off, then he could...

No! He refused even to consider that. It would only bring heartache. He pushed the thought from his mind before he completed it.

When Mother was feeling more the thing, they would all depart this place. Mother would return to her home on Park Street, he to his rooms in Oxford, and Robert would surely revel in his newfound wealth and be discovered more often at the club than at home. And, eventually, Mother might come to understand him and his need for personal honour.

Where was that doctor? How much time must he spend telling Mother that she was making a cake of herself by pretending to be ill? This must be yet another of her ruses to elicit sympathy from her sons and to manipulate them into, well, into something. His sister, Fanny, would have fine words for this when they returned and told her what had transpired.

With a sigh and a final deep breath, Edward turned his back on the newly verdant fields and re-entered the house. Just as he stepped across the threshold, the parlour door opened and the doctor walked through. His face was blank.

"Mr. Ferrars, Mr. Robert Ferrars..." He looked from one brother to the other.

"I have sad news. I regret to inform you that your mother has just died."

Chapter One

At the Sign of the Phoenix

March 23, 1814

Mary Bennet could not name how many times she had walked past this particular shop on the corner. From the outside, it was an unassuming establishment, mere steps from the Bond Street Bazaar. Whilst walking down the street, one could see a small display of books in a window, but there was no apparent door, and a passerby might well believe the shop merely to be another of the booths in an arcade near The Exchange. But if one were to take a few strides down that other street—little more than a laneway, really—there one would find the green painted door that said *At the Sign of the Phoenix*.

Every time in the past, Mary would stare at the door and wonder what was inside, but had never entered. She was always on some errand for her aunt, or expected somewhere, or simply too unsure of herself to walk unescorted into an unknown establishment. She ought, she told herself, to know better. She was Mary Bennet! She had solved—with some help, of course—three murders! She was not some simpering and helpless chit to be scared of a bookshop. And yet she always found some reason not to take that final step and enter the establishment.

Today, however, was to be different. Aunt Gardiner had told her in no uncertain terms to go and enjoy herself, and had even given her a whole guinea to spend "on matters completely frivolous." When added to the ten pounds her brother-in-law Darcy had sent her for her stay in London, she felt as rich as the Prince himself. Yes! Today she would enter the Phoenix and buy herself a book!

She turned the corner and reached for the door. It swung open easily in her hand and she stepped through. And then her eyes widened and she gasped. Never had she expected this!

The room, though not large, was larger than the outside promised, and was stacked from the floor to ceiling with books! More shelves than she could count crossed the floor from the side walls, all filled almost to bursting with every manner of tome. Here and there, scattered with no seeming sense of pattern, a chair leaned near a wall, a few occupied by an avid reader, and in the scant open space between shelves, a handful of small tables supported piles of what looked to be several copies of the same title. As Mary gaped, a ginger cat wound itself about her ankles and drew her forward a few steps, where she could now see, at the far end of the shop, a staircase leading upwards, with a sign that read *More Upstairs*. It was an emporium of books!

Heaven, Mary mused, must be exactly like this, and then she chastised herself for having such improper thoughts about the nature of God's heaven.

The cat rubbed itself up the backs of her shins and she stepped forward again. Now she could see a little desk in one corner, behind which sat a man of indeterminate years, neither young nor old, with thinning hair and spectacles. He peered at her through narrow eyes and gave a brief nod. He must be the bookshop's proprietor. She nodded in return and hoped she looked friendly and trustworthy enough to be allowed in his establishment.

"May I help you?" the man asked in hushed tones.

She swallowed and her face flushed hot. Could she voice her request to this unknown man? He would surely judge her most lacking. A serious, sensible young woman like herself ought to be reading a certain sort of literature. Improving manuals, for example, or sermons on the proper deportment of young ladies, or edifying poetry perhaps. But what Mary really wanted, and what she was going to buy with her small fortune of coins if her courage did not fail her, was a novel. Perhaps something horrid, like Regina Maria Roche's *The Monastery of St. Columb*. Or Mary Brunton's *Discipline*, perhaps. She had heard this latter had all manner of Highland scenes, which interested her greatly, although it really ought not to do so at all.

She should, of course, put all thoughts of the Highlands firmly out of her mind. It was not proper and would only lead to future disappointment. More disappointment. For a while, when she believed a certain man still had some affection for her, she discovered a great interest in Scotland and in its various regions and history. *He* was a Scot, after all. Or was he? Did his other associations negate his Scottishness? Could one be a Hebrew and a Scot at the same time? Mr. Benjamin Goldsmid was Hebrew and English, after all, but not quite the right sort of English... or was he? Even Mary knew that the banker had enjoyed a friendship with the late Lord Nelson and had even entertained the Prince Regent once. That was surely the right sort of English, wasn't it? Oh bother! This was too vexing for her to contemplate when she should, instead, be choosing a book.

Besides, it mattered not, and she tried to put her not-quite-Scotsman out of her head. She had discovered she loved him, and believed he had loved her. Foolishly, she believed they had an understanding, and he had kissed her and worked his way into her heart, but he had never offered for her. She had expected a proposal that had never come. Even now, so many months later, her heart ached at the memory.

Stop it, Mary! She chastised herself. This was no time to stew about Alexander Lyons, handsome though he might be. She was here in this marvellous shop full of books, and she would not leave until she had found something to buy. She blinked at the shopkeeper behind his desk as he repeated his question, and this time she answered him, asking directions to where she might find popular novels. He gestured with his head and listed a few of the titles he had for sale, which pleased her, and she wandered in that direction, stopping every three steps to examine a volume here and a pamphlet there, until at last, she stood before the display she sought.

Now all thoughts of Alexander did flee from her brain, for in front of her, on this small table not too near the window, was the selection of novels she had been hoping to find. A smile worked its way across her face as she took in the glorious sight.

There was Mrs. Roche's book. She picked up a copy and turned to the first page. Was it horrible, like *Clermont*? Or worse, like *The Mysteries of Udolfo*? She had never dared to read something as scandalous as *Udolfo*, but she had heard so much about it... Still, she could not stop herself from reading the first page or two, or perhaps five, oblivious to the rest of the world.

Perhaps she would do better with Mrs. Brunton's *Discipline*. She replaced the copy of *The Monastery of St. Columb* and reached for

Discipline instead, her eyes full of the stacks about her. But rather than her hand alighting upon the cool hard cover of a book, she touched soft flesh instead. She pulled her hand back as if burned, only to see another young woman do exactly the same thing.

"Please forgive me," Mary blurted out, as the other woman exclaimed, "Oh, I am so sorry!"

Then both of them smiled and both began to laugh, which brought the shopkeeper around to ask them to please be a little quieter.

"Have you read Mrs. Brunton's book?" Mary asked the other lady, her voice now low.

"No, although I do wish to. But I must hide it from my sister. She thinks me far too serious to read novels! I saw you looking at *The Monastery*. Do you like the Gothick stories?"

Mary felt herself blush and hoped the red did not go badly with her mustard yellow pelisse. "Oh no! That is, I ought not... I dare not. I am far too sober-minded for that! Although I must confess, I would like to see what it is about..."

The other lady began to laugh again and then quickly quietened down to a delicate titter. "We are much alike then. Which shall you buy?"

Mary pinched her lips together and frowned. "I cannot say! I would like to read both, but really must not spend that amount of money."

"And I likewise." Her companion shook her head and sighed.

"Ah, wait! I have a grand idea." Mary beamed. She felt a great connection with this unknown lady, who seemed so similar to her and who had such excellent taste in books. "Perhaps I can buy the one and you the other, and when we have read them through, we might meet and lend each other our books so we can read both."

"How very clever! Here, may I introduce myself? It is not quite the thing, and yet there is no one else to do the honours, and we are hardly at a ball or an at-home. It must be excusable. My name is Elinor Dashwood, and I am staying in town with my cousin for some months."

"A pleasure to meet you, Miss Dashwood. I am Mary Bennet and I am staying with my aunt and uncle. What fun this is!"

Before long, the two ladies had made their purchases and, seeing there was ample time before either needed to return home, they decided to take tea at an elegant tea shop by The Exchange. They talked of this and that and the other, and by the time both had to depart, they had become fast friends.

Over the next weeks, they met at the galleries and museums, and when the weather was pleasant, for walks in the park. Soon Miss Dashwood became Elinor, and Miss Bennet became Mary. Elinor was almost exactly Mary's age of one-and-twenty. She was reserved in nature, but felt deeply, and was determined to do the right thing by her family and friends. It was Elinor who, after her father died just a year past, had consoled her mother and sisters despite her own broken heart, and who strove to find a situation for her family that fit within their limited income. Reason and measure meant everything to her, even when they went against her own desires.

As the oft-forgotten middle child in a family of five daughters, Mary well understood her new friend. Mary had never been able to compete with her elegant and witty older sisters, nor did she wish to match the silliness of the younger two. She was the serious one, the studious one the others had so often deemed best to ignore. It was only during the last three years that Mary had grown particularly close to her next older sister, Elizabeth. But such a thing was a natural consequence of Mary having saved Elizabeth from the horrible charge of murder! Elinor, too, was close to her younger sister Marianne, but the two were as different as sisters could be. Like her, she felt that Elinor cherished having a friend who understood her completely.

They soon found another commonality which strengthened their growing friendship. In a moment of shared confidence, which Elinor begged Mary never to divulge, she confessed to a great disappointment of the heart. Without providing the particulars or the gentleman's name, Elinor lamented that the man she thought cared for her was, in fact, engaged to somebody else.

"I cannot fault him at all," Elinor cried out. "I would hate for you to think he acted poorly, for he never gave me any particular encouragement. And yet we found so much similarity of opinion, such agreement on so many matters, our friendship was immediate. I had thought, once... but no, I was mistaken. The memory of it pains me still."

Mary placed a hand on her friend's forearm. "I am grieved for you, indeed. My father jested once that a woman enjoys being crossed in love, but there is little truth to it. I understand all too well the pain of giving one's heart and receiving nothing in return."

Elinor's brow wrinkled and Mary, having kept her own counsel for far too long, felt at last able to unburden herself.

"I have told nobody until now. Indeed, there is no one who would truly understand, for I am expected to be the sensible and unromantic one in my family. But I, too, have experienced such a disappointment. His name is Mr. Lyons, and I thought he loved me."

And, with as little display of sentiment as she could manage, Mary told Elinor about her strange relationship with her private investigator, and how she had expected an offer from him despite their very different standings in the world. "But instead of coming to speak with my father," she concluded, "he merely returned to his accustomed life in London, as if our... our meeting of hearts and minds had never occurred."

"You poor dear," Elinor sighed. "We do indeed understand each other perfectly."

These two ladies were everything complementary; they had similar characters and similar tastes, and both were silently nursing broken hearts. Their friendship now was complete.

It was not long before Elinor became known to Mary's Aunt Gardiner, and then it was a matter of hours before Mary was introduced to Miss Dashwood's cousin Mrs. Jennings. Mrs. Jennings was a lady of mature years, not quite a cousin by blood, but related somehow by marriage and therefore granted the esteemed status of 'family.' She possessed a great love of laughter and teasing, and a greater love of inserting herself in other people's concerns, always eager to involve herself in her nieces' affairs, and by extension, Mary's. She had a good heart, despite being a bit vulgar, and welcomed Mary into her home at once.

With Easter on the way, Mary's aunt and uncle were very busy at their place of business, and whilst Mary had offered to help care for the family's four children, they were now of an age where they were engaged all day at their schools and did not need her to be hovering about. No matter that her stay in London was ostensibly for the benefit of her aunt and uncle, she knew that the real reason was to allow her some time to enjoy the city and all it offered.

Therefore, her aunt was pleased to allow Mary to visit her new friends as often as the two wished. Uncle Gardiner, it seemed, had known Mrs. Jennings' late husband through matters of business, for that man, too, had been in trade, and spoke highly of him. He had met Mrs. Jennings once or twice and was happy with her character, thereby having no reservations about committing his niece to Mrs. Jennings' chaperonage any time she wished. And so Mary became an almost daily visitor at that lady's home near Portman Square.

Of the great many people who graced Mrs. Jennings' parlour, the first Mary met was Elinor's younger sister, Marianne. She was as much absent as she was present, frequently preferring the solitude of her rooms to the society of the tea table. Marianne was seventeen years old and very pretty, with a summery freshness to her looks, rather than Jane Bingley's alabaster elegance. But the dewy glow of her flawless complexion was not matched by a spark in her dark eyes, and from what Elinor had said, Mary suspected that she was a third member of the Club of Broken Hearts.

Marianne did not speak much, but did spend a great deal of time sighing Romantically and gazing out of windows. With these exaggerated shows of despair, and the effort she put into reminding her sister of her piteous state, Mary began to wonder how much of Marianne's woe was real and how much affected. The younger Dashwood sister also had a habit of carrying about some volume or other, which Mary soon learned were books of sentimental poetry. Every so often, and not always in any matter related to the conversation in the room, she would begin to read aloud some passage that struck her fancy, with the same fervour that Mary herself used to devote to her books of sermons. She had, she now realised with the wisdom of another three years on the earth, been using these moralistic works to carve out a place for herself somewhere between her older sisters' wit and elegance and her younger sisters' high spirits and silliness. If Alexander Lyons had not arrived and placed her, for a short time, at the centre of his world, would she still be skulking around the fringes of society, clamouring for a moment of glory or the attention of her elders? Alexander...

She banished him from her thoughts and resolved to be a bit more understanding of Marianne Dashwood's melancholic cast of mind.

In stark relief to Marianne's artful air of gloom was the presence of a frequent visitor, a most gentlemanlike man named Colonel Brandon. He, too, was quiet and grave by nature, but he seemed to place a great deal of effort into appearing sociable to disguise his own quiet distress. He was, in that way, much like Elinor, for the two seemed quite at peace with the world until, in unguarded moments, an observant companion might detect that look in the eye that suggested quite the opposite. Mary was, she had learned of herself, such an observant companion.

This secret pain aside, the colonel was pleasant company and was already well known to the residents of the house. He was about five-and-thirty—a little older than Mr. Darcy—with an appealing if not handsome face, and very fine manners. He was mostly satisfied to let others speak, but when he did insert himself into a conversation, he betrayed an excellent education and well-considered opinions. Mary wondered if he knew Mr. Darcy's cousin, Colonel Fitzwilliam, for the two would likely get along quite well, she imagined.

Upon asking exactly this, she was delighted to learn that the two were, indeed, acquainted, upon which her liking for the man increased even more. She enjoyed talking with Colonel Brandon about this common acquaintance, as well as his years in India and of his estate in Delaford, and time spent in his company was never wasted, despite the suggestion of unhappiness that lurked behind his smiles.

That look in his eye kept calling for Mary's attention, however, and after a few of his visits, she began to devote herself to determining what, exactly, it meant. He seemed an unlikely sort to come so frequently to spend his time with Mrs. Jennings, for she was grandmotherly and a bit crude, and he was younger and of a very different character. And thus, Mary watched his eyes, that darted so often to where Elinor sat beside her sister. Could the colonel be in love with Elinor? They would likely make a good match, if a quiet and reserved one. But no. For even when Elinor rose to help with the tea or greet a new guest, Colonel Brandon's eyes still turned to that settee… Could it be? It must be so indeed. Serious and sedate Colonel Brandon was in love with the very young and very Romantic Marianne Dashwood!

There was, from time to time, another visitor to the house whose presence Mary did not initially understand. This was a rather young man—no more than a year or two older than herself— by the name of Edward Ferrars.

He came the first time with Colonel Brandon, but was clearly already known to the residents of the household, for both Elinor and Marianne greeted him warmly by his given name rather than the expected "Mr. Ferrars." Despite this familiarity, he seemed uncomfortable in his surroundings and shifted a great deal in his chair. He was ordinary in appearance, with mild manners and a certain sweetness of expression in his face that suggested a gentle nature. He did not initially impress with his personal graces or wit of conversation, but as Mary grew to know him better over several such visits, she found his character improved greatly.

Mary could not, at first, determine why Mr. Ferrars came about to visit so often when he seemed so ill at ease. He did not always come with Colonel Brandon, and he certainly did not visit for the pleasure of Mrs. Jennings' company. Could he hold a *tendre* for Elinor? It hardly seemed creditable, could it? There must be some history between the families that Mary did not yet know. But Mrs. Jennings was always so warm and welcoming to the young man that she, alone, could be the incentive for his frequent visits.

Still, the notion of an attraction to Elinor never quite left Mary's thoughts. This was something else Mary must observe closely and contemplate later. As for Elinor, her expression was always controlled when in company, and Mary had no way of understanding her friend's opinions of Mr. Ferrars, nor would she ask, for Elinor had not chosen to disclose anything and prying would be unladylike. Still, if Mr. Ferrars were, indeed, smitten with her friend, it might help take Elinor's mind off the other young man who plagued her thoughts.

However, no matter his feelings towards Elinor, Edward Ferrars was not of a mind for courting, for he had recently suffered a great misfortune. It came out at his very first visit, when Colonel Brandon dropped a quiet word in Mrs. Jennings' ear as the younger man and Elinor stared at each other. Mary had noticed the colonel's actions and watched as Mrs. Jennings' eyes opened wide, and her mouth, a second later, opened wider. She blinked twice and then addressed her new guest in a voice that could surely be heard across the street.

"Oh, poor Mr. Ferrars!" she exclaimed. "I had not heard. Lud! what sad and unexpected news. Why, when last I saw her, not quite three weeks ago I believe, she seemed as hale and vigorous as any woman ever I have known. I can hardly believe it. You poor lad." Then, glancing about to take in the other expressions around her, added, "Oh, friends, forgive me. May I speak, Mr. Ferrars? Yes, of course. It is no secret, after all. Ladies, poor Mr. Ferrars has recently lost his mother! How terribly unfortunate. If I had known I would have paid a call. It must have been in the newspapers while we were travelling. Here, let me call for some more tea."

There followed an outpouring of condolences and words of sympathy. It was evident that this was news to all present. Edward hemmed and hawed and shuffled his feet and had to be coaxed several times to speak.

"Thank you," he blushed at last, "for your kind words. My brother... that is, we decided not to publish the news. We were too distressed to contemplate it, but perhaps, now, thinking back, we ought to have done. It really was a great shock. Mother had not been ill at all, although I do not know why she was up at the Norfolk estate. She called both Robert—that is my brother, Miss Bennet—and me to attend her there. I admit to being rather surprised since we had had a falling out just days before. But I hoped to do the right thing by my mother and came." His voice now took on a dirgeful note. "I had long thought of the church for my career, and a clergyman must practise the Christian charity of which he speaks."

This Mary agreed with completely. She was devout in her beliefs and, despite some moments of unsettled confusion, a firm believer in the steadfastness and rightness of the Church and its ministers. Mr. Ferrars was quickly rising in her estimation.

The young man had not finished his tale, and spoke on, now that the subject had been broached and deemed suitable for conversation with this intimate group. "Mother was well the first night. We did not arrive until almost dinner time and she refused to discuss whatever she wished to talk about until the next day. But shortly after breakfast on the second day, she became ill. We thought it a trifle, perhaps something in the kippers or some other inconsequential indisposition, but when she was no better by noon, we called in the doctor from the town. And then, almost before we knew it, she was dead! She had been perfectly well not a day before!"

"My dear Mr. Ferrars, how dreadful!" Mrs. Jennings' emotions were writ large upon her fleshy face. She was formed for good humour, but must feel sadness strongly too. Her dismay was sincere to Mary's eyes. "My poor boy! And what caused this sudden event?"

Edward's sad eyes grew sadder still, and he pushed a lock of hair off his forehead. "I cannot rightly say. The doctor told us these things do happen, that it must have been a condition of her heart that we knew nothing about until far too late. My grandfather died suddenly as well, so perhaps it is something in the family." He looked down at the floor and studied the carpet with great intensity.

A frisson of something tickled its way up Mary's spine. Whilst she was certain there was nothing at all untoward in this sad story, she had seen too much of unexpected death recently to accept it without question. She must think of a way to pry without seeming rude.

"Were you and your brother the only ones in the house, Mr. Ferrars? Were there other guests?" She hoped she sounded genuinely concerned.

The young man closed his eyes and sighed. "In truth, we were the only ones there, except for Mother, of course. She never went to the estate, preferring to spend all her time in Town, and has no circle of friends there. The house, indeed, is not prepared for guests. It has been so long since anybody stayed there. Robert shall have a fine time repairing it to its former state." He shook his head, dejection etched upon his sagging shoulders.

"And the doctor had nothing more to say? He gave no indication of some other cause of her sudden illness?" She was being too bold. She must excuse herself. "I only ask in the hopes of assuring you of your own good health," she fumbled for words.

Edward shuffled his feet and mumbled a few false starts before addressing himself to her. "I thank you for your concern. No, he thought only that it was a sudden seizure of the heart. Such things happen, even in relatively young and healthy people. He advised me and Robert, although he is younger than me, to take care not to indulge too much and to take regular exercise. These are principles with which I hold regardless, and so I shall obey them without a problem." He sighed again.

"I am sorry, Edward." Elinor reached out to put a comforting hand on Edward's arm. Mary's brows rose in surprise. That they were familiar enough to use each other's Christian names was established, but this public display of physical touch betrayed a greater intimacy still. Surely not...

For his part, Edward looked even more uncomfortable than usual and mumbled something before begging everyone's pardon, but he must be going. When next he appeared for a visit, the subject of his mother's passing was left unmentioned, and whatever association there might have been between him and Elinor was likewise left silent.

There was one other person whom Mary saw often at Mrs. Jennings' house. This was a young woman, perhaps two or three years her senior, named Lucy Steele. She often came with her older sister Anne, for both were cousins of a sort to Mrs. Jennings. Mary had started to wonder if Mrs. Jennings were somehow related to every unmarried lady in England, but tamed her musings with the understanding that a heart as generous as Mrs. Jennings' must surely find a good selection of young women upon whom to bestow her goodness and beneficence.

Mary's first impression of Lucy Steele was good. Hers was a pretty face, with intelligent eyes and a ready smile. Her hair was neither blonde nor brown, but was of a similar shade to Elinor's, and she had a smartness in her air that gave her a sort of distinction. But despite her civil manners and natural intelligence, Mary soon found that Lucy had little education and less natural understanding, and whilst she was grand company for a half an hour or so, her actions were designed more to better herself in the world than to generally please others.

Anne, often called Nancy by her sister, was a rather different sort of a person. She was older than Lucy by several years, nearly thirty by Mary's reckoning, and as plain as Lucy was pretty. If Lucy was poorly tutored, Anne was less so, and she seemed almost simple. She seldom spoke, but to utter some unwelcome comment, and her thoughts were disordered. But she was kind beneath her awkwardness, and doted upon her sister, always offering to bring her tea or to open or close a window, the better to serve Lucy's comfort.

More interesting to Mary's eye was the undercurrent of antipathy between Lucy and Elinor. They were very civil and polite to each other and engaged in conversation on a variety of unchallenging topics, but to one such as Mary, who had learned from early childhood to observe the world around her, the tension between them was palpable.

Elinor seemed to dislike Lucy a great deal, for what reason Mary hoped soon to learn. In consideration of Elinor's natural good taste, this intimation of dislike might have been the result of a meeting with an uncouth mind, but Mary felt there was something more. Was it Lucy's obvious desire to ingratiate herself to those who might help her rise in society? Or was it some insult from their earliest days of acquaintanceship? Mary recalled with clarity how her own sister Elizabeth had taken umbrage with Mr. Darcy for an insult he uttered in her hearing. It was only by luck and a great effort on Mr. Darcy's part that Elizabeth had learned to give up her pride and start to like the man. Indeed, she had eventually married him, and seemed very happy in her choice! Could Elinor be holding such a grudge against Lucy, based on a long-past slight?

Lucy's demeanour towards Elinor was stranger still. There was a look of triumph on her face when she spoke to Mary's new friend. She was, to be blunt, smug. What victory had she won? Perhaps, Mary considered, if she were fortunate to have a moment with Mrs. Jennings, that lady might deign to tell her what she knew. For if there was a story, Mrs. Jennings would surely have all of it!

Chapter Two

Brothers

"I must ask you," Mary whispered to Elinor during one morning's visit, "about Mr. Ferrars. I sense some sad tale there, although you need not answer."

Mrs. Jennings was busy with her housekeeper and Marianne had pleaded a headache and was lying down in her bedroom, leaving the two young women in privacy. There was rain in the air, forbidding a walk, and it was the perfect day for an intimate chat. Mary glanced at Elinor, trying hard not to stare too directly at her friend, thereby intimidating her. Being a civil and sociable creature required so much work!

For her part, Elinor turned pale and muttered something unintelligible before letting out a great sigh. "You had better hear it, and from me, since who knows how the tale will be distorted by the time it reaches your ears otherwise? As it surely will, in time.

My sister is a loving soul, but hers is not a mind to keep a secret when she feels a passion. Come, let us sit by the window." She rose and drifted across the room with Mary in her wake.

For a moment, Elinor remained silent, her eyes closed, dark lashes against pale cheeks. Then, with another deep exhalation of breath, she spoke. "As you know, my own dear father died a year ago. We had just come out of mourning when you and I met each other at the bookshop. It might have been my first day in clothing not black or lavender. After Papa's death, my brother John and his wife moved to Norland. I do not believe Fanny—that is, John's wife—wished us to remain at all, but John is not cruel even if he is weak, and he permitted us to stay for as long as we required. During those long months, Fanny's brother came to visit, and we found we had a great deal in common."

"Her brother?" Mary's eyebrows rose.

"Edward. Edward Ferrars is John's brother-in-law. But we had never previously met. John's mother died some years before Papa married my own mother, and Fanny never pretended any love for my side of the family."

Mary nodded, but said nothing, allowing Elinor to continue.

"Edward is everything that Fanny is not—kind, gentle, with a generous soul and a sense of honour—and his presence made the ordeal of being a guest in my own home more tolerable. I grew to lo... to like him a great deal."

She turned to Mary with pleading eyes. "Nobody knows this, save Marianne. I must beg you not to tell a soul!"

Mary regarded her friend with serious eyes. "Of course! You may depend upon it entirely!"

Elinor's eyes met hers for a moment, as if assessing Mary's discretion. With a slight dip of her head, she went on. "I grew to esteem him greatly. You have met him; you know what he is like. Perhaps, at first, his manners are not open and he is diffident amongst those he does not know well, but as I came to know him better, I found more and more to admire in him. And, to be honest, I thought he liked me too. After we found our current home at Barton Cottage, just as we were about to depart Norland, he begged to tell me something, and I thought he was going to speak of his feelings. But we were interrupted and he never did say what he had planned.

"He came to visit us in Devonshire, and there too, I hoped... we all hoped... But it came to nothing and he departed again. I felt it was his humility that stopped him and admired him the more for it. But then..."

She stopped and took a great breath, as if trying to fortify herself. Mary reached out a hand, and Elinor took it, gripping back with surprising strength.

"But then Miss Lucy Steele came to the area and, under the guise of friendship, confessed to me that she had been engaged to a certain man for the last four years. Four years, Mary! Can you believe that? And this man was none other than Edward! Oh, I hoped at first that there was some other Edward Ferrars, that she was mistaken, but it was true. They had met whilst she was visiting her uncle Mr. Pratt, at whose school Edward had been studying. They kept the engagement a secret, for fear that Mrs. Ferrars would disapprove and disallow the engagement." She swallowed and her eyes went wide. "Four years!"

She took another shuddering breath before speaking on.

"That part is my own secret, the millstone I wear about my neck. The rest is more commonly known, for it happened only last March seventh, mere weeks ago. Edward's mother met and took a liking to Lucy, although she knew not of the connection with her son. Feeling emboldened, Lucy confessed to being engaged to Edward and a great row ensued. Lucy was sent from the house and Edward was called to rescind his word and cast her off. He refused and his mother, upon whose good graces his inheritance depended, changed her will to settle the entire estate upon Robert, his younger brother."

"La! That is a muddle!" Mary grimaced. She sounded exactly like her sister Lydia. "And now everybody knows that Edward and Lucy are engaged, and that Edward has no fortune at all upon which to live. And you..."

"My complete secret!"

"And you are bereft of the man you love and have to see him with a woman you thought was your friend."

Elinor blinked, but allowed not a tear to fall. "It is my lot and I must live with it."

Mary dared to put a hand on her friend's shoulder. "I am very sorry."

"It would not be so difficult, but that I see them here so often. And despite Edward's insistence upon honouring his engagement, I still believe by his glances, his kind words, that he cares for me, and has long since abandoned any affection for Lucy."

"And Miss Steele?"

"She looks upon me with triumph, although what manner of prize it is to have won a man who does not care for you, I cannot think."

"She does not behave like a woman engaged."

Elinor's only response was to shake her head again. And to this, there was nothing left to say.

The weeks went by in a pleasant manner. Easter came and went and the air grew warmer with every passing day. Shortly after the holiday, Mary's Mama and younger sisters came to London for a week, there to visit with the Gardiners (for Uncle Gardiner was Mama's brother). When Mrs. Jennings learned of this, she horrified Mary by inviting Mr. and Mrs. Gardiner, whom she knew somewhat, as well as Mary's family, for a visit. How much Mary dreaded this event cannot be put into words, but she spent more than one night with little sleep in trepidation.

But, to her amazement, the visit was tolerable. Mrs. Bennet had been in her finest manners and had immediately found a wealth of commonalities with Mrs. Jennings. In retrospect, Mary considered, she ought to have expected such. Both were ladies of a similar age, with two daughters married very well and with grandchildren to crow about (although it went without saying that each lady's grandchildren were the best that ever there were), and with a further interest in involving themselves in the lives of any other unmarried ladies of their acquaintance so as to rid them of that status.

Mama was not of the sharpest wit, but she was charming in her own way and was a sociable creature, and in this she and Mrs. Jennings were very well matched, and Mary knew at once that a fifteen-minute visit would soon become a three-hour-long tea.

Likewise, Elinor's sister Marianne and Mary's youngest sister Lydia took an immediate liking to each other. Marianne was seventeen and Lydia eighteen, and if Marianne had the more refined judgement of the two, Lydia's guilelessness and high spirits seemed to draw Marianne out.

Elinor had told Mary of her sister's disappointment. Marianne had met and been wooed by a young man in Devonshire, and everybody had expected an engagement. But this man, Willoughby, had departed with hardly a word and was now engaged to be married to a very wealthy woman he had met in London. Marianne was sensible and clever but her emotions had no moderation, and she allowed these Romantic sensibilities to take full possession of her moods. "My sister," Elinor had confided to Mary, "is very earnest in all she does, but she is not often really merry."

Lydia, on the other hand, was everything merry, and just as well as two like souls may find great pleasure in each other, sometimes there is truth in the notion that opposites attract. Lydia and Marianne, therefore, soon began their own conference in the one corner of the room. Only Kitty, Mary's next younger sister, sat silent and morose at her mother's side, waiting for someone to entertain her.

Great was Mary's surprise, therefore, when there came a knock at the front door and shortly thereafter Edward Ferrars walked in, with another man accompanying him.

"If you please," Edward mumbled in his self-deprecating way, "my brother Robert."

Introductions were made all around, and Mary took stock of the newcomer. He was taller than Edward and more handsome, although with a look of hauteur in his eye where Edward's mien was mild and pleasing. Robert seemed about twenty-one years old, and after saying his how-do-you-dos around the room, sat down and spoke not a word, although his eyes roved freely over the young ladies present.

"I heard you were to have visitors of a most charming nature," Edward explained, "and when I happened to meet Robert on my way here, I prevailed upon him to join me. It is kind of you, Mrs. Jennings, to permit him to join us."

"Always a pleasure, always a pleasure! Lud, if there isn't always room for one more around our table, and you being all but family. Mr. Robert Ferrars, you are very welcome."

There was a moment of general small talk and then the gathering broke once more into smaller groups. Mary watched as Robert surveyed the room once more before his eyes alit on the one female not seemingly engaged with any group. Her sister Kitty!

Kitty had always been in Lydia's shadow, despite being two years older, but she had of late emerged to become more of her own person. She was not the most beautiful of the Bennet sisters—that was undoubtedly Jane—but all five were considered very pretty girls and Kitty was more than handsome enough to capture an interested man's roving eye. And Robert's eye, so Mary considered, was very interested.

He edged over to where Kitty sat, presumably to pay his respects to Mrs. Jennings, but soon left the two matrons to chat together whilst engaging Kitty in conversation. He looked quite pleased with himself, and Kitty cast a triumphant eye over to where Lydia scowled at her, and thus a half hour passed before anybody looked at the time and declared that they had all stayed far too long.

Such a happy assembly, however, must not be so quickly given up and plans were made for a similar gathering to form the very next day, and possibly even for a walk in the park or a trip to a tea shop for an ice, if the weather should hold.

During the time that the Bennets were in London, Mary saw a great deal of Robert Ferrars. He arranged to be present every time Mary's sisters were visiting Mrs. Jennings. He looked askance at Edward, when he was present, uttered meaningless pleasantries to the other ladies, and danced attendance upon Kitty. Mary watched as carefully as she could whilst not neglecting her friend. Was Robert Ferrars truly taken by her sister? He certainly hovered about her like a bee at a flower. He offered his arm when the group walked out, solicited her opinion on all manner of topics, and was eager to draw her into conversation.

But at no time did Mary believe he was developing any real affection for her. His attentions were too obvious, and seemed even to Mary's eyes, designed for show. It occurred to her that his aim was not to fall in love with Kitty or make her fall in love with him, but rather to find someone who, by being the focus of his attention, would in turn focus all of her attention upon him. Robert, Mary considered, thrived on his vanity, and this doting upon Kitty was merely a means to bolster that aspect of his character. For her part, Kitty seemed equally pleased to be the centre of attention, with little regard for the man himself, which matter soothed Mary's concerns for her sister.

How suitable such behaviour was so shortly after his mother's untimely demise, Mary could not say. Men were held to such very different standards of mourning than were women, and the first month after Mrs. Ferrars' burial was completed. Still, it would have been more becoming for the young man to have at least affected some restraint in his demeanour.

But instead, the only time Mary saw him exhibit even the smallest degree of restraint was one very uncomfortable afternoon when, as well as the expected visit by Colonel Brandon and the Ferrars brothers, Lucy and Nancy Steele stopped to pay a visit.

As they entered the room, the whole mood changed. Edward stiffened and took in a sharp breath before attempting a smile and some kind words for his betrothed bride. Lucy fluttered her eyes and smiled coyly at Edward before sliding up to him and pulling him to sit by her on the settee. Her eyes roved slowly around the room, taking each person in, one after the other, before moving back to Edward, upon whom she made a great show of bestowing her charms.

Robert, who was sitting with Kitty, stopped quite still in his place as Lucy's eyes met his. Mary was uncertain whether he was merely taken aback upon having a new member join their little group, or whether there was some prior acquaintance between the two. Nevertheless, when introductions were made, he bowed politely and said all the words one says upon meeting somebody for the first time.

The two said nothing in particular to each other more than the expected civilities and utterances of polite conversation, but all through that morning, the mood never quite returned to its previous ease. Robert continued his conversation with Kitty, of which Mary heard mere snips and exclamations, but whenever she looked up to observe them, she noticed Robert's eyes flit more often than not to Lucy, where she sat in discussion with Edward and Elinor.

Lucy herself seemed to pay little attention to Robert, striving, so Mary thought, to avoid his eye and pay all her attention to Edward. Had Edward told her something ill about his brother that Lucy wished so little to do with him? Perhaps so, and perhaps she had confessed this to her sister Nancy, for Nancy's glare in Robert's direction was all animosity, which she hid very ill, to Mary's keen eyes, at least.

When, after their visit to London was over, the Bennets returned to Hertfordshire, it was with only a small amount of regret on Kitty's part, for the loss of the attention more than the loss of the beau, but with no glum glances at all on Robert's. His little flirtation was over, and he might now return to his comfortable life, leaving Kitty with nothing more than a few stories of "that handsome young man who spoke to me."

Now the summer was approaching fast, and the weather changed from the tentative warmth of early spring to the full heat of early summer. It was the middle of June, almost the time when Mary must say goodbye to her London relations and new friends and return to the bosom of her family in Hertfordshire. Only a fortnight remained of her stay in the city, and she was determined to enjoy each day to its fullest.

She walked with Elinor in the parks and took tea with her at the popular spots, and returned often to their favourite bookshop near The Exchange. Mrs. Jennings had offered more than once to invite Mary to join her when she returned to her daughter's home in Devonshire, where Elinor too was soon to return. It was a most tempting offer; a month on the coast, amongst people she knew and liked, was a great inducement. But her family feelings were strong, and she knew her mother and father would be expecting her home.

Still, she spent every moment she could with Elinor and Marianne. Thus it was that she was present quite early one morning when, to everybody's shock, Colonel Brandon burst through the parlour doors without a by-your-leave and gasped out, "Terrible, terrible news! I am loath even to say it, but you must know the worst of it!"

He collapsed into a chair and Mrs. Jennings called out to a maid to bring some coffee at once.

"No, no, I shall be well. I am well," he insisted. "But not all is well. Robert Ferrars, Edward's brother, did not return home last night. He was found this morning near Hyde Park. He had been beaten and robbed. I am afraid to say it, but he is dead."

Chapter Three

Alexander

"You must understand our concern." The red-coated colonel paced up and down Alexander Lyons' small office. He paused when he reached the offered chair once more, but did not sit down. He glanced down at the stack of cards on the desk that read *Alexander Lyons, Investigator,* and gave a brief bob of his head, as if reassuring himself he was in the proper place. Then he resumed pacing.

Alexander considered the man who had come calling a few minutes before. He had not written ahead, but had knocked at the door and hoped that the investigator was available. "You come highly recommended by a fellow officer, name of Fitzwilliam," the colonel had explained. "He said you had done great service to the family. I hope you can help us, too."

The colonel had then introduced himself as Nicholas Brandon of Delaford in Dorsetshire. He was requesting Alexander's services, he said, not on his own behalf but on that of a certain gentleman whom he knew, but who was too uncertain of matters to make the call himself. He took the offered seat and explained the situation, then rose and began pacing as Alexander considered what he had heard.

"Let me repeat this." Alexander spoke slowly as thoughts swirled in his head. He knew his broad Scots accent would not deter this stalwart colonel, but poorly chosen words and stumbling sentences might. "Your friend had a falling out with his mother three months ago and was disinherited in favour of his younger brother, Robert Ferrars. That brother had a will that he made last year, upon turning twenty-one." Alexander looked up for confirmation. Seeing Brandon's nod, he continued. "That document left everything to his brother Edward. This seems reasonable and quite unexceptionable. Very well. Now this is where matters get sticky.

"This same Robert Ferrars was killed three days ago. To all accounts, he was returning home very late through Hyde Park from a rather exclusive gaming establishment. That is of little import right now, although it may become vital later. What does matter at this moment is that he was beaten, robbed, and left dead at the scene. His estate ought, therefore, to have passed to his brother Edward with no concerns raised.

"But..." There was always a 'but.' "But on the day that the terms of the will were announced, a certain person, a lady, came forward claiming that she was, in fact, Robert Ferrars' wife and that Ferrars' considerable wealth ought rightly to be hers."

Alexander rose and moved to a shelf of books that sat against the far wall. He selected a tome and brought it to his desk, where he proceeded to open it and turn the pages until he found the one he wanted. Without looking at the words before him, he continued. "But there is no evidence of a marriage, and even if there were, the rule from *Lugg v Lugg* from 1696 is that it requires marriage *and* the birth of children to effect a revocation of a will."

Here Brandon interrupted him. "On what grounds would the extant will be revoked? Does the state of marriage annul a previous legal document? Yes, I know from Fitzwilliam that you are a lawyer by training. This is one of the considerations that brought me here today."

Alexander gave a nod and hoped he looked sufficiently scholarly. Not many men took him seriously, what with his strong brogue (that became stronger or weaker, depending on how annoying he found his company) and his mop of coppery-red hair. He knew he appeared and sounded like a kilt-wearing heathen from the braes, and this was an image he rather cultivated, no matter that it might cost him some business. Now, however, he preferred to project the image of a learned and capable man of letters.

"Just so. I read law at Glasgow, where I did my degree. I do not practise that profession, but I follow the latest judgments. My qualifications remain valid."

Brandon looked satisfied.

"Marriage," Alexander returned to the colonel's question, "is a fundamental change in circumstance. It is assumed that upon taking a wife and having children, a man necessarily wishes to provide for his family. Therefore, the court should take notice of what is—or ought to be—a clear and obvious intent."

"But that requires marriage *and* children..."

"And as you have told me, Lucy Steele, or Lucy Ferrars, should her tale be true, claims to be *enceinte*."

"Mmmm." Brandon was a man not given to unnecessary speech.

"And the question arises as to whether an unborn child has the status of a living child. This has been much about the courts these last ten or fifteen years. In *Doe v Lancashire*, it was ruled that a posthumous child does indeed hold the same status as a living child, on the condition that the father knew of that expectation. It is understood that he would wish to provide for the child, hence the material change in circumstance. But if he did not know..."

"Then the previous will stands."

"Just so. Just so."

Alexander sought another thinner volume and flipped through some pages. "Look here." He pointed to a passage and beckoned the colonel, who came and glanced at the lines. "There is a case presently before a judge, *White v Barford*, where neither husband nor wife knew of the impending birth of an heir. This might be relevant at some point, depending on how long we are at this investigation. I am interested to see how he will rule on the matter."

"And thus our predicament," Brandon looked up from the pamphlet on the desk and took his seat once more.

"Yes. We have two questions that require answers. The first: were Robert Ferrars and Lucy Steele really married? We have only her word that they were so, and that this marriage occurred within the last three months, after Mrs. Ferrars died and after Robert inherited her wealth. The second question: Assuming that Miss Steele is, indeed, with child, and assuming the child's father is Robert, did he know of her condition before he died?"

"I have come to the right man." Brandon dipped his head in respect.

"I shall do what I can to discover the answers." Alexander took a moment to make a series of notes on the sheet of paper before him. "I need not impress upon you the import of this last point. I can trust your discretion? I must speak to her before she discovers how key this is to her case. But now I have some questions of my own. Perhaps you will have some information for me."

"Please." Brandon waved an open palm in invitation.

"What were Miss Steele's circumstances before this possible marriage?"

Brandon thought. "She is not wealthy. Her mother is deceased and her father is not a rich man. She and her sister Anne—Nancy—stay with a variety of friends and relations around the country. Most recently they have been visiting a distant relation in Devonshire, a friend of mine by the name of Mrs. Jennings, but whilst in London, they stay with other relations."

"So, she would not have had a large dowry; Robert would not have gained by this marriage."

"No, indeed. She would have been the one to benefit."

"Then it is greatly to her detriment that this marriage—if it occurred—is not documented, for she may lose a great deal."

Brandon, terse as always, merely nodded.

"I also wish to learn more of the brother, Edward. If Miss Steele's claim is not upheld, he will regain what he lost by his mother's actions and will become a wealthy man again."

"You suspect him of ill-doing?" Brandon looked shocked and his shoulders stiffened under his uniform coat. "I could hardly believe that of Edward Ferrars! A more modest, self-effacing and sincere man I cannot imagine. I have offered him the living at Delaford, for he wishes to take orders. He was beyond grateful and appreciative of the offer, for all that the living will provide only two hundred and fifty a year. Surely such a man would never be involved in anything improper..."

Alexander shrugged. "I mean no disrespect. I merely have questions that I must ask."

Brandon relaxed. "Yes. Of course."

"Did the Runners have any concerns about Mr. Robert's death? There was nothing untoward? They had no suspicions other than theft?"

Another shake of the head. "No. Robert was not circumspect about making his new circumstances known. He was a young man still, and not so wise. He had begun spending freely and, according to people I know, was becoming a regular patron at gaming tables around London. If some footpads were looking for a man to rob, they would not have to look hard to find Robert Ferrars. The Runners were confident the motive was theft. He was found all but naked. Every coin, his watch, everything of value was gone. Even his boots."

"How did they know who it was?" Another question that had to be asked.

"He was well enough known. As badly beaten as he was, he was not disfigured. I was walking by when the Runners were seeking someone to put a name to him. It was undoubtedly him."

"I am sorry. That cannot have been easy."

Brandon seemed to shrink. "No. And I was the unhappy one to tell his—" He stopped. "Oh my God."

Alexander snapped his head up. "What is it? What is wrong, Colonel?"

"There is something you ought to know. The import of it only occurred to me now." He took a great breath. "It came as a great shock to us all. Assuming her claims are correct, before she married Mr. Robert Ferrars, Lucy Steele was engaged to Robert's brother Edward."

That very day, Alexander joined Colonel Brandon on a visit to Mrs. Jennings, where Edward was so often to be found. As Colonel Brandon explained, Edward had no lodgings in London, other than a room at an inn, and few close friends. Mrs. Jennings was kind hearted and sympathetic, and for all manner of reasons Edward chose to sit out his mourning in her matronly presence rather than in his lonely chamber. Alexander was pleased to begin this case, which might prove to be most ordinary, or quite unusual indeed, depending on what he learned.

Mrs. Jennings met the two men at the front door. "Colonel," she gushed. "So very good of you to come, and to bring your guest. Mr. Lyons," she lowered her voice, "very sad, very sad! And those girls, just sitting here like so many glum turtles, what a pity. You know," she whispered in a conspiratorial voice, "when I first met Mr. Ferrars, I thought he had a *tendre* for Miss Dashwood and she for him, but of course, that wasn't so. Still, with them thrown together now the way they are... But this is hardly the time for that! Not with the poor boy just having lost everything. His mother, his brother, his betrothed... Isn't it simply shocking about Lucy and Robert? We had only learned that she was engaged to Edward and look what happened! I had imagined Nancy would have told us, but for once, she didn't breathe a word. Strange one, is Nancy. Well, never mind that. Come in, lads, come in."

Alexander stayed back for a moment, watching Brandon and Mrs. Jennings as they moved towards the parlour. Mrs. Jennings was a round woman with a pink face that looked better designed to laugh than to mourn. But her generosity of spirit was clear and if Edward needed a place to condole, she would offer him all he required. He imagined for a moment how her own children had fared as they grew up. They must have been lucky to have a mother who so obviously loved and acted in the best interest of her offspring. Elegance and style might be lacking in her manner, but genuine affection was not, and in the end, children thrived on love.

He walked into the parlour a step or two behind his hostess. A small group of people rose to greet him. His eyes roved over the faces, taking in the gathering of strangers, and...

"Mary!"

What was she doing here? He had no notion at all of Mary Bennet being an intimate of Mrs. Jennings. Dash it all! He had no notion of her being anywhere other than in Hertfordshire at her family's house. How long had she been in London, and without telling him? He had thought they had a particular connection. What had happened that she would mislead him like this?

"Mr. Lyons." Her curtsey was everything polite, her voice everything cold. Oh Lord, what had he done this time?

Introductions were made. He bowed to Miss Dashwood, whom Mary called Elinor, said proper words to Miss Marianne Dashwood, a very pretty thing of about seventeen, and scratched the ears of a small pug that ran into the room from some doorway, only to be shooed out at once. And then, with a serious face and a sympathetic eye, he walked over to shake the hand of the man at the centre of all of this: Edward Ferrars.

"I am not certain what, exactly, we need you to find," Edward breathed when approached as to his wishes. "Before this very week, I would never have imagined Lucy to have told a mistruth. It is true that our engagement was formed a very long time ago, whilst we were too young, perhaps, to have fully established our characters, still she was not the sort to mislead... Or perhaps," he blinked as his forehead creased, "I was not the sort to see that."

From the corner of his eye, Alexander saw Elinor Dashwood's face tense up. Mary seemed to have noticed it too, but there was a look in Mary's eye... she knew something that Alexander did not. He would have to ask about that later. For now, he still needed to hear from Edward.

"What happened, Mr. Ferrars? If you prefer to adjourn to a private room...?"

Edward looked around him wildly, a drowning man seeking a piece of flotsam to grasp. Mrs. Jennings walked over and whispered something to him, and he breathed again. "No, thank you. I have nothing to hide and am more at ease surrounded by friends."

"Then, let us sit, and I will hear your end of things."

The young man stared at him, unblinking. He could not have been more than twenty-three or four, but at this moment he looked eighty, such was the weight of the world upon his shoulders. He stumbled backwards into a chair and all but fell onto it.

"Yes. Very well. Lucy... Miss Steele... I am still in disbelief. One day she told me how happy she was with me and how well we would manage on a small income from a church living, and the very next thing I knew she walked into our solicitor's office with her sister behind her, claiming that Robert's will was null because she was his wife. Was she cooing and flirting with me whilst already married to my brother? I can hardly account for it! And then... and then the news about the babe!"

He stiffened at once and his eyes flashed to the other side of the room. "The women... I ought not to have said that."

For their part, Mary and Elinor affected not having heard him, but Marianne looked partly shocked and partly intrigued.

"Did Robert know about the child?" Alexander kept his voice low, and Edward and Colonel Brandon leaned closer in their chairs so as not to be overheard when they spoke.

"I... I honestly cannot say." Edward shook his head. "He certainly said nothing of it to me, but we were not as close as some brothers are. And we frequently disagreed."

"About what?"

Edward's expression went blank. "On several matters." He did not explain, and sat back in his chair, lips a tight line across his white face.

Chapter Four

Willoughby

Mary fought to maintain her composure. She smiled at Elinor and tried to give all due attention to her words, but her mind was full of only one thing: Alexander.

Whatever was he doing here? When Colonel Brandon suggested bringing in an expert to assess Lucy's claims on Robert's estate, she never imagined that man would be Alexander. She had pictured an elderly solicitor, or some crusty pedant in clothes from the last century and whose vowels could cut glass. Not this young, disturbingly handsome, redheaded Scot who had torn out a piece of her heart.

But of course it made sense. Alexander was a brilliant investigator and a trained lawyer; he was the perfect person to determine whether Lucy's claims were valid. She wondered if Colonel Brandon had his direction from her brother Darcy's cousin, also a colonel, or if Alexander were merely that well known amongst the first circles of society. It mattered not. He was here and she must confront him. Again.

She had a brief reprieve. He had chosen first to address himself to Edward, as she herself would have done. Edward had been the presumed beneficiary of Robert's will, after all, before Lucy appeared. From Mary's scant understanding of the law, even had Robert not made a will, Edward would likely inherit his wealth anyway, being the most immediate living male family member.

But if Lucy had actually married Robert, what was she owed as his wife? Alexander would know! She must ask him... It was such a pity they did not like each other again.

Then Mary caught a word from the men's conversation. "...the news about the babe."

Her eyebrows rose on her forehead. This was something she had not heard before. Was there a child? Whose? Not Lucy's, surely! That would be most scandalous! It hardly seemed like that lady, who put on such a show of innocence. But then, she had been engaged to one man before, supposedly, marrying his brother! However had they contrived that?

How she wished anew that she were a man who could talk of such matters and not be expected to swoon or collapse from the impropriety of it. No, as distasteful as it might be, she must find time to ask Alexander about all he had learned!

"You know this man." Elinor's hand on her arm and subsequent question roused Mary from her reveries. "He called you by name."

Mary pulled her friend to the window seat, where they might talk in some semblance of privacy. "I told you of the man who raised my hopes and then abandoned me," she began. Elinor's brow furrowed in concern. "This is he."

"But, Mary, he hardly seemed to disdain you when he entered. He seemed, well, shocked at first, but then pleased to see you here. Surely, he did not leave with his own heart cold."

How could one explain? "We have known each other for some time. We met when he was asked to investigate a murder in which my own sister was a suspect. We have battled and made peace time and again, and I have grown to like him very much. When last we saw each other in October of last year, he..." she turned to ensure they were not being overheard. Then she leaned close to her friend so she might whisper. "He kissed me! Or, if I am quite honest, I kissed him. But I assure you, he did not object! That is when I thought he would declare himself and join with the Church and marry me. But he did not; he merely allowed me to return to my family whilst he came back to London, as if it had never happened."

"Join with the church?" Elinor sounded confused. "Oh, yes. He is a Scot. He must be a Papist. Or a Presbyterian."

"Worse!" Mary shuddered. "He is a Hebrew!" She really ought not to be so alarmed by this, for she had known it for many months, but it was still something so strange to her accustomed view of the world.

To her surprise, Elinor's face lit up. "Oh, that is not all bad! Our village doctor at Norland was of that faith. He trained in Scotland, where such is permitted, and he was the best doctor we had. He was ever so clever; he was always making up rhymes and charades to amuse the children. Is Mr. Lyons good at making up rhymes?"

"I... that is... I do not know! He has never spoken of it. But his father was a doctor, near Glasgow. Alexander knows as much of medicine as most of the medical men I know, although he read law at university. He has saved more than one life with his knowledge."

"He has? How remarkable! What a fine friend you have."

Such support from Elinor was unexpected. Her new friend was a lady of such sense and prudence, it was almost incredible that she would not insist upon the proper faith in all of her associates. But perhaps that sense allowed her to see past the first rush of emotion and instinct.

"Did Mr. Lyons give any indication of why he left?" The half smile was still on Elinor's face and her eyes flickered to where Alexander sat with Edward and the colonel as she continued.

Mary considered this. "He did not leave so much as not continue forward. I do believe he hoped for a continuation of our friendship, or whatever it is we have."

"Did he write to you?"

This was shocking. "No! Of course not! We are not engaged. It would not be proper. But he did send his warmest regards through my sister, who is married to a great friend of his. But... well, I did not respond."

"You have not sent him a word since you last saw him? Nothing since October last?"

Mary swallowed in shame. "No. I expected him to come to speak with my Papa. And then it was Christmas, and then I was invited to spend some months with my aunt and uncle here in Town, and then..." She trailed off.

"Had he any notion that you have been in London since March?"

Mary hung her head. "No. None. Or, none from me." She looked up at her friend in embarrassment. "Oh, I have done him wrong, have I not?"

Elinor patted her hand. "It is not, perchance, the finest way one should treat those one cares about. But I believe the man still likes you a great deal. Perhaps you might rebuild your friendship."

Across the room, Alexander looked to be concluding his conversation with Edward Ferrars. He tucked his pencil behind an ear and was closing his notebook. Perhaps she might take a moment to speak with him and request that he call at the

Gardiners, so they might speak. She really did miss his sharp mind and his deep conversation. He was not a man to engage in lengthy discussions about nothing. There was always meat on the bones of what he said, and she had learned to appreciate that greatly.

But as she sought an excuse to make such a move, there came a tap at the door and the housekeeper appeared with a man in her shadow.

Having achieved Mrs. Jennings' attention, the housekeeper announced, "Mr. John Willoughby."

If Lucy's appearance so many weeks before had occasioned a sudden shift in mood, how much more so did Mr. Willoughby's.

Marianne, where she sat on her sofa reading, dropped her book and went completely white. Mary feared for the young woman's health, and she noticed the alarmed look in Alexander's eye as he saw Marianne's reaction. Colonel Brandon, sitting beside him, flushed a deep red and his face turned dark. If he could have killed with a look, Mr. Willoughby would already be lying dead on the floor.

Elinor too went stiff, with an expression upon her face more full of dislike than Mary had seen even when confronted with Lucy Steele, and Mrs. Jennings' normally welcoming and affable countenance went cold and disapproving. Only Edward Ferrars seemed not to be alarmed at Mr. Willoughby's appearance. He rose to his feet and bowed.

"Forgive my intrusion," the newcomer spoke. He had a well-modulated voice that fit his handsome appearance. There was nothing in his face or civil address that could, to Mary's mind, account for the antipathy she felt in the room. "I heard some distressing news about an acquaintance of mine and upon learning that his brother might be here, I came to offer my condolences."

He was everything charming and spoke so prettily. But did a man pay a call upon another whom he had never met? Perhaps in

London circles these things were done, and he clearly was acquainted with Mrs. Jennings and the Dashwood sisters. Mary sat back to observe. It was, after all, what she did best.

Mrs. Jennings recovered herself at once. From what Mary could see, she was not happy to see this man, but for all of her occasional crassness, she was never rude. "Mr. Willoughby," she extended a hand to be shaken. "It is an honour to have you in my home. I believe you know everybody here save Mr. Ferrars, Mr. Lyons, and Miss Bennet, of course." She introduced the newcomer to Mary, and he said all the proper things with the finest of manners. Then Mrs. Jennings took him over to where Edward and Alexander now stood. The men all shook hands and sat down. Mrs. Jennings did not mention that Alexander was not there as a guest, but as a matter of business.

Willoughby addressed himself to Edward, his voice clear enough in the small room that Mary did not have to strain to hear him. "I did not know your brother well, Mr. Ferrars, but I was often, of late, thrown in his way, or rather, he in mine. We had begun to engage in a friendship, and I mourn the man I wish I had known better. I felt the need to meet you, his closest relation."

Edward mumbled something that Mary could not hear, and Mr. Willoughby replied in a stronger voice.

"Oh no, not that at all. It turned out we were members at the same club—he only recently joined, and I, too, am newly listed on its rolls. Being of a similar age and of similar tastes, it was natural that we should find ourselves often in each other's company. Indeed, I was with him on that fateful night. Oh, I shudder to think of it! We parted company at two o'clock, I believe. I called for my carriage to take me home, but your brother insisted upon walking. It was not far, he assured me, and the air was fresh. I have berated myself time and again for not insisting that I drive him home."

Again Edward muttered something in return, and the conversation became quiet enough that Mary could not hear what was said. Alexander looked quite interested in what he was hearing, but Mary noticed he did not bring out his ubiquitous notepad and pencil.

Beside her, Elinor all but hissed. "I cannot believe he dared to appear here! Not after what he has done. Surely, he must have known that we were still in Town. It is quite imprudent of me to say so, but I am unimpressed by his performance."

"Whatever can you mean?"

"He is the cause of poor Marianne's broken heart. I have not wanted to talk of it before, it not being my tale to tell, but everybody knows it. It will be a familiar tale, I am afraid." She dropped her voice so Mary alone could hear her. "When we arrived at Barton Cottage, Mr. Willoughby quickly became a regular visitor. He is very similar in many ways to Marianne, and when they met, they formed an immediate attachment. He displays the heightened emotions and affectations that so please her, and when he rescued her from a fall, her heart was lost."

Elinor glanced around to ensure she was not being overheard. Satisfied, she went on.

"Like you with Mr. Lyons, Marianne believed herself all but engaged to him, such were his attentions. The entire neighbourhood believed the engagement to be a real thing. But unlike your situation, where it seems there is still affection on both sides and where your beau did not so much abandon you as not press his suit, for Marianne it was final.

"Willoughby departed the neighbourhood with hardly a word and when next we saw him, he was engaged to another woman! The very next day he wrote Marianne a most horrid letter explaining that he had never really cared for her, that it was all a mere dalliance and that his affections were already engaged elsewhere. It quite broke her heart. She has not recovered, despite all our best efforts."

Enlightenment opened Mary's eyes. So this was the cause for Marianne's constant low spirits and frequent headaches. The poor girl, who felt so strongly, had been all but destroyed by a callous lover. Perhaps, Mary considered, her own anger at Alexander was a better response. She, too, felt abandoned, but she would not let a man reduce her to such abject misery. She pursed her lips and let out a soft sigh.

Elinor's stoic eyes glistened with restrained tears. "And now that he is married, how can my poor sister sit there and look at him and not feel her heart rent in two as if for the first time?"

If Willoughby was ill advised to come by Mrs. Jennings' house to visit Edward, he was even more so in what he did next, for he moved across the room and took the empty seat next to Marianne's. She sat there as still and pale as a corpse as he spoke to her in tones Mary could not hear. His manner was gentle and caring, almost as if he were trying to console the girl.

This was most perplexing; it certainly did not fit with the picture Elinor had just now painted, of a man who so callously toyed with a young girl's heart and then tossed her away like yesterday's cheese rinds. Could he wish to re-engage her affections, as Robert had flattered Kitty for his own benefit? No, surely not! He was a married man. It must be kindness and nothing else that motivated him. Willoughby did not stay much longer, and Marianne said hardly a word to him, but when he departed with compliments to all, Mary saw her eyes follow him out of the room.

Poor Marianne, it seemed, was still in love with John Willoughby, and had no hopes at all.

It was now the middle of the afternoon and Mary was expected back at her aunt and uncle's house for dinner. She must find a way to speak quickly with Alexander. It would not be amiss to approach him and ask after his mother and sisters, would it? Mary had never met those ladies, but she had heard enough about them to make her interest sincere.

She mentioned something of this to Elinor and waited until Alexander was no longer intently busy, but before she could rise to speak to him, the door opened once again. How busy this house was! There were more people coming and going than at the largest coaching inns in Town.

This time the housekeeper looked quite flustered and not at all happy about the person she must announce. "Mrs. Jennings..." she whispered, hoping to attract her mistress' attention. This was most unusual in a house as well-run as Mrs. Jennings'. Whatever could cause the housekeeper to interrupt a gathering? It must be dire indeed. Mrs. Jennings excused herself and went to confer with her housekeeper. Mary saw her face fall.

"Mr. Ferrars," Mrs. Jennings called to her guest, her voice tight. "There is a... a man here to speak to you. You might wish to see him privately."

From where she sat, Mary saw only the shadow of a man beyond the open door. Whether he was large or small, Mary could not discern. He waited patiently for Mrs. Jennings to lift herself from her chair and cross the room. As he spoke to her, the lady's face grew pale and the expression alarmed. She turned about and stared into the room, concern etched on her visage.

Alexander must have noticed this as well, for he rose and crossed the floor to where she stood. He also listened for a moment and then hurried back to whisper to Edward before returning to the door. He murmured something to the person beyond it, and then Mary heard him say, "I shall be joining Mr. Ferrars in your discussion as his lawyer." The shadow behind the door seemed to debate with himself briefly before nodding his head.

As the two men prepared to leave for this interview, Alexander turned to look at Mary. Their eyes met, and Mary saw as many questions in his as there must be in her own. She walked towards him, one hand turned palm-up in supplication. Whether he saw it or not, he took that last step towards her, letting him speak in a voice low enough that only she could hear. "Please, I wish to talk. May I call on you? Where?"

"I am staying with my aunt and uncle." There was no time for more, for he was needed elsewhere, but she hoped it was enough.

He held her gaze with his for just a moment more before he bowed and strode out the door after the shadow and Edward Ferrars.

Chapter Five

The First Conference

The rap at the door came as the family were finishing their dinner. It was early by town hours, but the children must eat at a reasonable time. Mary heard the door open and the quiet tones of the maid, presumably requesting the visitor to wait in the front salon. Her aunt and uncle raised their eyebrows at each other, but concluded the meal as if nothing were amiss.

"Up you go." Mary's aunt kissed each of her children in turn. "Be sure to complete all your schoolwork and then you may read or ask Miss Boyd to take you to the square. I shall be up later." The four young Gardiners responded in kind, hugging their parents before disappearing up the back stairs. This was an affectionate family, elegant and sensible. The oldest child, a girl of eleven, was a great reader already and she and Mary had spent a great many hours discussing all the books neither of them ought to have read.

When the children were gone, Mr. Gardiner stepped out of the dining room for a moment. "The visitor is for you, Mary. A young man whom I have seen before but not met, but who says he knows you. He calls himself Alexander Lyons. A Scot, by his hair and his speech. Are you willing to speak to him?"

Mary could not keep the smile from touching her lips. "Yes, I will see him."

"And I shall sit in the corner," her aunt supplied. "I will not have you returned to my sister with your reputation blemished."

Mary hid a laugh. If only her aunt knew how many times Mary and Alexander had conferred completely in private, and for how long! Mary had previously mentioned her association with Alexander, for the tale of how Lizzy was absolved of a charge of murder was famous in the family now, but the details, well, those she preferred to keep private.

"By all means, Aunt. Please, allow me to introduce Mr. Lyons to you."

The introductions were performed and Mary and Alexander made themselves comfortable before the bright window in the back parlour. Mary's aunt sat in a chair on the other side of the room, working at some sewing. Her uncle was in his study, the next room over, with both doors open. Mama would be pleased at the prodigious care her brother and sister took of Mary's reputation.

"Mary," Alexander began, his voice low enough that his words would not reach unintended ears. The crease on his brow betrayed his unease. "How long have you been in London? Why did you not tell me you were here? I have done something to displease you, but I cannot think what. I thought we were better friends than this. Please, can we talk?"

Mary's face grew warm. Her earlier feelings of injury had been tempered by Elinor's words, and embarrassment blossomed where indignation had once been. She opened her mouth, unsure of what to say, but the sight of her aunt by the door stopped her attempts.

"Later. When we are alone."

Alexander's eyes flickered to their chaperone, and he nodded. "Yes. Of course." The words were all but a whisper. Then, in a somewhat stronger voice, he added, "I have something else I wish to confer about."

Mary let out a rush of breath. "Something about Edward Ferrars?"

"Just so." The copper head bounced in a short nod. "How came you to be associated with him?"

"I am friends with Elinor Dashwood; I met Mr. Ferrars later." She recounted the story of their meeting and of the people she had encountered in Mrs. Jennings' parlour. "But what of you? What brought you to her house?"

"There has been a contestation of Mr. Robert Ferrars' will. Colonel Brandon asked me to investigate the nature and truth of the claims on Edward's behalf. But I am here for a slightly different reason. The man who upset the gathering earlier today was from the Runners. He came to take Edward Ferrars into custody on suspicion of the murder of his brother."

Mary's eyes grew wide. "What? That cannot be!"

Across the room, Aunt Gardiner looked up from her sewing. Mary apologised and tried to keep her voice low. "I can hardly credit Edward with such a vile deed. Why, he is so unassuming, I do not believe he was even so terribly distressed by the loss of his inheritance. You do know about that, I assume."

Alexander nodded. "Colonel Brandon apprised me of much of the story. There will, I am certain, still be a great deal to learn."

"Then what is the Runners' cause for their accusation?"

Across the low table from her, Alexander pinched his lips. Mary felt her eyes drawn to them, those lips that she had kissed. She had enjoyed that kiss very much, no matter that she should have been shocked by it instead. Shocked by her own brazen actions. What would it be like to kiss him now? Would he ever kiss her again?

He seemed to notice the direction of her gaze, and his face softened. In that instant, she brought her eyes back up to meet his own. They were conferring now on a serious concern! This was no time to lapse into reverie and musing, no matter how much his eyes drew her into their depths.

"Yes, Edward Ferrars," the investigator stated. Only a moment had lapsed, but it might have been an hour, and Mary had to force her attention back to the case at hand. "At first, the Runner said, they had no suspicion of Robert's death being anything other than a robbery ending in tragedy. But Atkins—the man who came to Mrs. Jennings this afternoon—said he had heard some rumblings that begged further investigation, and he did not like what he found. It seems that Edward was left with almost nothing upon being disinherited. He has two thousand pounds of his own and not a penny more. There are no gifts, no other sources of income, and he has no career. Without the generosity of friends, he cannot even continue his studies at Oxford, which seems to have been his one joy in life, and his path to a place in the clergy, which is his professed desire."

"Yes, perhaps, but it hardly seems an incentive to murder. For one of Edward's status, it is a great loss to be sure, but he will not want for the necessities. A great many men live on nothing. A gentleman, after all, can do much better on nothing than a working man. He can visit first this friend for a month or two, and then that one, until a whole year has gone by without the need for him to part with a penny."

"And so he seems to have done in his younger days after finishing school. But nonetheless, a fortune of a thousand a year is nothing inconsiderable, especially when you believed it ought always to have been yours."

Mary peered at him. "This can hardly be all the proof they have."

"No, indeed not. It transpires that Robert Ferrars had, in the three months since he inherited his fortune and his estate, amassed a great deal of debts. At least one of the men to whom he owed money—the owner of a gaming house, it turns out—had been threatening Edward for repayment, believing that he had influence over his brother, or possibly believing that Edward was the wealthy man, being the older of the two."

"What does this man say upon questioning?"

"I paid a quick visit to his establishment after leaving Mrs. Jennings' home. The gaming house is not far away, just near Hyde Park. He was not pleased to speak with me, but he did grant me some time. He assured me that he knew full well that it was Robert who owed the debt, not Edward, and he denied all attempts to intimidate Edward. Still, it seems somebody had been bothering Edward, and he might have decided it better to rid himself of his brother for his own peace of mind."

"You work quickly."

Alexander bobbed his head. "I must. But there is more. A footman out late claimed to have been near the street when Robert was attacked. Atkins believes this servant was dallying with his sweetheart in an alleyway. Whatever his cause for being there, he says he heard a to-do which caught his attention. The noise did not last long, however, and when he stepped out into the street, he saw nothing. But he did report seeing a gentleman leaving the area at great speed."

"What made him believe the other man a gentleman? All men look the same in the dark."

Alexander gave her a strange look, but continued in a steady voice.

"Atkins is a good investigator. He asked that question, and was told that the man wore the clothes of a gentleman, by the shape he made in the patches of light, and had on expensive boots. The footman knew the sounds of solid boots as compared to those of rougher wear for working men."

Mary turned up her nose. "You know as well as I that a prosperous businessman can and does dress as well as a gentleman. My uncle, for example, turns a fine image, and you, too, do not embarrass yourself by your dress."

"Thank you, Mary. And you are correct. Still, this particular gentleman happened to drop something which gave Atkins the notion of who he was, namely a handkerchief embroidered with the monogram EF."

Once more, Mary sniffed. "And he is the only man in London with those initials, of course."

"There is, further, the rift between the brothers on Miss Steele's account. How much have you heard of that matter?"

"Only that Lucy, who was engaged to Edward, surprised everybody by marrying Robert instead, or so she says, and with no notice or announcement. And that she is claiming Robert's wealth as his wife." She stopped for a moment as the import of her words filtered through her unhappy thoughts. "Oh. I see... this establishes a great motive of jealousy." She frowned and thought further on this. Alexander pursed his lips again and this time, Mary did not look at them.

"There was one more piece of evidence pointing against our friend," Alexander said after a moment. "The staff at the Ferrars house were forthcoming about a grand argument between the brothers the night that Robert died. Nobody heard the entirety of the fight, for the library doors were heavy and shut tight, but the butler and several maids all insist that at the end of it, Edward stormed out of the room and shouted, 'I will not and cannot tolerate this. You have brought shame on the family, and there will be a reckoning.'"

"You remembered those words?" Mary was the one who had perfect recall, not Alexander.

"Ah, but remember, I have my ways!" He reached into his pocket and withdrew his notebook. He turned to the correct page, where Mary could see the words inscribed with his pencil.

"With the handkerchief, the betrayal, and the fight, Atkins felt he had good cause to arrest Edward." Alexander let out a rush of breath.

"These are damning events when taken together, are they not?" Mary sighed. She had known almost none of this and it did not cast Edward as an innocent man. "Where is he now? Elinor will be most distressed! She is very fond of him."

Now Alexander smiled. "My legal training has been to some advantage. Whilst it is most rare for a judge to grant bail for a felony, there are some precedents. I told Mr. Atkins about the Habeas Corpus act of 1689, and how when there is the surety of property, a gentleman is from time to time released on a bond. I also suggested that Colonel Brandon would pledge for Mr. Ferrars' appearance in court should matters come to a trial. And," he looked sheepish and pushed a hand through his unruly red hair, "I invoked the name of the Earl of Matlock."

"Richard Fitzwilliam's father?"

"And Darcy's uncle. The very same. I hope I am not required to act upon that tenuous connection. Still, I have sent a note to Colonel Fitzwilliam begging his, and his father's, forgiveness. But all to good effect: Edward Ferrars is not yet under arrest. He must remain in London, or give ample notice of his intentions to travel and full details of his destination, and he must stay with a reputable personage such as Colonel Brandon himself. Brandon's rooms are surely superior to those Edward now calls home. Atkins, in the meantime, will continue his investigations, as shall I. When I presented my credentials as a lawyer as well as an investigator, he was generous enough to agree to my participation."

"I am pleased to hear this." Mary was most relieved indeed. Elinor would be devastated to learn of this crushing blow, and anything that might alleviate her distress was welcome. Mary had no notion whether her friend still thought of a future as Mrs. Ferrars, but that she cared deeply for the man was unquestioned. Both Dashwood daughters, it seemed, had given their hearts to unsuitable men. As, Mary considered with an inward grimace, had she herself. This handsome investigator was in all ways inappropriate for her, but he was the only man she could ever imagine herself wanting.

"I appreciate you coming here to tell me this, Alexander, but surely you have another purpose for your visit. This all could have waited till the morning or been sent in a message through my uncle."

"Aye, so it could." Alexander's mild brown eyes bored into Mary's own dark ones, teasing emotions that were wholly out of place in a murder investigation. "You are clever, Mary, with a first-rate mind. You hear things others do not, and you understand what you hear. I, too, do not believe Mr. Ferrars capable of murdering his brother, but I do not believe I can get all the information I need myself. Miss Steele—or Mrs. Ferrars should her claims be true—will tell me only part of what I need to know. She is the one claiming Robert's fortune, after all, and knows that I am engaged to disprove her claims. She has more to gain by refusing my questions or by misleading me than by telling the truth."

"But I, on the other hand, might be able to learn something you cannot."

"Aye, you're my smart one, you are. Will you help me? You are already in Miss Dashwood's confidence; could you find a way to a similar intimacy with Lucy Steele?"

How she had missed this! She had not even known that she missed it, but this request made her feel ten feet tall, with wings on her feet. These investigations, begun so much by necessity, and then by happenstance, gave her life purpose. She had heard Alexander grumble about the useless upper class, which notion gnawed at her. She was of that class, after all. Her father was a gentleman who derived his income from the rents and produce of his land. It was how things were and had always been.

How dare Alexander, that misplaced Scot, take grievance with the very foundation of English society? Did the man not know his place? His words, when he dared voice them, were an insult to her and to her family.

And yet a small part of her suspected there was truth in his words. What value was the upper class? A good landlord could do well by his tenants. With fertile land and competent management, the fields could prosper and local industry flourish, and all could benefit. But she also knew that not all landlords were good and industrious leaders, and that a trained steward from the middle classes could do as well, if not better, than a gentleman or nobleman. Her own father, she confessed to herself, was no more than a middling and indolent manager of his land. He would not let his tenants starve, nor would he allow their homes to collapse about their ears, but he was satisfied with the adequate. There would be no great improvements on Longbourn's estate whilst he was the master.

And what of her and her sisters? They were skilled at nothing, were trained at no profession. Even the sons of the gentry went to university, where they might study for law or for the church, or purchase a military commission and serve their country. But a gentlewoman? What use were her accomplishments? Of what real significance were being able to paint a table or speak Italian in a world where women did not travel to Italy?

But by helping Alexander in his inquiries, Mary finally felt she had value. Her abilities were useful. She could help discover the truth and save people's lives! Having met Edward Ferrars, she could hardly believe him to have killed his brother; this time the life she saved might be his. What better way to employ the natural gifts that God had given her?

The small smile that had crept upon her when Alexander arrived now widened to a grand beam. "I shall do my best! On that, sir, you can depend!"

Chapter Six

Talking to Lucy

It was early in the morning when Alexander appeared at Lucy Steele's door. She and her sister Nancy stayed in London with a cousin in Holborn, no more than a mile from his own offices. It was not a fashionable part of town, but neither was it disreputable. Still, should she succeed in claiming Robert's estate, Lucy would move upwards in the world.

Interesting! Like Edward, she had elected not to lay claim to the Ferrars' house on Park Street, both seeming to feel that it was not yet theirs to possess. And thus, Lucy still resided with her cousins. Where, if she had been married in fact to young Ferrars, had the two of them lived? Or had they maintained a fiction of being unattached? Certainly, this marriage, should it be real, had been an utter surprise to everybody. Had Lucy never departed the walls of her cousins' home?

The cousins, whom Alexander learned were called Richardson, had only a maid to answer his rap on the door. She did not seem pleased to have a caller at such an early hour and only Alexander's offer—or threat—to wait in the front hall until Miss Steele was available to talk with him convinced the maid to see if the lady might have a moment.

He waited for fifteen minutes before Lucy appeared at the top of the stairs, Nancy in her wake. This was not a large residence; there were two main rooms on the ground floor and he imagined two or three upstairs, with more in the second storey where the nursery might have been. In his mind, he contrasted the place with the Gardiners' residence near Cheapside. That was a most elegant house of fine proportions that could accommodate one or more visiting cousins with ease. The Richardsons, on the other hand, would have been most aware of two permanent guests. In his mind, Alexander congratulated them on opening their home to the two Steele sisters.

Lucy conducted Alexander to the room at the back of the house. Through an open door he could see a small dining room, and there beyond an ell in the space, the stairs down to the kitchens. The room was sunny and welcoming, if outdated in its decoration. Lucy did not call for tea. This was very much a matter of business. Nancy sat in the corner by the door, an unexpected chaperone. This was an interesting choice for a married matron (or was she?) who claimed to be expecting her late husband's child. Speaking alone with a man of business could hardly damage her reputation now. A chaperone seemed unnecessary.

Alexander offered his card, excused his early arrival once more, and set to his task.

"You must know why I am here."

Miss Steele looked at him.

"Robert Ferrars left a will naming his brother Edward as heir to his estate and personal fortune, and you have contested that. You cannot imagine such a claim would go uninvestigated."

"But I am... I was his wife. We were married. What was his is now mine." Her stare dared him to naysay her. In the corner, Nancy nodded her silent agreement.

"You must surely recognise our concerns. If you were married, why did you not tell of it before Mr. Ferrars died? It seems most unusual."

A glint appeared in Lucy's eye. Was it a tear? Or something else? The girl was clearly a skilled actress.

"We had our reasons."

"What reasons might these be? You carried on toward Mr. Edward Ferrars as if nothing had changed, as if you were still engaged to him, this being the very reason for his disinheritance. Had you been honest, he might have regained his mother's favour."

She stared at him. "As I said, we had our reasons."

"Come now, Miss Steele. Answers like these will not convince any judge of the veracity of your claims. There were no banns called here in London, neither at your family's church, nor at the one Mr. Ferrars frequented. There are no marriage lines. How can you expect anybody to believe you? There is no evidence at all that this marriage took place."

Lucy's pretty features took on a determined look and her eyes narrowed. "If you must have it, we eloped. It was immediately after his mother's death. Robert came to talk to me, to convince me to release Edward from his promise to me, and as we spoke, we fell in love."

Alexander's pencil hovered above his notebook. A question burned in his mind, which he proceeded to ask.

"Why did Robert wish for you to break with Edward? I have heard that he was disinherited because of your engagement, but with his mother already deceased, there was no remedy for that."

Lucy glared at him. "I cannot think what you mean, sir."

Alexander gazed at her from beneath lowered eyelids until she continued. "Robert was not particularly close to his brother, but he did care for him. He believed that Edward's affections for me had... had faded over time, but that he was too honourable to suggest we part ways. It was only with Edward's best interests in mind."

"Indeed?"

"So it was, too!" Nancy exclaimed from her chair near the door. "That's exactly what he said when he came to talk to you those three months ago. He said he had seen you about, and knew that you wouldn't be happy with Edward. He was fresh in mourning then, but he was sweet to think of another so unknown to him."

Lucy scowled at her sister for a moment, but then turned back to Alexander with a false smile.

"Indeed, it was very caring of him. And, as I have mentioned, as he tried to convince me to release his brother, we found we had a great deal to talk about, and we fell in love in an instant."

"In an instant? How many of these meetings did you have?"

"Two," came Nancy's reply from the doorway.

"Two! That is... that is a very sudden change of heart. Then when, exactly, did you marry, and where?"

She looked like a petulant schoolgirl. Alexander was reminded of his sisters when they were younger, but Lucy's glower held an edge of hardness that his sisters never showed. "Very well. It was six days after Mrs. Ferrars died, three days after Robert and Edward arrived back in London. We had talked for the two days prior, and on the third we left to marry. We eloped. There. I said it. We ran off to Scotland and married there. That is why there is no record of our marriage in London. It is easy to marry in Scotland.

You need no banns or licence. It is a simple thing to arrange, and in almost no time, it is done." She punctuated her statement with a sharp dip of her chin.

"This tale hardly sounds credible. Please, I need more."

She inflicted him with another scowl. "Robert left London saying he had business to attend to at the family estate. I told my cousins and sister that I was going to stay in the country with a friend for a week. The friend was Robert's upstairs maid who can talk like a lady. That is how we did it."

"And all the while, when you returned, you pretended that nothing was changed. You continued to speak to Edward as you had when you were engaged and allowed him to believe you still intended to marry him. You allowed everyone of your acquaintance to believe you were still engaged to Edward. I cannot imagine why."

Now, at last, Lucy began to look sheepish.

"It was Robert's fault. Or rather, his idea. He thought it would be looked at amiss if he were known to have married so soon after his loss. He wanted to wait a full year for appropriate mourning to be observed. Then we were to pretend to have a proper English wedding, and nobody would be the wiser."

"And yet he did not do that."

"No. We wished to marry, and so we did. That is all I have to say."

"Why, then, continue with the pretence of your engagement to Edward?"

"It gave us the excuse to see each other," she returned in a childish voice. "Otherwise, we had little reason to meet. Often, after a visit to Mrs. Jennings' house or some other parlour, he would offer to walk me home or such, and we would... we would spend some time together. In private." She clamped her mouth shut with these words.

"And I went home by myself," Nancy supplied. "No one bothered to ask why I was alone."

Alexander now returned to his initial series of questions and faced Lucy once more. "I will need to know where you married: the name of the town, the places you stayed, the people who were your witnesses."

Lucy cocked her head. Alexander could imagine her thinking up how to arrange this.

"If I cannot locate any witnesses, I will have to testify that I cannot prove you to be married to Mr. Robert Ferrars. If you still wish to press your contestation of the will, I shall require this information. I can send a messenger off at first light tomorrow to verify what you tell me."

She smiled. She had taken his bait. "Very well. I shall tell you the names. But I cannot promise they will remember us. It was three months ago, and I am certain many people pass through."

"Still, perhaps one may remember you. Was there no register? Even at Gretna Green, the couple often enter their names into the marriage register. Mr. Lang, who performs many of the marriages there, has a book, this I know."

Lucy gave a sad smile. "We did not wed at Gretna. It was our aim, but as we neared, Robert wished to go elsewhere, so he would not be known by anyone we might encounter. There is a small village further along the road." She stared at him. "In my excitement of being wed, I forgot the name."

Alexander met her gaze, but continued his questions with no pause.

"And you did not sign the register, then?"

Lucy shook her head and thought for a moment. "But there was such a document. A certificate of sorts with our names and the names of the witnesses. Robert took it with him when we left. He must have it in his belongings at the family's house. I am certain he would have kept it safe."

If he kept it at all, Alexander thought. Still, he would have to make a thorough examination of the late Robert Ferrars' effects.

"I have one more thing that might be of value!" Lucy's voice brightened, as if she had just now recalled something. "A letter, a letter from Robert. It arrived only recently, just before..." she gave a great and exaggerated sniff, "just before he died. May I?"

She departed the room for a few minutes, leaving Alexander to write his notes in the notebook he always carried with him. He was completing the last line when she returned with a letter. Alexander took it and examined the envelope. The imprint on the seal looked to be genuine; he would have to find Robert's signet ring—if it had not been stolen with his other belongings that fateful night—or his writing implements. Another reason to make an examination of the man's quarters. He drew a quick sketch of the stamp in his notebook and opened the paper to peruse the contents.

It was a very short letter, more of a note.

"Yes, you know about that." Lucy went red. "We were married... it was not improper!"

The note indicated that Robert knew about the unborn babe.

Lucy,
I know that the elopement to Gretna did not meet your expectations. I shall visit with my solicitor soon to make provisions for our child.
Yrs,
RF

It said nothing more.

Alexander read the note again, hoping to find more meaning in these few words. Something had clearly happened between the two, if the letter was to be believed. But why would Robert use such unromantic language? This was hardly a love letter to a new wife, and the mother of one's future bairn. Whatever had occurred to make the elopement unsatisfactory was not explained, nor was it a cause for regret, it seemed. Neither did it imply that Robert wished to make arrangements for Lucy herself, only for the child. What sort of newlywed husband would write such an impersonal letter?

Furthermore, why did he write to her at all? Could he not simply have called upon her or contrived to meet, and spoken to her, as Alexander was doing now? And he mentioned Gretna, although Lucy had said they went elsewhere. Rather than satisfying Alexander to the validity of the marriage, the letter raised more questions, many of which revolved around Robert Ferrars' true relationship with the lady. For it hardly seemed, by his words or actions, that he thought of her as his wife at all.

If this was true, Robert's death was a great loss to Lucy, not just because it deprived her of a husband, but because it also deprived her of any means of proving her status. Sad luck indeed!

As Mary had planned, she and Elinor went to pay a call upon Lucy later that morning. The lady, however, was not accepting visitors.

"I'm sorry, Miss Dashwood and Miss Bennet. Miss Steele is indisposed," the maid informed them. "If you wish to leave a card, I'll make certain she knows of it."

This was disappointing! Mary had a great explanation for her visit in mind and she had hoped to find out some interesting information. But such was not to be. Having the morning now at their disposal, she and Elinor opted for a visit to the bookshop where they had met before returning to Mrs. Jennings' house.

They enjoyed a pleasant morning and an ice cream at the nearby tea house and made their way back home a little after one o'clock. Mrs. Jennings was out visiting, the housekeeper told them, but Miss Marianne was in the front parlour. The two young women went in search of her, only to find her in obvious distress on the sofa. Her eyes were red and she was rocking back and forth with her arms about her knees. A piece of paper lay half crumpled on the table at her side.

"Marianne!" Elinor's concern was clear in her voice. "Whatever is the matter? What has happened, dearest? Is it Mama? Is she well? Margaret?" She mentioned a younger sister still in Devonshire.

Marianne turned her stricken face to her sister. She shook her head, then voiced, "The letter is not from them. It is not from anyone at Barton Park. It is... Oh!" Her head fell into her hands and she began to weep.

"Who is it, then? Has somebody died? Not John, or Fanny, or.. No, not little Harry?"

"Everybody is well, to my knowledge." Marianne choked out the syllables between tears. "It is from him. He wants... but I cannot! I simply cannot! Now that I know what he is." With these words, she grabbed at the crumpled note and ran from the room. Her sobs could be heard through the house until the sound of a door closing indicated she had achieved her bedroom upstairs.

Elinor's shoulders sagged as she gaped at the stairs where Marianne had disappeared. "Whatever can she mean? What can that be about?" Mary had never seen Elinor so concerned. "Please excuse my sister." She addressed herself once more to Mary. "She is, perhaps, too much in thrall to her sensibilities, but I can hardly account for this." Her face was a picture of agony; how greatly she must care for her sister.

"Do not apologise on my account. I have four sisters. When one is troubled, the others must feel it acutely. I recall when Lizzy was accused of killing our cousin. I could not rest until I had done everything in my power and more to absolve her. And poor Miss Marianne is clearly sorely distressed."

Elinor nodded, lines of worry between her eyes. "I must see to her. Perhaps there is something I can do."

"May I join you? Will she talk to me? I have had some success solving other people's troubles in the past. Perhaps now I may be of use."

Elinor nodded again. "We can ask. What she will respond, I cannot say."

The two walked up the stairs and knocked at Marianne's door. A whimper from within might have been permission to enter, which the friends did.

"Marianne, dearest?" Elinor moved closer to where Marianne lay sprawled across her counterpane. She lay on her stomach, her head buried in her arms. "Will you talk to me? Or perhaps to Miss Bennet? She is terribly clever and might be able to help."

"Oh, it's no use!" the pile on the bed wailed. "He will not give up. I know now what he is and what he is capable of. Oh, how deceived I was in him! What fortune I discovered his true nature. But now... He knows where I am! Oh, Elinor, it is too horrible!"

"What is this, Marianne? Who is importuning you?"

But there was no answer from Marianne, only a new series of sobs and wails and pleas to be left alone.

"Let us return to the parlour, then. There is little we can do until she will talk to us." Mary gave Elinor's arm a gentle tug. Elinor cast a last glance at her crying sister and followed Mary out of the room.

"It must be Mr. Willoughby," Elinor said as they crept down the stairs. "I cannot imagine who else it would be. But what I cannot fathom is what he has done. Why will Marianne not talk to us?"

"Talk about what?" A familiar voice sounded from the parlour as they entered the room.

"Colonel Brandon." Elinor dropped a curtsey to his bow, but the slight smile that crept across her face was one of deep friendship.

"Miss Dashwood, Miss Bennet," he greeted the ladies. "What has happened? Am I too late to help?" At Elinor's gesture, he stepped back to his chair and waited for the two friends to sit before doing likewise.

"'Tis Marianne," Elinor told him. "Something happened today. She received a letter that distressed her greatly. She will not tell me what it read, but I can only imagine it is from Mr. Willoughby."

At the mention of that name, Colonel Brandon's face grew dark again and his jaw clenched. Whatever could be the history between those two, Mary wondered.

"What has the man done to her? What new insults has he added?"

"New insults?" Mary could not help but ask the question.

"After he departed Devonshire so hurriedly last autumn, he came to London, where he met and became engaged to Miss Grey," the colonel explained.

"Yes," Elinor added. "Miss Grey and her fifty thousand pounds!"

"Indeed! I see why she is upset by him."

"But there is more. The day after she discovered his treachery, he came to the house to tell her that he never cared, that it was a mere dalliance, and he returned two notes to her. She wept for days."

"And you believe he has sent a letter with more harsh words?"

Elinor agreed.

"But," Mary spoke slowly, "she seemed not so angry or hurt as worried. Terrified, even. She spoke of it being horrible. She said he will not give up. What can that mean, I wonder? Is he threatening her?"

The colonel's frown deepened and he rested his chin on steepled hands. "I have heard rumours... but I ought not to mention them. It is not my place to speak ill of others."

"Please, Colonel. I shall forgive any lapse of manners. Your words might allow us to help Miss Marianne." Mary sought the firmest voice she could find, attempting to sound like the serious investigator she wished to be, and not another silly girl just out of the schoolroom. It must have worked, for the colonel's eyes softened.

"Very well, Miss Bennet. Forgive me. I have heard rumours that Mr. Willoughby's marriage is not a happy one. It is no secret that he wed Miss Grey only for her fortune, but they are not suited and she holds sway over him for, by the nature of her inheritance, contrived in what way I cannot know, she retains control over the disposal of her wealth. It was a clever bit of work, that inheritance. I have never heard of the like. A trust, perhaps? It matters little. Regardless, the rumours suggest he seeks his entertainment—and his pleasure—elsewhere. Could he be attempting to regain your sister's favours?"

Elinor's face went white. "No! He could not! I cannot believe it!"

"Until we can convince her to speak, we cannot know. Perhaps, Elinor," Mary suggested, "you might prevail upon her to confess to you. Then, once we know the truth, we might help."

"Yes, yes, so I see. I shall do what I can."

But her face, when Mary departed a short time later, was almost as etched with distress as was Marianne's.

Chapter Seven

The Ferrars' Residence

After his interview with Lucy Steele, Alexander paid a call on the Bow Street Runner, Mr. Atkins. It was just a short walk from the Richardson's' house to the organisation's buildings, and mere steps from the site of his own offices and rooms, and he knew the way well. To his pleasure, Atkins was available to meet with him.

The Runner heard Alexander's request and agreed. He, too, had news he wished to discuss with the investigator. He talked as they made their way across London to the Ferrars' house on Park Street.

"I have not been settled with this killing," the Runner confided. "The witnesses' reports, the evidence at the scene, and Mr. Edward Ferrars' disinheritance all seem to point so neatly to him as the ultimate culprit. But they point too neatly. It is rare that a killer leaves his calling card at the scene. And we have discovered other evidence that the murder and robbery itself were perpetrated by two men known to us from Seven Dials. Why would Edward Ferrars have been present if he had hired some cutthroats to do his work for him? A far better plan would be for him to have spent the night playing cards in the company of dozens at some popular venue."

Alexander's eyebrows shot up. "What ho? This is news. You have discovered the culprits who did the deed? Tell me more." Had they not been on foot, Alexander would have taken out his notebook to record this information. He would have to remember it until they had arrived.

"We set some men asking questions up and down the streets and the alleyway where he was found. Servants as well as the toffs. We found a young maid, not more than seventeen or eighteen, I'd say, who was awake due to a severe stomach cramp. The servants' quarters at the house open into that alley, and she witnessed the whole event. Naturally, she was too terrified to call out to stop them, or even to speak of it until we promised her name would never be known. Quite shaken she was, could hardly even say what she had seen. It was full dark when it happened, being near on a new moon, but there was enough reflected from the gas lamps on the close-by road for her to see the size of the men."

"Distinctive enough for identification?"

Atkins grunted. "Aye. Enough so. There were two of them. They must have accosted Ferrars on the main street, for this girl only heard them as they dragged the blighter into the alley. She watched them beat him senseless and strip him bare."

"A horrid thing to behold, poor creature!" Alexander shuddered to think of his sisters witnessing such brutality. No wonder the girl had uttered not a sound.

"Indeed. But when we got her to talk, her description was good and sounded familiar to a few of us chaps. They were the terrors of St. Giles, and we knew them well. We went to inquire, and it turns out these two vanished the night after the death. One fellow's sister said he was flush with blunt the two or three days ahead. Must have been paid for his efforts, and then told he could keep what he found on Ferrars' body. We are fairly confident they're our men."

"That was good work!"

"'Twas luck as much as hard work, but we take what we find." They walked a few paces in silence. The heat of the day was growing, and dark clouds were starting to form at the horizon. It would be a close afternoon with storms in the evening, if Alexander's experience with London weather held true. Then Atkins added, "We learned something else, something that does not help our lad Edward."

"No?"

"Turns out he was known in St. Giles as well. Often seen in the area. Seems he worked with a charity for the poor that ministered to the worst-off in the stews. Came with the parson and a package of ladies and gents distributing alms and morals on the regular. He knew these two men. I have a score of witnesses who will attest to that."

"Alas for Edward! And so, all the evidence points to him."

"But I still do not like it," Atkins shook his head. "It is too neat. It is too clear. And yet he is all I have."

"Then let us see what we can discover in Robert's rooms. Perhaps something there will illuminate some of the shadows."

The house on Park Street was closed up. After Robert's death, Edward had elected not to move in—he felt it improper, he had said—and then, within days, he had been compelled to stay with Colonel Brandon. Likewise, Lucy had chosen to remain at the Richardsons. Had she not, Atkins suggested she would be asked to remove herself there regardless, until the matter was cleared. Until such time as the estate was settled, therefore, the staff had been sent on their holidays and the doors locked. But Atkins had a key from Edward, and Alexander had ways of entry that did not rely on such implements.

They let themselves in and set about exploring the premises. It was a house typical of the area: fine and elegant enough, but not on one of the most fashionable of the streets. It was where one of some wealth lived when wishing to be amongst one's betters, but not quite able to achieve that stratum. The entrance hall led into several rooms for entertaining, with stairs leading up to the first storey, and a second set at the back leading down. On the first storey were a drawing room with a pianoforte and some elegant-looking furniture and two or three other rooms for less formal entertaining or for the family's private use. A quick examination of this space revealed nothing of interest. This was no surprise; Robert would hardly keep any personal or private papers in such communal space, nor had he moved any of his own papers into the small and dark study. That room seemed to have been unused for a great deal of time. Any papers of interest must, therefore, be elsewhere.

The bedrooms were on the floor above. Here Alexander found a large suite decorated in such a manner that it must have been Mrs. Ferrars' rooms. He observed that in the months since her death, these rooms had not been changed, for the colours and fashions were of a decade or more past. This, Alexander knew from his own sisters, who were always quick to inform him of the latest fashions for clothing and decorating. There seemed to have been no effort undertaken to update the rooms for a new Mrs. Ferrars, namely, Lucy. This musing, he scratched down in his notebook, and then tucked his pencil behind one ear, where he could reach it when next he had need of it.

There were three other rooms on the floor, including one that looked impersonal enough to be a guest room, one that looked, by the personal items on some shelves but the empty wardrobe, to be an abandoned family member's room—this must be Edward's—and one that looked to be recently inhabited. Robert's. When he had planned to redo the main suite to make it his own, Alexander could not guess. Presuming his marriage to Lucy was real, it seemed unusual that he had made no attempt to move into the main suite in anticipation of her joining him. As the new master of the house, even without the expectation of a mistress, such a move would occasion no surprise on the part of the staff. But such musings were mere fantasy. There was work to be done at hand.

"Shall we?" Alexander held the door open. Atkins strode in, drew open the heavy draperies and flung the window wide. Despite the warmth of the day, Alexander also lit a lamp to better examine the space. "I shall start with the desk; perhaps you would like the closet or the shelves."

The hunt began. Both men settled into their task with a particular focus, commenting here and there on something that might be of interest. They worked thus for some time when Atkins let out an "oh ho!"

"What have you there?" Alexander straightened up from the desk and stretched to relieve the stiffness in his back. He was only eight-and-twenty: far too young for such complaints! He stretched again and let out a small groan of relief when something in his neck clicked.

"A diary," Atkins replied, holding the small booklet high for Alexander to see. "Not a great one. It seems to have been started only on the seventh of March last."

"Three months ago?"

"So it seems."

"Right when Lucy and Edward's engagement was made known and Edward was sent from the house. Is it Robert's for certain?"

"So it says in the front. Let me read it." Atkins brought the slim volume to the desk closer to the window and scanned the entries.

"Hmmm... He recounts the day. Mrs. Ferrars had taken a liking to Lucy, it seems, as much to slight Miss Elinor Dashwood to whom she suspected Edward had taken a fancy. Seems she invited the girl to this very house. Here, let me read."

Mother expects Edward to marry very well and only Miss Morton will do, being the daughter of some lord or another. What a bore! Edward shall do very well with Mother's fortune; why should he not marry where he wishes? I am the one who must choose my bride for her fortune.

"He goes on in this vein for a while. Then there is this."

Miss Steele was invited to visit at Park Street, and perhaps sensing Mother's favour, confessed to something which was a great shock to us all: that rather than Edward being somehow attached to Miss Dashwood, he has been for these past four years engaged to Miss Steele. I have never seen Mama in such a wild fury! It was quite a display to watch. Within moments Miss Steele was sent out with a flea in her ear and warned never to return, and Edward was all but dragged in to be thoroughly castigated by our martinet of a mother. I sat in my corner listening to the whole display.

When Edward refused for the tenth time to end his engagement and marry Miss Morton as Mother insisted, she informed him in as cold a voice as ever I have heard that she would forthwith remove all his hopes from him and deny him his share in Father's fortune, it being hers to bestow. And—to my surprise and delight—she would settle it all upon me!

"Did she now?" Atkins pursed his lips. "But this we already knew. Still, this corroboration is interesting. Here is more."

Edward seemed less bothered by this than either of us had expected. He had, until now, been a gentleman of leisure, which he called useless idleness. Now he must find a career and toil for his supper. But perhaps he is not as sanguine about his fate as appearances let on, for as he left the room, I distinctly heard him mutter, "I shall have my revenge! She will pay." And three days later she was dead.

"What is this?" Alexander leaned over Atkins' shoulder to reread the entry. "Did Robert suspect his brother of having a hand in Mrs. Ferrars' death? She did pass on most unexpectedly. What else does the diary say? Anything else of Miss Steele?"

The two men scanned the later entries. There were only six or seven of them, as if Robert had decided to start a diary and then quickly grew bored with the endeavour.

"Here is something about Robert attempting to dissuade Lucy from continuing the engagement, and another hinting at a more pleasurable meeting, and then this one, alluding to plans to 'travel north together.' But nothing about an actual marriage."

"Perhaps he could not risk one of the servants discovering it," Atkins suggested.

"Aye, that could be so. Still, one would think a man would make some mention of such a point in his life, especially when the last entry is three days after their return. But he only mentions a new gaming hall he had discovered, there to go with his friend W. And the good Lord knows there are plenty of men in London whose names start with W."

"Sadly," Atkins agreed.

They put the diary aside to be examined further at some later point and brought as evidence, and continued their search. Somewhere there must be the record of the marriage that Lucy had mentioned. If it existed.

Alexander made his notes and returned to his examination of the contents of the desk. Here was something. A set of papers, neatly folded and held together with a string, lay tucked below a stack of clean new writing paper. Somebody wished to keep this safe and hidden from the prying eyes of servants. But Robert had never expected an investigator to be searching through these drawers!

"Find something?" Atkins asked from the other side of the room, where he was back at the shelves.

"I do not know. It is a ledger of sorts, with a column of dates, a column of figures, a column of letters, and a column of spaces or checks. A list of debts, perhaps, paid and unpaid?"

Atkins crossed the room again and glanced at the papers. "Looks that way to me. Some of these figures are quite large. Here, they start accumulating on March 14th, immediately after the brothers returned from burying their mother in Norfolk."

"So our man inherited a fortune, or was set to inherit a fortune, and immediately set about losing it at the gaming tables. Here," Alexander pointed to some figures with a small plus sign before them, "he seems to have made some gains, but most of these look like losses. Fifty pounds here, seventy there, a hundred, and more and more. He owed a lot of people a lot of money. A great deal of money. This amount itself would be enough to kill for. Let us see... NB, FM, JP, JW, GH... and so many others. We might have to spend some time trying to discover who these men are, but it will be no easy task."

"No. Completely fruitless, I should think. Still..."

Alexander sighed. "I have a number of, er, associates in my business. I shall set them to the task of discovering what they can of who frequents the gaming houses and who might be owe or be owed money. Perhaps, then, we can assign names to the initials."

"A good plan." Atkins blew out a puff of air and Alexander returned to his search. This drawer held nothing new, nor the one below it. Then he opened the third drawer down.

"Atkins! Here, what is this?" Alexander unfolded a thin letter, written and signed and folded, but unsealed and unsent. "To his solicitor, Messr William Hollings, ESQ.

> *Sir,*
> *It has come to my attention through means I would prefer not to commit to paper that my brother, Edward Ferrars, was complicit in the untimely death of our mother, Mrs. Henrietta Ferrars, on Wednesday, the sixteenth of March of this year. I would talk to you concerning this matter and how to proceed. Please call upon me at my home.*
> *Robert Ferrars*

"I wonder why this was not sent. It is, after all, three months since these events." Atkins frowned as he reread the letter.

"More than a long time to keep it sitting in his desk, is it not?" There must have been something in Alexander's voice, for Atkins turned his head to look directly at him. "Was there enough fraternal affection left between them that he did not wish to see his brother accused of this crime?"

"Then why write it down at all?" the Runner demanded.

82

Alexander pursed his lips. "It is almost as if he wished for this to be kept for some later time." He paused. "Or to be found."

Atkins thought for a long moment. "Do you believe the insinuation?"

This was an excellent question. Alexander wished he did not have to consider it, for he liked Edward Ferrars and would be most distressed to see the man guilty of murder. Or, rather, two murders. Could a man as meek and unassuming as he really be responsible for the deaths of both his mother and brother? How much evil would have to lurk in a man's heart to commit such a heinous pair of crimes? It scarcely seemed credible. And yet there was too much evidence to discount the notion.

"I wish I knew what to believe," Alexander replied at last. "These things we have found raise more questions than supply answers. I do wish I knew more about Mrs. Ferrars' death."

"As do I." Atkins shook his head. "And yet she died at the estate in Norfolk, far beyond my jurisdiction. I have no authority to travel there, and no authority to act should I do so."

"Perhaps not," Alexander returned. "But I do."

Chapter Eight

Talking to Edward

Colonel Brandon had stayed with Elinor and Mary long enough for a cup of coffee and then, claiming business elsewhere, departed. The afternoon was progressing and soon Mary must take her leave to return to her aunt and uncle. But no sooner had she resolved to depart when there came a knock at the door and Alexander appeared.

"Excuse me," he bowed to the ladies. "Miss Dashwood, Mary." There was a warmth to his voice when he said her name that Mary could not resist. What was it about this infuriating man that drew her so? Like a moth at a flame, she had hovered about him and been singed, but still could not turn away. Even now, the urge to run to him and touch his bare skin was almost too strong to ignore. She wished for nothing more than to enfold him in her arms and beg for another kiss to make the world fade away to nothing. Oh, if her thoughts were words, how shamed she would be! Her face was growing warm merely from thinking of it.

Oh! How horrified she would be if Elinor and Alexander were privy to her scandalous imaginings. But her musings, she assured herself, were her own, even if her flushed face betrayed something of their matter.

If Alexander noticed her red cheeks, he mentioned not a word, and merely said, "I had hoped to find Mr. Ferrars. I have just come from Colonel Brandon's home where he is residing and the maid informed me he is not in. I wondered if he is not receiving visitors, or if he had stopped here to visit, as I know he does often."

Mary took a calming breath and was thankful when Elinor replied. "I am sorry, Mr. Lyons. We have not had the pleasure of his company today. Colonel Brandon was here—he departed only minutes ago. Did you, perchance, pass him in the street? He was off to his club, I believe. Poor Edward! Perhaps your initial supposition was correct. Shall we accompany you to his rooms? The maid might have a different response to two ladies."

This was deemed a good idea, and the three set out. Soon they were knocking at Colonel Brandon's front door, and after a quick consultation within, were led to a small and very masculine sitting room. The colonel's London abode was not large, being more a comfortable set of rooms in a building of the same, than a house in any real sense of the word. There were three rooms downstairs and, presumably, three up. One must be the colonel's own, another where Edward was staying.

"Pardon me while I see if the gentleman is available." The maid dropped a curtsey and scuttled towards the stairs whilst Mary and her companions sat in silence.

Soon, the door opened and Edward entered. "Forgive me," he greeted them. "I had not known... If I had known earlier... Miss Dashwood." His eyes lingered on her, and hers on him. It was clear to Mary that they were in love, but she doubted Edward would ever have the fortitude to offer for her. Perhaps she ought to convince Elinor to speak first. It was unconventional, of course, but in this case it must be done!

It was another few seconds before Edward seemed to become aware of the others in the room. He blinked and cleared his throat before greeting Mary and Alexander and taking his own seat.

"Mr. Ferrars, I am most pleased to find you in. May we talk further? I have a great many things to ask you." Alexander's Glaswegian tones seemed somehow fitting in this dark wood and leather-filled room, more reminiscent of a hunting lodge than of a modern and bright society salon.

"Yes, yes, of course. Er... whatever you need. I shall answer what I can." He shifted on the settee, closer, perhaps, to Elinor than was strictly necessary, but Mary then realised that she was closer to Alexander than the confines of the room dictated as well. She mentioned neither.

"I have to ask you again about some of the objects we discovered near where your brother was found." Edward blinked again as Alexander continued. "The handkerchief, for example." He reached into a pocket and withdrew a piece of white fabric. Edward took it and stared at it with a blank expression. Beside him, Elinor frowned.

"Is it yours?" she asked. "It is, for I recall seeing it at Norland." She referred, Mary recalled, to the Sussex estate where she grew up. "I remember Marianne commenting on how a gentleman should have an excess of flourishes on his linens, whereas I prefer a simpler monogram. And when I saw this handkerchief, I remembered that conversation. It is yours, is it not?"

Edward gulped. "Yes. I have to say it is. I had a set of three from when I was at school and lost two. They were embroidered by... by the cousin of my tutor, and I was distressed to have only one left.

And then, some months ago, I lost that one as well. I had it at my mother's funeral, that I know. I held it in my hands and promised myself I would not shed a tear, for men do not cry. And I crushed it so hard in my hand I thought it would tear. I remember coming home to the house and looking at it with all its creases and as it lay on my bed to be laundered, but I never saw it again." He looked up with that same dazed expression and shook his head. "I cannot account for it at all."

Alexander took a few moments to add some lines to his notebook. Mary's eyes were riveted to the motion of his pencil on the page and the careless sweep of his letters. It was an educated hand, so out of keeping with his outward appearance. When he spoke, his voice was quiet, as if inviting a confidence.

"That day must have been very distressing."

Edward nodded and sat forward in his seat, and as he did so, Mary watched Elinor move ever so slightly closer to him. "I cannot tell you how distressing, Mr. Lyons. It was not like when Father died. He was old, much older than Mother, and he had been ill for a great amount of time. We had expected his death for weeks when he finally passed. It was difficult, to be certain, but it was not shocking. But Mother..." He opened his hands wide in bewilderment.

"Tell me about the day of her death." Alexander's pencil hovered above the paper. "Every detail you can recall will be helpful."

"Why?" Edward's eyes widened in alarm. "What possible import can Mother's death have on Robert's murder, or his marriage, for I assume you need to discuss that as well? Why do you need to know this?" He looked wildly about him. "And the ladies... It is not fitting talk for delicate ears."

Mary could not stifle a snort. "I am made of sterner stuff than you might imagine, Mr. Ferrars. We females are not so feeble as men like to make out. I cannot speak for my friend, but I have heard and seen more horrible things than you can imagine, and yet I am strong and undamaged and able to carry on perfectly well."

"And I, Edward," Elinor added. "I have every bit of confidence in my rational mind. Hearing of distressing things will not harm me."

Alexander explained himself. "Every piece of information we have, sir, might have some bearing on the case. Or, rather, the cases. Remember, I am investigating Miss Steele's claims on your brother's estate, and your own possible role in Robert's death. Do not forget that. Because this latter is inextricably linked to the former, I must know everything."

"But that cannot be!" Edward exclaimed. "How can Robert's death be connected to Mother's?"

Mary had to interject. It was so simple. How could the man not see it? "It seems most probable," she explained, "that Robert's murder was associated somehow with his new wealth. Even if the Runners are mistaken and it was a simple case of a violent robbery, Robert would not have been the victim were he not known to be wealthy, and newly so."

"Yes, I see. I see. Very well." He sank back against the soft settee once more. "The first night we were at the Norfolk estate, I recall nothing amiss. Robert and I came together. We arrived late and discussed no business. Mother said we would talk in the morning. I suspected she wished to dissuade me from marrying Miss Steele." Again, Mary saw that sad sidelong glance at Elinor.

"To what end? Had she not already drawn up her new will, leaving everything to Robert?"

The young man shrugged. "I believe so. She had said it. But Mother was never one to be completely forthcoming. And every will can be superseded, can it not?"

Alexander scratched something in his notebook. "The first night, then, was unremarkable. You ate nothing unusual? Heard nothing strange? No? Very well, then. What next?"

Another shrug. "In the morning, Mother came down for breakfast but soon left, complaining of feeling indisposed. I believe it was a complaint of the stomach. She remained ill all day, and we called for the village doctor. When next we saw him, she was dead."

This all accorded exactly with what Mary already knew. From Alexander's bland expression, he too had heard nothing illuminating.

"What was the cause of death? The doctor must have said something."

Edward sighed. "He could tell us very little. It is mostly men, he told us, who meet such sudden ends. Their hearts, you know... But it is not unknown for a lady to have such a seizure and die from it. He was distressed but not alarmed. Or, at least, not that he mentioned to us. He arranged for the local parson to come and the next thing we knew, she was cold and buried. And Robert and I returned to London that very same day as her funeral."

"So you had no suspicions?"

"No. None at all."

"I have sent a message already, asking to speak with the doctor who tended her." Alexander's words produced no alarm or great reaction in Edward, and he continued writing his notes.

Now Mary sat forward. "Did you spend a great deal of time at the Norfolk estate, Mr. Ferrars?" Everybody seemed very interested in what had happened there, but she knew nothing of the estate itself.

"Oh, not at all. No. Our home was always in London, and all the more so after Father died. Mother hated the estate."

"Why so? Is it not pleasant there?" Mary could not help but think of her own beloved family estate in Hertfordshire. It was not particularly grand or elegant, but it was her home. As exciting and interesting as London was, she was never sad to return to the pleasures of the country. How strange, then, that the Ferrars should prefer Town to their own land.

Edward was noncommittal. "It is pleasant, I suppose, but has little in particular to recommend it. The land is not particularly prosperous, there being too much water in too many places to farm it efficiently, and the house is in disrepair. It brings in a thousand a year—enough for comfort, but no great fortune. It was not the main source of our family's wealth."

"Then why were you there?" Mary had to ask that question.

"I cannot say!" Edward looked quite bewildered. "Robert sent me the summons; he said Mother demanded it. I had thought she wished to make me understand all that I was to lose, but it was most unlike her. Indeed, it was all most odd. To me, it seemed as if she herself was uncertain as to why we were there." He lapsed into a deep and gloomy silence.

"She said nothing of her decision? Nothing of the will?"

"No. Not a word. She hardly had time. But Robert seemed to think she might be reconsidering her actions. I cannot say why he thought that. Perhaps he only wished to cheer me with the saying of it."

"What, if I may ask," Alexander's voice was low and gentle, "was your reaction to the news of her death?"

Edward started and his eyelids fluttered rapidly. "I was shocked! I could hardly understand what he told us. He must be wrong! I thought it all a terrible joke, and that Mother would walk in a moment later and laugh at us. She was not a warm woman, but she enjoyed a joke at others' expense. I still cannot believe it. Until that very last morning, she was strong and hale. There was nothing the matter with her, nothing at all. For her to take ill so suddenly and die seemed... well, impossible."

Mary thought that Alexander had concluded his interview, but the Scot, instead of rising, settled further into his seat.

"My next question regards Miss Steele."

Edward's face drained of all colour, and Elinor's hands went white as she squeezed her fingers together. "She tells me," Alexander said, "that Robert had the record of their marriage on some papers he carried back with him. Do you have any knowledge of where those papers might be?"

At this question, Mary saw Edward's eyes flutter in relief. Beside him, Elinor's jaw lost its tight line. Had they been expecting a different question?

"I cannot say," Edward answered. "I... that is, we... we were not close. We were never close, Robert and I, and since these events..."

He did not state which events, but Mary understood. Since his mother learned about the ill-advised engagement to Lucy, since he was disinherited in favour of his younger brother, since his mother died, and since his betrothed eloped with his brother. That brother who had stolen his fortune and his wife.

"Robert never suggested where he might have put those papers? Did he have a place where he kept such important documents?"

Edward shook his head. "None that I know. He had grown different of late. I have no understanding of the man he had become. Any hiding place I might once have known of was surely changed." He paused and furrowed his brow for a moment. "Have you asked his solicitor? Might he have entrusted him with the papers?"

Mary saw Alexander nod. "Aye. I have sent a message to that gentleman, a Mr. William Hollings, I believe."

"He was Mother's lawyer. Yes. That makes some sense. Robert was not one to make such strides into independence as finding a new solicitor."

"This is the man who drew up the new will?" Silence, that might have been agreement. "And he managed your brother's financial affairs?" Edward shrugged and nodded. "Very well. I shall wait to receive word from him."

Alexander paused. He had another matter to query. "Many of the staff at Robert's house report hearing a row between you the night he died."

Edward stared at him.

"Can you tell me what it concerned?"

The young man looked from Elinor to Mary and then back to Elinor. At last, he cleared his throat. "I cannot say. It was... that is, I cannot think... surely, it was nothing in particular. Merely a minor disagreement. I can hardly recall."

"And yet the housekeeper recalls you leaving in anger and uttering threats. Do you deny that?"

Edward's eyes narrowed. "I thought you were here on my behalf. You are asking questions as if you wish to discredit me. I have answered all of these questions already when that Runner—what is his name? Atkins?—asked me. I would rather not repeat myself."

Alexander's eyes fixed Edward to his seat. "Mr. Ferrars, you must understand that I have been retained to discover the truth. I would like to believe that the truth frees you from all blame in this sad affair, but I cannot disregard evidence merely because I wish it not to exist. But never mind. Perhaps I can ask Mr. Atkins for his notes, or perhaps you will choose to answer me at another time."

Alexander did shift in his seat now. He slid his notebook back into his pocket and put his pencil away. As Mary and Elinor began to rise, Alexander commented in a most offhand manner, "It must be almost a blessing to have your poor brother deceased."

Once more, Edward sounded affronted. It was no easy task to rile him to emotion, but when angered, he could speak. "I beg your pardon, sir! That is a most cruel thing to say! It is true, my brother and I had our differences, but to suggest I had reason to celebrate his death is unconscionable."

"And yet his passing leaves you in far better circumstances. You must see that."

Edward's nostrils flared. "I have no wish for glory, sir! My sister sees her worth in pounds, and my mother and brother did as well, but not I! Wealth means little to me. Even without my inheritance, I am in no danger of starvation. I have friends I can visit, whose generosity will allow me to complete my studies. I can take orders and live comfortably with a small living. If I desired a fortune, I need only have listened to my mother's urging and married Miss Morton and her fifty thousand pounds. But that is not what I want. I want a quiet life with E..." He stopped as if frozen into stone for a moment. "A quiet life with everything in order and without the weight of society's expectations upon my shoulders. That is what I want." He stood up straighter than ever Mary had seen him. "Now, if you will excuse me."

And with scarcely a nod of his head, he stomped from the room, leaving Mary and her two companions staring at each other.

Chapter Nine

Marianne's Letter

"That was unnecessary." Mary turned on Alexander the moment they had descended the few steps back down to the street. "There was no cause to say such hurtful things. I have never seen him so upset." She stomped a few paces down the pavement, not trusting herself to remain civil. Whatever had she liked in this infuriating man?

"Mary..." She heard his footsteps as he hurried after her. "It was deliberate. You must see that. Mr. Ferrars is so quiet, so reticent. He spoke hardly a word that we did not have to coax out of him. That accusation was the only thing that brought him to spontaneous speech. And I had wondered if, in his anger, he might say something he would otherwise choose to keep hidden."

Oh. She had done it again. She had allowed her indignation to colour her thinking. She had judged without full understanding.

Her feet stilled, and she stopped on the street. Elinor was a few paces behind; Mary could not see her friend, but sensed her standing far enough back not to interfere.

The air rushed out of her. "I apologise. I felt Edward's anger, and I felt my own, and I did not stop to consider whether this was a ruse. But it was badly done, nonetheless. How cruel you sounded, how unfeeling. That is not the manner of a gentleman, to manipulate another thus. It is manipulative and deceptive. It is un-Christian."

He stiffened his jaw and expelled a short breath. "Mary..."

"I am sorry. That was uncalled for. But is it justified, to bring a man to such distress in order to learn his secrets?"

"In this instance, I am trying to save his life. I do not enjoy this manner of questioning, but if it helps to uncover the truth, I will resort to such measures, again and again."

"You are rather Machiavellian." She still refused to look directly into his eyes, but she thought she detected... a hint of a grin? Was he laughing at her?

"You are too clever for your own good. Sometimes the end does, indeed, justify the means. Please, let us talk about this at another time. I really do wish to hear your thoughts. But your friend is waiting." His head flicked in the direction of Elinor, who still stood a few feet behind them.

The rigid indignation in Mary's spine softened. "Very well. Did you, then? Did you learn something?"

He gave a short nod. "I might have done so, yes."

Mary started walking again, now with Alexander at her side and Elinor a few steps behind.

"I discovered that there was some ongoing trouble between the brothers. I learned that Edward was left poor but not destitute. And I learned that he had means to a far greater fortune than his mother might have left him had he wanted it. Some of this we knew already, but it was grand to hear it from his lips." He dropped his voice so only Mary could hear it. "And I learned that he still wishes to marry your friend."

Mary slowed her steps again to allow Elinor to catch up, and Alexander offered an arm to each lady. It was not a long walk back to Mrs. Jennings' house, and Mary was pleased to see him act the gentleman for a change, even if he protested he was none.

"I must see to Marianne," Elinor mentioned as they approached the house. "I hope she is improved, but I fear she will keep to her rooms."

"Is Miss Marianne ill?" Alexander asked.

Of course. He did not know about the letter and whatever it contained.

Elinor told him in a few words about her sister's distress.

"You did not see this letter?"

Elinor shook her head. "She would not show us. She was so distraught, I could not trouble her more by demanding it. When she is calmer, I hope to discover what it said."

"I believe it was from Mr. Willoughby," Mary explained. "When he came to pay his respects earlier this week, he paid a great deal of attention to Miss Marianne, and she seemed quite distressed by it. I cannot think of another man whose actions would trouble her so."

"Nor I," Elinor added. "Since we have been in London—nay, since we left our home at Norland—there has been no other man to whom she has paid the first bit of attention. It must be him. Him or Colonel Brandon, and the colonel is far too much a gentleman to write to a lady unrelated to him, or ever send a lady into such misery."

"Did she say anything?" he asked again. They were now in front of the house, and the trio stopped and stood by the door.

"No, it is all supposition," Elinor sighed.

Mary could do a little better. "I do recall her words. She said, 'He will not give up. I know now what he is and what he is capable of.' And then she said, 'He knows where I am!'"

Elinor gaped at her. "You remember her every word?"

Mary blushed, "I am blessed with a good memory," at the same time as Alexander blurted, "It is phenomenal!"

Then he grew more serious. "He knows where she is... what a strange thing to say." A frown formed on his broad forehead. "Have you no idea what she meant by it? Surely her presence in town was not kept hidden."

Mary shrugged. "Not at all. But the poor girl clearly feels in some sort of danger."

Elinor suddenly started. "I must speak to Mrs. Jennings about returning to Devonshire. Perhaps if Colonel Brandon has concluded his business in Town, he will accompany us. I must write to Mama... But..." Her face fell. "No, that will not do. Mrs. Jennings' daughter has a new babe and does not wish to travel, and Mrs. Jennings will not leave her grandson so soon. Oh, what can I do to help Marianne be safe?"

An idea began to form in Mary's head. It might not work. There were a great many questions that must be asked, and a great set of favours, all of which depended upon others' goodwill. But it just might be possible.

"Will you allow me until tomorrow before you take any action, Elinor? I have thought of something I dare not mention now, but that may help."

"Why yes! Yes, of course." Her friend gave her a quick hug before disappearing into the house, leaving Mary and Alexander together on the pavement.

"What is your idea, Mary? Come, let me call for a hackney and I shall accompany you home, and I shall tell you all I learned today."

She thanked him and they stood at the busy main street, talking about the case, until a suitable carriage rolled to a stop.

"I am concerned about Marianne. If she is afraid that he knows where she is, whoever 'he' may be, it only makes sense for her to be somewhere else."

"And if that somewhere else is kept a great secret…"

"Then she will be safe, for now at least."

"And you wish to prevail upon your aunt and uncle to allow her to stay at their house?"

She cocked her head at him. "I can think of nowhere better. He will not expect her to leave Mrs. Jennings' home, but even were she to do so, he would expect her to remain in the fashionable parts of London. But my aunt and uncle's house, while fine and elegant, is in a part of town where the middle class lives…"

"Such as myself?"

She snorted at him. "And my dear relations, and I as well! Really, Alexander, you can be as much a bore as my brother Darcy." Then she started laughing.

He joined her, and encouraged thus, she laughed harder still until tears ran down her face. Beside her in the carriage, Alexander reached into one of his bottomless pockets and found a handkerchief which he used to dab at her flushed cheeks.

He was so close, inches away, and his fingers grazed her skin with the piece of linen. Then he disposed entirely with the handkerchief and ran his fingers across her cheek until he cradled her face in one hand, and then he was kissing her. Or she was kissing him. Oh, why was this so lovely, when she ought to be shocked at herself? Why could she not pull away and slap him when she found him so infuriating? If only he were not so handsome and so perfectly suited to her! Vexatious man!

For these short minutes, she abandoned all claims to sense and reason, and allowed herself the luxury of the moment. Edward,

Elinor, Marianne, they could all wait. The soft touch of Alexander's lips upon hers, his hand on her cheek, the scent of him so very close, was all she needed in the world right now. She gave a gentle sigh and hoped that no one could see through the thin curtains at the windows.

All too soon, the carriage slowed to a stop. Mary pulled herself out of Alexander's arms and put a hand up to feel her hair. "Is it...?" She asked half a question.

Alexander gave her a great grin and neatened a few stray wisps and replaced a pin. "My sisters taught me to help with their hair," he explained. "Your fichu..."

Another few tugs and adjustment set Mary's dress to rights. She hoped she might explain her burning cheeks and kiss-reddened lips to her aunt. Perhaps if she let herself in and hurried up the stairs and then washed her face...

Luck was with her. There were her aunt and the children in the square across the street, talking to some neighbours. If she hurried, she could avoid being spotted! With a quick goodbye to Alexander, she dashed from the carriage and into the house, wondering what they would need to discover next. Or, more truthfully, when he would call on her next. The months of separation had only increased her liking for this annoying investigator, and no amount of peevish anger would stop her from aching to see him again.

By the time she descended the stairs to join her family for dinner, she was calm and in perfect order once more. She chatted merrily with her aunt and uncle about her day with Elinor, leaving out most of the details about poor Marianne and the visit to Edward. She listened with pronounced, if feigned, interest to the children's tales of sailing boats on the pond and Mrs. Greenberg's new puppy. She heard her uncle's recitation of the recent shipment of textiles he had received at his warehouses, and engaged in a conversation as to the most fashionable colours for the summer.

But the entire time, all she could think of was Alexander's arms around her and the soft press of his lips on hers and she wondered how her thoughts were not so loud that the whole house could hear them.

When, at last, the children were kissed on the head and sent up to do their reading, and the adults retired to the parlour, Mary finally broached the subject she wished to discuss.

"I told you at dinner of Elinor's sister, Marianne." She toyed with a sweet biscuit upon her plate.

"Yes. The poor girl had an unwelcome letter, it seemed." Aunt Gardiner poured herself a cup of fragrant tea. Was that clove and cinnamon in the mix? Uncle had access to the best teas in London, and it smelled delightful! Mary accepted a cup but put it aside until she had made her request.

"She was most distressed. I have never seen her so afraid. She believes the writer of the letter will find her somehow and importune her, although I know not how or with what. I was wondering..." she trailed off. How could she make such a bold demand on the kind relations who had offered to host her for all these months?

"You wish," Uncle Gardiner completed, "for her to stay here where she is safe and cannot be found."

Mary beamed at him. Not for the first time did she wonder how this astute and elegant man could be her mother's brother! Mama had been a beauty in her youth—indeed, even now with five grown daughters and two grandchildren, there were few in Meryton who could match her for looks—but she had never astounded the town with her wit. But her brother, Mary's uncle, was a different creature, and her aunt, likewise, had an excellent understanding. He knew what she wanted!

"I hate to ask, but I am so concerned for her."

"She will have to share your room," Aunt Gardiner looked over her teacup. "We have not the luxury to give Miss Dashwood her own chambers."

"Yes, yes, of course! She is so very elegant, and she plays the pianoforte beautifully. Perhaps she would agree to tutor Julia and Sam."

"Perhaps. When will we meet this young lady? Have you made your offer to her yet?"

"Oh, no, Uncle! I would never dare without asking you first. But tomorrow, as soon as it is suitable, I shall tell her of the invitation."

Any further words were interrupted by a knock at the door. Once again, Alexander was ushered inside, and Mary fought in vain to hide her smile. It had been only a few hours since last she had seen him—kissed him in the hackney coach—but she could never get enough of his company. He met her gaze and his lips twitched in a secret greeting, but he turned at once to his hosts.

"Mr. Gardiner, Mrs. Gardiner, how kind of you to admit me once more, and at such an awkward time of day. I would never think to importune you, if not for the needs of business." What considerate words, and his every manner suggested he meant them sincerely.

"Please do come in, Mr. Lyons." Aunt Gardiner welcomed him in kind, and offered him a cup of tea, which he accepted with obvious pleasure.

"Delicious!" he exclaimed, taking a sip of the fragrant spiced tea. "Something new?"

Uncle Gardiner grinned. "Fresh in my warehouse today, off a boat from India. Fine blend, is it not? The tea and spices were sent separately, with instructions on how to combine them. I have half a mind to keep the lot for myself, never mind the profits." He chuckled, and Mary knew at once what she would buy Lizzy and brother Darcy for their Christmas present this year.

They spent a moment discussing the merits of different blends of tea before Alexander turned to the reason for his call.

"Mr. and Mrs. Gardiner, permit me to turn to matters of business. I have come to ask you something quite unusual. I must travel to Norfolk as a part of my investigations. Mrs. Jennings and Miss Elinor Dashwood also need to travel there, to sort through the late Mrs. Ferrars' belongings, at Edward and his sister Fanny's request. Fanny," he explained to the couple, "is Elinor's brother's wife. Naturally, we are all to go together."

Both the Gardiners responded suitably and Alexander continued. "May I be so bold as to assume that Miss Marianne Dashwood will be invited here to stay for some days? Yes? Very good! I had hoped you had already made that request, Mary." He smiled at her and her heart sped up. "With her sister hidden away, as it were, in this safest of places, Miss Elinor Dashwood will have no company of her age on the trip to Norfolk. She has asked me to be her envoy in requesting that Mary be permitted to accompany the group as her companion. Mary? Does that suit?"

"Norfolk?" Uncle Gardiner's eyes widened. "That is a fair distance, my lad."

"Aye. That it is. We must travel a little over a hundred miles there, and a hundred back. You can understand why Miss Dashwood wishes so much to have a friend with her, somebody useful and sensible."

Mary's uncle nodded. "Yes I can. I have travelled the length and breadth of England and beyond for my business, and those miles do get very lonely. Will Mrs. Jennings be with you for the entire journey?"

"Of course! I would hardly think of having the ladies travel without her."

"And a suitable number of footmen and servants?"

"Tell me your requirements and I shall ensure it."

"Mary? Do you wish to go?"

Mary could hardly sit still, such was her excitement. At last, she might discover something that would be of use, and see a new place at the same time. London was wonderful, but a change of location was to be anticipated with joy. "Yes, very much! I must thank Elinor for the invitation."

Her aunt and uncle looked at each other and conducted a thorough and silent conversation with their eyes. Then Aunt Gardiner turned to her and uttered, "Yes, you may go. Mr. Lyons, when do you propose to leave?"

"At first light, if we may."

"Then, my dear," to Mary, "you must send a message to your friend Miss Marianne, and then you had best go and start to pack."

Chapter Ten

The Norfolk Estate

Alexander was most relieved that, for once, every plan was carried out without trouble. By the time the sun was above the horizon, Marianne had taken possession of Mary's room on Gracechurch Street and Mrs. Jennings' carriage was well on the road to Norfolk.

Mrs. Jennings and Elinor sat facing forward; across from them, Alexander sat on his bench with Mary beside him. She was so close. A bump in the road or a shift of the carriage would send her falling against him, and it would be a moment's work to move his arm and pull her to his side. He could not help but recall that short hackney ride only yesterday when her tears of laughter had led to the kiss he had been dreaming of since last they met the previous autumn. What had possessed him to kiss her? What had taken him

DEATH IN SENSIBLE CIRCUMSTANCES

so long to do it again? And she had not protested or pulled away, but had thrown her arms about him and pulled him even closer.

What ought he to do about her? In a different world, if they were different people, he would be down on bended knee in a moment. She was everything he hoped for in a woman. She was both intelligent and sensible—not a combination found as often as one might hope—with a keen understanding and a fine sense of humour, when she chose to engage it. She understood him perfectly and they worked so well together it could not have been better planned. And that she was very pretty was not to be denied!

But they were too different in circumstance. There was too wide a gulf between them, both in situation and belief. Mary was a daughter of privilege, born into the gentry with no expectation that she would ever have to soil her hands to live; he was the son of a country doctor who himself had scrambled his way up to a respectable career by a great deal of toil and sheer luck. She was English as a rose, as natural a part of the local society as a leaf was on a tree; he was a perennial outsider, with his flame-red hair, broad Scottish accent and country upbringing. And as for their different faiths, he could not imagine how to reconcile those!

A wise man had once told him to give Mary time to mature and become more comfortable with her own place in the world before dragging her into his, but would she ever be ready to accept something so foreign and different from anything she had ever known? Perhaps during this journey to Norfolk, they would find some opportunity to talk openly and out of earshot of their travelling companions.

The journey to the estate was a long one. It was a hundred miles there and a hundred miles back, far too long to complete in a single day, almost too long for two. They changed horses more than once and stayed one night on the road at a fine inn that Mr.

Gardiner had suggested, and by late afternoon on the second day they finally drew up to the house.

He had not, until the night before, known the name of the estate. Edward had always referred to it as "the Norfolk estate," and nobody else referred to it at all. Now, he discovered, the house and lands were known as Deer Park, although to Edward's knowledge there had never been deer in the neighbourhood, neither was there any sort of grand park worthy of the name.

Alexander had hoped that Edward might join them on this journey. He knew the land and the people, even if only slightly, and his presence might have smoothed their way. But Edward was still angry with Alexander for the insult he had given during their conversation, and Colonel Brandon insisted that by the terms agreed to with Mr. Atkins, Edward must stay with him in London. Furthermore, Alexander conceded, there was no room for a fifth person in the carriage. One of them would have had to ride, and that would, of necessity, be him. He far preferred sitting here with Mary nestled against his side.

Now Deer Park stood before them. As Edward had described, it was not a large or grand house, and was in some disrepair. There were tiles missing from the roof, at least one window was boarded up, and the gardens were overgrown and unkempt. Some minor efforts had been made to keep the place from becoming completely disreputable, but there was little evidence that anybody cared for it enough to bring it back to order.

The housekeeper, a sharp-eyed woman named Mrs. Pavy, was not pleased with the intrusion of four unwanted guests. At Alexander's insistence, Edward had sent an express to inform her of the visitors, requesting that they be made welcome and comfortable. Such could not be denied, although the inconvenience of it all was writ large on the lady's face. Still, a clean bedroom had been prepared for each, with fresh linens and open windows, and a warm meal was waiting for them in the dining room. The housekeeper saw to each guest's immediate comfort and then excused herself for the evening, informing the party that a maid and footman would be available to see to their needs.

There was little to be done this evening. Alexander had hoped to interview the housekeeper to hear her recollections of that fateful day, but that would not be possible. She had quite refused his entreaties, saying she might find some time on the morrow. There was no use pressing his point; he required her cooperation if he hoped to get any useful knowledge from her, and so he bid her a good night. Instead, he called for some paper and ink and sat down to write a note to the village doctor and some others in the neighbourhood before seeking out the library to sit with a book and his thoughts.

He had just selected a volume—a history that his tutor at University had mentioned once—and settled himself in a worn leather chair near the fireplace when the wooden door creaked open and Mary's shape emerged from the dark hallway beyond.

"May I come in? Elinor and Mrs. Jennings have both retired for the night. I said I would do likewise, but..." She spread her hands, palms up. "Perhaps I am more accustomed to travel. I am not fatigued. I was hoping—"

"—to talk?"

She nodded.

"As was I. And not about this case." He pushed himself up from the chair and found another that he pulled right beside his own. There was no fire in the grate since the weather was warm, but some lamps on the mantel and on the small table to one side shed ample light to cut through the growing darkness. Mary slid into the offered chair but did not relax against the tall back. She sat upright, hands clasped in her lap. Alexander ached to reach out and gather those soft hands in his own, but they were not alone in the house.

One of the servants, or Elinor or Mrs. Jennings, for that matter, might walk in at any moment. Propriety must reign, for now at least.

For a second their eyes met and Alexander almost forgot his conviction of a moment before, but then Mary dropped her gaze and spoke. "When I heard nothing from you for so long, I thought you had decided you were best rid of me."

"What? Never! I could not write directly, you know that! People would talk... The whole of Hertfordshire would know in a day. Your father would have disallowed my correspondence. But I sent you my regards through Darcy. Surely, he passed them to you by means of your sister's letters."

Her gaze shifted to the side. "I thought... I thought you would come yourself, to speak to my father. I..." She went red. "I ought not to have presumed anything. Please, forgive me."

"Ach, Mary! Do not be saying that. You know it is not that easy. He would send me off at once, forbid me to see you ever again. Would he not? And, for that matter, why did you never inform me that you were in London? We might have contrived some manner to meet."

"Other than over another body? Perhaps it was I who killed Robert, merely to have an excuse to meet you once more."

"Do not tease like that. Somebody might not take your words as jest. In truth, Mary, I would have moved heaven and earth to see you again, to call at your aunt and uncle. But it is one matter to come as an investigator in the course of business, and another entirely to come as a suitor."

She looked up at him and he was lost at once in the depths of her deep eyes. "You would have done that?"

"You doubt me?"

Once more, her gaze dropped to her lap. "Perhaps I did, which was most unkind of me. But I thought... you did not come." She raised her once more, confusion and sadness in their depths. "I imagined... I presumed we had some sort of understanding, even if it was unspoken. Was I mistaken?"

If he could have declared himself with his adoring gaze alone, he would have been a lost man, but she deserved more than the empty promises he could offer her now. Her eyes met his and fixed him to his chair with the intensity of her expression. "I am not dallying with you," he managed to say. "But if I present myself and am sent away, with no chance of seeing you again, how could I live? Perhaps I have chosen the coward's path, but that path, at least, leads me to you from time to time."

Mary's luminous eyes fluttered closed. "I did not think how it would be for you. And I am sorry I did not let you know I was in town. I was hurt, and unfairly so. All those weeks we have lost, we might have enjoyed in conversation."

"We are together now. I am not the man you wish me to be, but I am not inconstant. Can that suffice, for the present, until... until circumstances are different?"

"It will. It must!" She reached her hand out towards him and he grabbed it. How easy it would be to lean forward in his chair, for her to do likewise, for his hand to move once more to her soft, rosy cheek, for her to incline her head towards his. Their eyes met and held each other's gaze, and Mary's lips parted, a mere crack, but enough to draw every ounce of his attention. A brush, a touch... it would never be enough.

The creak of footsteps in the hallway outside threw him back to reality. There were servants about. This would not do. Instead of pulling Mary towards him as he longed to do, Alexander raised her hand in his and pressed a soft kiss to the back of it.

"We ought to retire."

She nodded. She, too, had heard the floorboards outside. She was no silly thing to take his words amiss. "Until morning, my friend."

She rose and departed, but despite his words, Alexander spent a great many minutes staring at the doorway after her.

Alexander rose early the next morning. Hot tea and coffee were waiting in the breakfast room, and the housekeeper greeted him with a friendlier face than she had shown the night before. To his relief, she also agreed to talk to him later, although she insisted she had nothing of value to tell him. Hopefully, this boded well for the day. No sooner had she left the room, when the maid entered and handed him a note from the doctor, offering to see him and discuss the matter. After taking a quick cup of coffee and a fresh roll with jam from a tray, Alexander asked for directions and set off for the village.

The village at Deer Park was no great distance from the manor house. Indeed, all the lands pertaining to the estate were spread out behind the house, leaving the building itself more a part of the village than separate from it. A short walk down the drive let him out almost at the edge of the settlement itself, and from there it was only another minute or two before he was at Doctor Peddleton's front door.

He was shown inside to where the doctor was still taking his morning tea in a bright room towards the back of the house.

"Morning, morning. You must be that investigator, Lyons. No one else calls this early with such a calm look upon his face. All desperate and troubled, they are. Come and sit. Tea? Ham?"

"Tea please. It is kind of you to see me."

"Och, a Scot! I never would have thought it. You write so well. Thought for certain you were a proper Englishman. Ah well, never you mind. A man's a man for all that, eh?"

Alexander felt his smile falter for a moment before he fixed it back on his face. There was no point in trying to speak; he had seen this situation too many times before, and there was no help for it. Of its own accord, his mouth began to open in anticipation of the barrage of argument that cried out to be spoken, but he mastered himself, as he always did, and tempered his words.

"Just so," was all he said. There seemed little point right now in mentioning that his own father was a doctor as well, and this man's equal. Perhaps this fact would emerge later. Instead, he accepted the tea and polished his finest society manners for the occasion before embarking on his set of questions.

"I have been engaged by the family of Mr. Robert Ferrars on an issue concerning his will. Part of that investigation has led me to questions about the death of his mother, Mrs. Ferrars. I was hoping you might have some thoughts to share with me about the same."

The doctor leaned back in his chair, teacup in one hand. "This is quite some time ago. Over three months, if my memory serves. A great many things happen even in a small village such as this during that length of time. You can hardly expect me to remember every detail of the day."

"And yet it is a rare enough event that the Ferrars family of Deer Park visit the neighbourhood, and rarer still—or so I hope—that one of them takes ill and dies whilst here. Those occasions alone must keep the day fresh in your mind."

"Mr. Lyons, if you knew the number of people who have been born, taken ill, broken bones, and died in the last three months... Oh, very well. It was a rather unusual set of circumstances. Perhaps I can recall enough to satisfy your curiosity."

"I thank you, Doctor, for any information you have. What can you tell me about Mrs. Ferrars' final illness and death?"

"It seemed ordinary enough. It is rare for a lady of her years to die without a preceding illness, but these things happen, even in people not greatly advanced in age. Stomach aches leading to shortness of breath and then a stoppage of the heart. It is sometimes known as *angina pectoris*. You are correct. Mrs. Ferrars did not visit Deer Park often, and the villagers were not well pleased when she did. *Angina pectoris* is often found in people who are quick to anger, and Mrs. Ferrars—forgive me—was a woman not known for her evenness of temper."

Alexander nodded. "I am familiar with the concept. My father was a doctor." It was satisfying to watch as Dr. Peddleton's brows rose on his forehead. "I learned a lot at his feet. My studies led me, instead, to the law, but I know more of the science of healing than do most men."

"Yes. Very well. I see." There was, perhaps, a new look of respect on Peddleton's face. "I see I have underestimated you, young man. You are, then, not happy with this pronouncement."

"I am not looking for what is not there. If her death was natural, I shall be pleased to find it so. But it does seem unusual, does it not?"

The doctor raised his teacup to his lips but replaced it on its saucer without drinking. "Yes. I was surprised. Not unduly so, and not shocked, but surprised."

"What else might it have been?"

"Do you accuse somebody of murder, sir?"

"I merely wish to discover the truth, whatever it turns out to be. I have my suspicions, but I was not present. Please, anything you can tell me might be of utmost importance."

"Very well." The doctor sighed and sat straight in his chair. "I was not happy with Mrs. Ferrars' death, but having no reason to believe otherwise, I put it down to some sort of seizure of the heart. But at night, when I cannot sleep, I muse about what might have been the ultimate cause. There are many poisons in a house, and especially an old one that is not well kept."

"Rat poison?"

"Yes. Mice, rats, various other creatures that ought not to live between the walls. Arsenic is a common enough such item. Gardeners use it against insects, some use it as a medicine, and it is even in cosmetics and dyes."

"And easy to procure, aye?"

"Yes. Every chemist and apothecary has a goodly supply. Every household larder likely contains as much as well, enough to kill a man in all likelihood. It causes stomach cramps, flux of the bowels, and death by shock, which without a proper examination is similar to a stoppage of the heart."

"I had wondered as much. Is there any way to be certain?"

The doctor's face went white and very serious. "You cannot mean to exhume her! I absolutely forbid it! And it would tell us nothing. Let me reread my notes on the case. Come with me to my office?"

Alexander rose and followed the doctor down the hallway of the house and into a rather cramped room filled with shelves and files and bookcases. Peddleton scanned one shelf and pulled out a thick tome. He put it on the desk and opened it about half the way through, then flipped through several pages until he found what he wanted.

"Most of my colleagues do not believe in keeping a record of each case," he explained, "but I find what happened to one might help in the treatment of another. Now if only I had a system to organise it, so it is not dependent on my memory. But I digress... here. Mrs. Henrietta Ferrars, age fifty-six. Not so very young, although not old. Not too young for a sudden and lethal bout of dropsy or angina. Hmmm…" He read through his notes. "It was as I said. She had felt mildly ill the night before, but put it down to the long drive up from London. At breakfast the next morning her stomach began to cramp—sorry, Lyons, if I am blunt with my descriptions, but needs must—followed by greater distress and violent and loose flux of the bowels. Then weakness of the muscles, disorientation, severe chest pains, and loss of consciousness, followed by death. Exactly what one might expect from a stoppage of the heart, or…"

"From arsenic poisoning."

The two men looked at each other.

"I fear," Alexander said after a moment, "that I may have more than one murder to investigate."

After leaving Dr. Peddleton, Alexander found and spoke to a few other people in the village, but none had anything of value to say. Mrs. Ferrars had not been in the village at all and none could account for her state of mind or relate anything unusual she might have said. Only the doctor's considerations were of use.

Alexander wandered back to the house in low spirits. He had not expected to learn anything to amaze him, but he was fighting a fit of blue devils, nonetheless. The single roll he had taken early this morning was not enough to sustain him and he hoped that a heartier breakfast might return him to his normal humour.

Mary was in the breakfast room when he slid inside. An empty teacup sat on the table before her, a plate with a few crumbs at its side. She was reading a book and looked up when he entered. After last night's talk in the library, he expected a gentle smile on her face, not the determined set of her jaw and disapproving look in her eyes.

"Alexander! I had hoped to accompany you on your outing today."

"It was no place for a woman, Mary." He knew as he spoke that he ought to measure his words, but he was hungry and in no good mood. He slunk to the sideboard with heavy steps and pushed some eggs onto a plate.

"No place for a woman?" There was iron in her words. "What do you believe me to be made of? I am not some wilting rose that swoons at the first mention of trouble." She was sitting, but Alexander was certain that had she been on her feet, her hands would have been balled into fists and planted firmly on her hips. "Now let me ask you again why you did not call me to join you. After our discussion last night, I expected it."

"Not now, Mary. I am in no mood to talk."

"That is unfortunate, because I am. Did you leave me here deliberately? Are you ashamed of sharing your knowledge with a mere woman? Or of admitting to those you met that I have been of assistance in the past?"

He set the plate of eggs and toast onto the table with a thud. "Mary, you are being unreasonable. This had nothing to do with you. I had questions that needed asking and I wished to ask them early. And you were not yet risen."

"You did not inquire after me."

He clenched his jaw. She was being most irrational. She was here to be with Elinor, after all, as her companion, and not as his assistant. "I met no servants to ask. Furthermore, some of the details I needed were of a delicate nature. You might be made of stern enough stuff to hear it, but the doctor would never have mentioned what he did in your presence."

Mary's face grew tighter still. "I see." Were the words directed at him or at the doctor, Alexander wondered? When she said nothing more, he turned to his eggs, eating in deafening silence. He imagined the tea in its china pot would turn cold from the ice in her demeanour, and he dared not look at her.

A sip of his coffee soothed his bad temper a degree, and he said, without looking up, "I will relate what I learned. I do not intend to keep matters from you." To which he received a grunt of an answer and nothing more.

He had almost cleared his plate when Mary asked, "And what did you learn?" Her voice was a bit warmer, and he raised his eyes once more.

Her expression remained hard, but there was less anger in her fine eyes now. He leaned forward so as to speak quietly, lest they be overheard. His intent must have been clear, for she did likewise. A wave of relief washed through him; she was still his ally, even if she was upset with him.

"What did I learn? A great deal, and nothing at all. Mrs. Ferrars did not visit the village on her last trip here, so none of the people had anything to tell me, save the doctor."

"He who attended her during her last moments." There was still a tinge of steel in her tone, but she was speaking sensibly, and he did value her insight, no matter that he had not sought her out for his morning visit to the doctor.

"Just so. He recalled the event, though it was many months ago, and at first reiterated his belief that the death was quite natural. But upon further questioning, he did admit to some unease at the conclusion. He re-examined his notes, and confessed that her death might have been due to arsenic poisoning."

Mary's eyes widened. "Oh my! How alarming! But you do not seem surprised. You had suspected as much?"

"That is, after all, why we are here." He rose to take more eggs and toast. This was no elegant breakfast, as one might find at a grand house where the family was in residence, but it was far superior to what he might have procured for himself in his small set of rooms in London. He would not allow this tasty if simple breakfast to go unappreciated, nor did he know whether he would be in the house again before dinner. The better to eat now, while there was food for the taking.

Mary's voice softened. "Sit and eat. I shall get you some more coffee. I know you prefer it." He took his chair and let Mary rise and busy herself with the pot and cups. "Sugar but no milk if I recall."

She did not hate him after all!

"What of Mrs. Jennings and Miss Dashwood? Are they risen? It is not so early." It was, he saw by the clock on the mantle, only shortly after ten o'clock, well into the work of the day for country folk, but an early hour yet for those accustomed to the hours of the *ton*.

"Elinor and I have taken our morning walk. Mrs. Jennings only recently called for her tray, for she is a late riser. She and Elinor will likely spend much of the day discharging Edward's requests to sort through his mother's belongings. This leaves me at your disposal." She looked at him expectantly. All traces of hostility were gone. "What are our plans?"

"You forgive me then! I am much relieved. Very well. I believe that as our companions are looking through Mrs. Ferrars' effects, we must examine her sons'. I propose to start with Robert's rooms. I do not know what, if anything, I might discover, but if there is something there, I shall find it."

"And I shall help you. When do we start?"

Chapter Eleven

A Search

Robert Ferrars' rooms in the manor house were at the end of the main hallway, where it turned along the courtyard. The building was not so large that there were separate wings for family and guests, but a small cluster of rooms at the top of the stairs seemed set aside for visitors, whilst the larger rooms and suites that lay along the passageway looked to be those of the family.

On the left were the master suite and chambers, and already Mary could hear Mrs. Jennings and Elinor at work inside, talking about this gown and that set of books. She had walked through the place earlier with Elinor and had found, as she had expected, a large bedroom with an attached alcove for a maid and a washing room, connected to a sitting room which in turn led to another bedroom on the other side, presumably for the master of the house. The rooms were all quite impersonal, betraying little of the people who lived there. Only a small shelf of books here or a set of playing cards there gave any indication that these belonged to individuals and were not merely a fine suite at some once-elegant hotel.

Next to the main suite there was a much smaller set of rooms which looked all but abandoned. Two or three amateurish watercolours on one wall and a doll on a chest suggested this must have been Fanny Ferrars' room before she married Elinor's brother John, but it seemed most likely that she had not passed through its threshold since that day.

On the other side were three other modest suites. The first, closest to the main stairs, had been made into a small sitting area. Beside it was a chamber that, by its simple decor and few books with nameplates, was seen to be Edwards, leaving Robert's room for the end, by Fanny's.

It was this room which Mary and Alexander now entered. It was more elaborately decorated than Edward's, displaying evidence of a man who enjoyed the physical luxuries of his status, without having matured into developing his own tastes. "Why do you think he had not moved into the master suite?" Mary mused. "It would seem that he would have enjoyed the large suite and fine furniture, the better to feel master of his demesne."

"Hmmm. Perhaps he wished to redo the rooms and had no desire to move in and then out again. Or perhaps he merely had not spent enough time here to consider it. From all I hear, he left the day of his mother's funeral and returned only once to see to some estate business." Alexander walked to the middle of the room and turned slowly about to take in the entirety of it. "With your agreement, I shall start there at the washstand and armoire. Will you look at the shelves?"

This was acceptable, and they set to work. Mary took out every volume and examined what she found most carefully. She looked over the titles and searched for name plates and shook each one open in case it hid some secret letter or lock of hair. But there was nothing of interest. Robert's tastes in reading were immature, and Mary doubted he ever opened a book for pleasure. The whole collection seemed designed more to add an element to the decor and to demonstrate what a young man ought to have read rather than to entertain him in his quiet hours.

From the bottom shelf, she pulled out a slim portfolio that contained a handful of pencil sketches of buildings and faces, but if Robert were the artist, he displayed little talent and less interest in developing his abilities.

"Any joy?" She stood straight and worked the aches out of her back. She had been hunched over for far too long.

"Nothing here," her companion replied. "I know that he favoured a certain make of shaving soap and liked his cravats folded just so, but nothing that gives any indication of the man himself or his actions. What ho? Wherever did he get this coat? It must have been his father's, for he was far too young ever to have worn something this out of fashion! No, I am afraid there is little in here for us."

They worked for a few minutes longer and then moved to Edward's rooms.

Once more, Alexander started with the washstand and cabinets whilst Mary went to the bookshelves. Edward was a greater reader than his brother, and his books all showed evidence of actually having been read. He was interested in matters of history and theology—which improved him in Mary's opinions, being of a similar bent herself—and seemed to enjoy a small collection of poetry, if the curled pages and faint grease marks were any indication. But again, she found nothing of any import regarding the investigations at hand.

She was about to suggest they take a rest and perhaps enjoy a walk outside when Alexander called out, "What is this?" Mary left her shelves and hurried to the far side of the room where he was peering into a small cabinet next to the armoire. It held a container of shaving soap, some bottles of perfume that reeked of sandalwood, some unidentifiable tubs of creams, and three small vials, all with the printed label, "arsenic in solution."

"Can he really have been so careless?" Alexander asked.

"Oh my!" This was shocking indeed. Could Edward truly have poisoned his mother? Between Alexander's interview with the doctor this morning and the discovery of these vials of poison, it seemed more and more likely. "I can hardly believe this of him."

Alexander took a clean handkerchief from a pocket and used it to pick up one of the small bottles. "If there is poison on the container," he explained, "I would prefer not to have it on my skin. This one has been leaking a bit. You can see where it has dried on the outside." He examined the vial and then peered once more into the cabinet. "See the small circle in the dust?" Mary looked closer and nodded. Clean wood showed through the fine dust exactly where the vial had stood. "This has been sitting here for some time. There is not so much dust there to suggest years, but when we consider that the cabinet has been closed but not sealed, enough to suggest months. See," he dragged a fingernail along the base of the cabinet, leaving a fine line, "there is enough to make a mark, but not enough to be deep."

Mary nodded again. She could see that it was so.

"Then this has been here since about the time of Mrs. Ferrars' death."

Alexander turned sad eyes on her. "So it seems. He must have thought it would be adequately safe from discovery. And he was not completely wrong. There is little enough staff here that a maid would not take the time to clean out the inside of a closed medicine box, and if one had, she would think it nothing more than another jar of some cosmetic preparation or medication. Heaven knows enough of our beauty treatments are lethal that even were she able to read, it would pass unnoticed."

"Might he have come back to retrieve it at a later time? The house was Robert's, but surely he would still request to visit. Further," she added, "Edward knew we were coming here. Would he not have made some effort to remove the vials? He did write to the staff to inform them of our arrival."

Alexander clucked. "A good thought. He is, recall, unable to leave London without a grand excuse, and this would be hard to pass by Mr. Atkins. He might have considered there to be more danger from alerting the housekeeper than by chancing our discovery of this evidence."

"Yes, of course. To inform the housekeeper would be an admission of guilt." She frowned, a hundred unhappy notions tumbling through her mind.

Alexander's expression matched her thoughts. "I admit I am dismayed. It points rather badly at Edward. Between the notes in Robert's diary and these vials, there is too much against him to ignore."

"What I do not understand," Mary shook her head, "is why Edward would do it? Had his mother not already assigned her fortune to Robert? Whatever could he gain?"

Still holding the vial, Alexander sighed. "I can think of several reasons. Perhaps he thought Mrs. Ferrars had not yet signed her new will. The very fact of the summons here suggests that she was still trying to work upon him to change his mind with respect to Miss Steele and Miss Morton. If she had made an irrevocable decision, such a bidding would be pointless."

"Oh. Yes, so I see."

"I have yet to speak to Mr. Hollings, the lawyer. I must ask about the exact nature of her will and when it was signed. But there is another possibility as well."

"Anger?"

"Just so. You are a smart one, Mary, and understand too well the failings of the human condition."

"So he might have been angry enough at being disinherited that he chose to take the ultimate revenge. If the will was signed and her mind was set, he would never be able to regain what he believed was rightfully his. In his anger, he chose murder. Or so a judge might reckon."

"I liked Edward, but I shall have more difficult questions for him when we return."

Further searches through the room provided nothing new, and eventually Mary followed Alexander out into the hallway. For the sake of pure form, they looked through Fanny's chamber as well, but there was nothing of any interest in there at all. They descended the stairs with glum expressions.

The salon was empty. The housekeeper informed them that Mrs. Jennings and Miss Dashwood had taken a ride to the village to procure some supplies to help them organise and package up Mrs. Ferrars' belongings, and then immediately excused herself to see to some undisclosed duties. It was now nearly two o'clock in the afternoon and Mary was in need of a cup of tea and perhaps something to eat.

Since Alexander seemed intent on writing down his observations in his notebook, Mary took it upon herself to visit the kitchens in hopes of procuring some food. Deer Park was not so different in design from Longbourn that she had much difficulty finding the servants' realms, making only two wrong turns on her way.

The space, when she found it, was all but void of life. Of the housekeeper, there was nothing to be seen, and Mary wondered if that lady had left the building entirely, perhaps to visit with friends or relations in the village.

A rack of fresh bread across from the fire and a pile of uncleaned vegetables on the large wooden table suggested that the cook had been in and then had left again, which opinion was substantiated by the sole occupant of the room. This was the maid that Mary had seen upstairs, the only one in the house, so it seemed. She was sitting at the table with a metal cup of something before her and some dried ends of yesterday's loaf on a plate.

"Begging your pardon, Miss. I finished the rooms and was only taking a short break till Cook returns. I'll be back to my duties."

She began to stand, but Mary bid her stay. "Enjoy your rest. It's Lottie, am I correct?" The maid bobbed her head. "I have only come to find something to eat myself. The house is very quiet right now."

Lottie relaxed, but did not pick up her bread.

"We must have caused quite a bother when Mr. Ferrars wrote to say there would be visitors."

This time, the maid nodded with less trepidation.

"I cannot imagine you have many guests here. From what Mr. Ferrars said, the family is seldom in residence."

"No, they are not." Lottie raised her head and pointed with her chin. "There are cakes in that cupboard. It's closed against the dog and flying things. Let me get them for you."

"Not at all. I am perfectly capable of opening a small door. Please, finish your meal." Mary found the cupboard and retrieved a small plate of shortbread and two sweet yeast buns. Then, after a quick glance to ensure no one was coming, she took a third bun and placed it on Lottie's plate. "This will be our secret!" she said with a wink.

The maid gave her a great grin and began to eat.

Mary found a pitcher of water and poured herself a glass, then sat down at another chair at the table. "Are you on the staff here, or were you brought in to see to us?"

The maid mumbled something with her full mouth, then blushed red. "Excuse me, ma'am." She swallowed. "I'm here all the time. I'm the only one, but there is always something what needs doing, even if nobody is coming. The curtains get dusty, or the floors need washing. The house is not grand, not from what Mrs. Pavy says, but the family might come up of a sudden and it must be somewhat ready."

"Yes, of course! When Mrs. Ferrars and her sons came in March, had they given you much notice? Or was their visit a surprise?"

The maid looked at her askance, but did not hesitate to answer.

"Mr. Robert wrote the day before. We hadn't seen them in near on a year, so it was unexpected, but as I told you, the house was ready for them."

"Oh, I do not doubt that at all. Our rooms have all been very well prepared. I have no complaints! But," she hoped she sounded unconcerned, "did Mrs. Ferrars not write herself? How odd that Mr. Robert should be the one to inform you. From the short time I knew him, he hardly seemed the sort to bother with such things." On a whim, Mary asked further, "Did you see much of the family whilst they were here? Did you notice anything unusual? I only ask," she lowered her voice, "because Mr. Robert was here for the first time as the heir. I imagine he saw the house differently, knowing it was to be his and not his brother's."

"'Tis funny you say so," the maid whispered back. She leaned in closer to Mary. "Mrs. Ferrars was as she always was, finding fault here and there. When she first took ill, we all thought it only her usual complaints about the food. Sad, that. And most unsettling. Mr. Edward was fine enough, but he always is a gentleman, so quiet and not at all demanding. But Mr. Robert was different. I cannot say how... excited, perhaps, or maybe nervous? It was like he had a secret he wanted no one to uncover. He even came to see about his mother's favourite sweet, saying it was a special day for her. I thought it was to celebrate his being named heir and wanting to thank his mother. So sad it was her last day."

"That was very considerate of him. What was the dish, this favourite sweet?"

"It was a sort of syllabub pudding that she liked, but the others didn't. She insisted upon eating it with a spoon so as not to get the froth on her face. The Misters Ferrars did not take any, for they preferred the lemon biscuits, but Mr. Robert insisted we make it special for his mother."

"What a kind son. He must have been most distressed when the very next day his mother was gone."

"I... oh!" A noise from the back door silenced her from whatever she was about to say. She put away her water and plate and rushed back to her tasks, whatever they might be, before the door could open. Mary did likewise and absconded with her shortbread and buns to carry them upstairs to where Alexander must surely be waiting for her.

She found him in the library, deep in thought and staring absently at his notes. He acknowledged her entrance with a nod, but said not a word, only grunting his thanks as she placed the plate of sweets beside him on a low table.

"I would like to re-examine the bedrooms." She took a nibble of a piece of shortbread. "Mmm, lavender."

Alexander stuffed an entire biscuit into his mouth and chewed. "The bedrooms again? Of course. Why?"

"Let us take another look, and then I shall tell you. If I am correct, this might change everything we believe."

Chapter Twelve

The Evidence of the Vials

Alexander followed Mary up the stairs and back down the long passageway to Edward's bedroom. What had she discovered that she would not tell him? She found meaning in the tiniest details and was able to piece together insignificant clues that would leave better men baffled. He ought, by some people's measure of the world, to take offence at being shown up by a slip of a girl hardly into womanhood, but that was not him. No! He was proud. Proud of her, proud of being her friend—and more, so he hoped—and proud of their association. What a brilliant investigator she would be, if only women were permitted such occupations.

He pulled the key to the door from the pocket in which he had stowed it and stepped aside as she entered. The curtains were still wide open from their earlier explorations, and the room was bathed in bright sunlight. Mary stood still in the centre of the space for a moment and breathed deeply. Did she imagine she could inhale the secrets this room held? The heavens only knew what she had noticed that might be the clue they needed. Then she turned and moved to the cabinet with the medicines and tubs where they had discovered the vials of arsenic in solution.

This cabinet did not lock, but the door closed with a small latch that opened at a finger's flick. She worked the mechanism and opened the door wide. Everything was as they had left it.

There was the shaving soap, there the perfumes, there the tubs of cream, and there the three vials of poison. Even that line in the dust where Alexander had drawn his fingernail was still there. He said as much to Mary, who listened with all due attention.

"When we discovered this earlier, you lifted the container with your handkerchief." It was part statement, part question.

"Aye. There was some residue on the outside of the vial where the liquid had leaked out and crystallised and I did not wish to have it on my bare skin."

"A very sensible precaution! But look," she pointed to the vial in question with the fine white powder trailing down its length to the surface on which it stood, "there is the impression of the bottle in the dust—"

"Which is how we know this was left here some months ago, most likely on Edward's last visit..."

"—but there is no ring of dried liquid on the base of the cabinet."

Alexander fixed her with a wondering stare.

"Let us, for the moment, assume Edward was the poisoner. Had he spilled some of the liquid whilst using the bottle, he would have wiped it clean. It is instinctual, and like you, I doubt he wished to have arsenic solution on his hands. At the least, there would be some blot or smudge from his hand as he handled the vial. But the trace of the poison on the side of the bottle runs uninterrupted from top to bottom, as if there was some liquid gathered at the top under a poor seal, which ran down the bottle after it was set down." She looked at him with confident eyes.

"Speak on."

"If the liquid ran down the side of the vial and dried, where is the ring of dried poison and residue on the shelf? There is none there, only the dry dust."

There was no stopping the great grin that spread across Alexander's face. "Clever girl! So, the bottles—or this one, at least— was placed here some time after it was used, after the liquid had evaporated to crystals. That would not take long—no more than some hours—so it could well have happened before the two Ferrars brothers left in March. If the one who moved it was in a hurry, he might not have noticed the residue. We were looking carefully. He might not have done."

"Do you think...?"

"Let us go to Robert's chamber. I suspect his own medicine shelves have something to tell us."

They locked the door and went to the other room. There, in Robert's cabinet, on the shelf beside his own collection of pomades and soap powders, was an empty space, also lightly flecked with dust. And there, under the dust but nonetheless distinct for one who looked for it, was a small ring where some liquid had pooled around the bottom of a small container and dried, staining the wood ever so slightly.

"Well! This is interesting! Good girl, Mary!" He beamed at her. "What gave you that idea?"

"The maid mentioned that Mrs. Ferrars had a very particular sweet special only to her after their meal on the night they arrived. Robert made his way to the kitchens to ensure it was prepared for her. It would have been easy for him to introduce the arsenic to the syllabub then, or when it was before her on the dinner table. I wondered, then, about the poison and the bottle, and I recalled the trace of sediment on the side. And from there, it was a natural conclusion that we should re-examine the cabinets."

Alexander held out a hand. She reached for it with her own and shook it like any friendly gentlemen would do.

"But how..."

"Oh, wait. There is the maid in the hallway now!"

Without waiting for him, Mary dashed out the door. Alexander had heard the quiet noises in the hallway, but had thought nothing of them, for even in a neglected house such as this one there was always a maid or servant about. But Mary had heard, and she had something to learn. With long strides, he followed her out the door, taking care to lock it on the way.

Mary had just finished making her request when he joined them.

"This is Lottie," she introduced the maid as if she were a lady. "Lottie, my friend Mr. Lyons." Alexander bowed and the maid's eyes went wide. "Lottie, will you please come with us and answer some questions? There are no wrong answers, and you will not get in any trouble at all, so please be as truthful as you can be. We just need to know something."

"Of course, miss." The maid dipped her head.

Alexander unlocked Edward's door again, and the three filed inside. Mary led the maid to the cabinet, which Alexander now opened again, and stepped aside to let the maid look inside.

"Do you happen to recall," she asked in a gentle voice, "whether those three bottles were there when last you cleaned this cabinet? Remember—I will not be angry no matter what you say. I wish only the truth, as best you recall it."

Lottie nodded with the same wide eyes. She cocked her head and seemed to be thinking very hard.

"It is a while past," she said after a while. "I cannot rightly say I remember everything like it was yesterday, but I do not recall seeing these in here. I knew the gentlemen would be returning to London right away and set about packing their belongings. Normally that sort of thing a valet would do, but the Mr. Ferrars didn't travel with valets, not then, anyway. Mrs. Ferrars held tight to her purse, she did, pardon me for saying. They did for themselves. So it was to me to pack their things. I needed to be certain they had left nothing behind and I came to make sure the only personal items they took with them were the ones they had brought. I would have remembered something I had not seen before, I think."

She frowned and looked at the vials again.

"But I did see them. Where did I see them? Oh, so sorry Miss, Sir. I cannot recall. They were not in here, but somewhere else."

"Hmmm." Mary made a non-committal noise. Then she asked, "How can you be certain they were not in here when last you cleaned the room?"

"I remember thinking how little Mr. Edward had with him. He brought his shaving soap and some beeswax lotion for an itch he gets on his hands, but nothing else. Not even Cologne water, which so many of the gentlemen favour. Not like Mr. Robert, who seemed to have his whole toilette case with him—" She stopped short for an instant. "Oh!"

"Yes, Lottie?" Mary's pointed glance kept Alexander quiet.

"I recall now. I recall where I saw those bottles before. Mr. Robert had them in his cabinet. Not all the time; they were not there when I unpacked him, but when I cleaned his room to pack him up, they were there. I remember now, thinking there were rats in the walls or something, and I wondered why he didn't talk to Mrs. Pavy about them. But I thought he was trying to be no bother, that he tried to sort it himself. But with all the ado of the funeral and the house being thrown into a fuss, I forgot all about it."

Mary thanked the maid and sent her back to her tasks.

"This changes matters, does it not?" Mary sat down on the bed and looked at him.

He replied with a nod. "Somebody went to a great deal of trouble to try to cast the blame on Edward."

"The entry in the diary, the letter to the solicitor, the poison in Edward's medicine cabinet..."

"Just so. All especially placed to lead us to think Edward had killed his mother."

"What I cannot understand is why. Why implicate Edward? If he had already lost his mother's favour, what reason could there be to have him implicated in her death?"

Alexander began to pace the room. His feet moved of their own accord, taking him from the door to the window, to the washstand, and back to the door. Sometimes the motion of his feet set into action the motion of his mind. He waited for inspiration, but none came.

"The letter and diary in his London rooms? Those were in Robert's own hand?" Mary's words interrupted his fruitless efforts at thought.

Alexander pursed his lips. "I shall have to look closer and perhaps set the papers before an expert in counterfeit and forgery, but I should say so, yes."

"And the party that came in March was small, only the three of them?"

"Aye. There was nobody else here. I have asked this of everybody I could find: Mrs. Pavy, the maid, the cook, the doctor at the village, the groom who came in from the village to care for the horses. Only Mrs. Ferrars and her two sons were here. There were no other rooms prepared, and nobody came to visit, even for a few moments, other than the doctor after she took ill."

"Then it must have been Robert."

"There seems to be nobody else."

There was further silence.

Then Mary gasped. "We have forgotten something."

"Aye? What is it?" A moment of hope flared in his breast.

"The handkerchief! Unless Edward was complicit in killing his brother, somebody tried to blame Edward for that death as well."

"And that could not possibly have been Robert." He let his head fall back on his shoulders and squeezed his eyes closed. "Oh, this is a muddle indeed."

Mrs. Jennings and Elinor were waiting in the parlour when Alexander and Mary returned downstairs. The older lady sat half-sprawled on the large settee, her face etched with exhaustion. There was not a trace of her customary good humour. Elinor looked slightly less fagged, although she too seemed to melt into her chair with no sign that she ever wished to move again. A book fell open in her hand, but her head lay back on the upholstery and Alexander doubted she had read a word.

"Children, you're back," Mrs. Jennings drawled. The words seemed to use up her reserves of energy. "Who would have thought Mrs. Ferrars would have so many possessions! Oh, that Fanny might have come and done this rather than us. But it had to be done, and if this is a duty I can do the dead, so be it." She closed her eyes and said nothing more.

Elinor roused herself from her cocooning chair.

"Please, sit. There is no ceremony here. You look as tired as I feel," Mary told her friend. She glanced at Alexander as she took a spot on the sofa, and he obeyed her request as he sat down beside her. "Have you completed your task?"

With a symphony of groans and anecdotes, the two ladies related everything they had done. Most of Mrs. Ferrars' clothing would be boxed up by Mrs. Pavy and Lottie to be stored in the attics in case they were ever needed. Those books which the ladies had deemed suitable would be shelved in the library, and her ornaments and *bric-à-brac* would be packed up to be sent to Fanny Dashwood, who would decide what to do with it. She had left very few letters, none of which involved more than acknowledgements of gifts or lists of proposed activities for house parties. These Fanny would get as well, but Elinor suspected they would be consigned to the fireplace. There remained only a few items of jewellery that were kept at the estate, to be returned to Edward.

"There is nothing here of any particular value," Mrs. Jennings yawned. "One or two very pretty pieces, though. I cannot imagine Mrs. Ferrars ever having worn them, but they would look quite fetching on Miss Dashwood." The spark was back in her eye. "Perhaps when this whole dreadful affair is over, she might see her way to a piece or two." She gave an exaggerated wink that left Elinor looking most uncomfortable and Mary on the verge of giggles.

The only task left to be done was an interview with Mrs. Pavy. Mary suggested to Alexander that she be the one to speak with the housekeeper, and to her surprise, he agreed. Perhaps he felt guilty for not inviting her along to talk to the doctor, or perhaps he thought she would elicit more useful answers than he would, with his notebook and pencil poised to write down every incriminating word. No matter, she was pleased for the task.

While she undertook this task, Alexander told her that he was off to find the local magistrate to inform him of the vials of poison and request that the room be sealed. This, too, was satisfactory. She would find that discussion interesting, but Alexander would relate anything of note later on. Thus, she set off in search of Mrs Pavy.

She found the housekeeper busy with a list of linens in her small office off the kitchen and begged a moment of her time.

"Mr. Lyons seems satisfied with what he has learned here," Mary explained, "but I hoped you might have a minute for me." She wished to put Mrs. Pavy at her ease and adopted a conversational tone. "I am so heartsore at all the tragedy this house has seen of late, with Mrs. Ferrars' passing, and then that of Mr. Robert. I knew him just a little, and her not at all, but still I feel the weight of their deaths. I thought if I heard some recollections of them, it might ease my mind."

"I am quite busy, Miss, if Mr. Lyons is not of a mind to speak to me." The housekeeper shuffled the lists in her hands and cast her gaze back at the top sheet.

"Can you not take a short break? I am certain Mr. Edward would not begrudge you a minute to yourself, and perhaps you will join me with some tea..."

Mrs. Pavy narrowed her eyes at Mary, glanced down at the inventory lists, and then looked back at Mary. "Very well. I can give you ten minutes. Come to the kitchen, if you will. There's hot water on the fire."

Shortly, Mary found herself at the large kitchen table once more, now with a steaming cup of tea and another piece of shortbread on a plate before her. "What can I tell you?" Mrs. Pavy asked.

"I suppose anything will do," Mary replied. "When did you last see Mr. Robert? Did he come up at all since... since he inherited the house?"

Mrs. Pavy picked up her own cup and sniffed at it as if it were boiled washing water. "Just the once, not long after his mother passed on. What a dreadful time that was, I tell you. The house was upside down, what with them arriving with all but no notice, and then with the fuss and bother of the funeral, and me not knowing which of the boys to listen to for my orders. That Edward, he's a sweet man, and I was happier when he was the one to inherit, but Robert insisted on things being done his way. Fortunately, they had her buried and ran back to London within a handful of days, and I was thankful that Mrs. Dashwood—their sister Fanny, that is—did not come as well."

Mary made some sympathetic murmurs, and the housekeeper huffed into her tea. "It was bad enough with Mr. Robert came back later with those two ladies with him. It was just for a day, on their way to visit friends, he said."

"Ladies?" Mary raised her eyebrows.

"Two sisters, one of them the lady that was the cause of Mrs. Ferrars disinheriting Mr. Edward. And to think that Mr. Robert would bring them here! Ordering me about like her own servant, that one was. And the other one poking about where she wasn't wanted, always with her head in a closed room, or opening cabinets that should be left alone. No manners at all. I was pleased to see the back of them."

"It was kind of Mr. Robert to see them to their destination." This was all Mary could think of to say.

"Well. Indeed. Now, I must be back to my tasks." She rose without another word and strode back to her office, leaving Mary with some answers, but more questions running through her mind.

Their tasks were now complete. There being little left to do at Deer Park, the quartet departed the next morning. It would be another two days of travel back to London, two days of enforced company in the confines of the bouncing carriage, but perhaps there would be a moment to sit with Alexander and read through his notes. They might help her make sense of what she had seen and heard. Because it was now clear that there was more going on with Robert's death than they had imagined.

Chapter Thirteen

An Unwanted Note

Mary and her friends arrived back in London in the late afternoon, after another night in an inn along the road. She wished she had been able to take some minutes in private with Alexander to talk, but the presence of Elinor, and more pointedly, Mrs. Jennings, had made that impossible. There would be time to speak soon. She had so much more to ask and so much more to say that she hardly knew where to begin.

For now, however, her task was to further pick apart the knot surrounding Edward Ferrars. The clues they had discovered at Deer Park were more than sufficient to convince her that somebody had tried to frame a plot against Edward. Somebody— almost certainly his brother Robert—had killed Mrs. Ferrars and then had contrived evidence to blame Edward. This much seemed quite clear.

What was still obscure was why. Why go to such lengths to point a finger at Edward? Robert was already the heir. He had nothing to gain if Edward swung for his own crimes... or did he? Mary itched to see the will Mrs. Ferrars had drawn up. But more troubling was a thought that had occurred to her as the carriage rolled into London. There had been a deliberate and concerted attempt to destroy Edward.

Had Robert not left the incriminating comments in his diary and in his unsent letter, nobody would have suspected anything to be amiss about his mother's death. The doctor had been satisfied, and the parson in the village as well, from what Alexander had told her, and to all accounts, that sad affair was settled. So why, then, bring to everybody's attention a crime which had heretofore gone unnoticed? After all, it was Robert himself who had perpetrated that vile deed, and until his damning words were found, he seemed quite certain to be forever free of suspicion. What possible reason could he have had to make such a criminal deed public?

By tacit agreement, she and Alexander had decided not to disclose their findings to the other ladies, or even to confess their suspicions, but there was too much unsaid to remain silent for long.

At last, the carriage rolled down a bumpy road, heading towards Upper Berkeley Street where Mrs. Jennings lived. They would rest there for a while and the horses would be relieved of their burden until such time as a hack or cart could be hired to transport Mary and her few belongings back to Gracechurch Street.

She thought then of Marianne Dashwood, now residing with the Gardiners and their family. How had she fit into this family, so different in every way from her own? The Gardiners, whilst everything elegant and refined, were nonetheless from the circles created by trade. For Marianne Dashwood, born into the luxury of a grand estate and a life of leisure, it must be most unsettling indeed to see her hostess send the children off to their school every day and then disappear herself to work a full day at her husband's warehouse. That her work was intellectual—for Aunt Gardiner managed the books and on occasion helped with a customer—and not physical, was of little import. She worked for her living, which placed her in a different world.

Moreover, would Marianne be pleased at Mary's return? Would she enjoy having another woman with whom to commiserate, almost like sisters? Did she have secrets to share and dreams to discuss? Or did she prefer her solitude wherein she might brood very Romantically about her tragic lot in life?

No matter! What was more important was that the young woman was safe, hidden away where no one might find her.

"Oh!"

Three sets of eyes turned to her.

"Mary?" Alexander blinked at her.

"I had a thought. That is... I was wondering about something." She looked at Mrs. Jennings and Elinor, who were watching her. "It is nothing of import. We are all too tired now for anything more than a meal and our beds. Perhaps when we meet at some later time, we might discuss it."

"Yes. At some later time."

Good. He understood her so well!

Soon the carriage rolled to a stop before Mrs. Jennings' townhouse and the occupants tumbled out. Two servants emerged from the house to wrestle with the trunks and bags whilst Mrs. Jennings led the others up the two stairs and into the house. Within moments, they were seated in her salon and a maid came in to inform them that tea would soon be ready.

"I am afraid that I must get back to my family soon. I have only my soft valise and can easily find a hackney." Mary pushed herself up to standing and started for the door.

Mrs. Jennings looked concerned.

"But after such a long drive, Miss Bennet! How tired you must be. I insist you rest and take dinner here." Despite the five days in each other's presence, Mrs. Jennings still thrived on all the company she could gather.

But Mary was insistent. "Thank you, ma'am. My aunt is expecting me. When Mr. Lyons sent his express message yesterday, he included a note to my family. I should very much enjoy dinner another evening."

"And I shall see her safely home," Alexander smiled.

"I promise to send a messenger with news of Marianne as soon as I am able."

Mrs. Jennings sat up. "Ah, Marianne! Yes. Here, I see the stack of letters that have arrived these last few days. Here is one for Miss Marianne. Will you take it to her?" She reached to the pile and extracted a thick envelope written with a fine man's hand. "She will be pleased to receive her correspondence."

Mary eyed the letter and thought that Marianne would likely not appreciate this particular note, but agreed nonetheless. She and Alexander rose and bid the others a good evening and then left the house with their light bags to find a conveyance to carry them across the city.

"You had a revelation." Alexander began his comment without preamble.

She looked straight ahead as the open carriage worked its way through the crowded streets. With all the horses and carts and people about, it might be faster to walk, but Mary was tired and was pleased not to carry her bag, light though it was, for the hour it would take to reach Cheapside.

"I did. Or, rather, I might have. I had been wondering," she explained, "why Robert had set all those clues about pointing towards Edward as their mother's murderer, when he had no reason to do so. Moreover, I was wondering why he set the clues at all, for until we found them everybody believed Mrs. Ferrars' death to be lamentable but arranged by no one but God. It was never thought to be murder until the diary and letter were found."

Alexander nodded. "I had considered that myself."

"But then I thought of Marianne Dashwood, hidden so no one could find her, and I realised that Robert might have hidden the clues so no one could find them. Or," she added after a pause, "not until he wished them to be found."

Alexander turned his head to look at her. "Until such time as he needed to find somebody else to blame. Or until he wished to be rid once and for all of his brother Edward."

"So I believe. When will you have a chance to examine Mrs. Ferrars' will?"

He let out a breath of air. "With luck, tomorrow morning. I sent my messages before we left; I hope to have a response sitting in my office when I return this evening."

She looked at him.

"No, you cannot join me. He will never speak to me if I bring you along. Mary... I must insist. I understand your valuable contributions, but I can only believe Mr. Hollings never will. If I am to convince him that I must see the will, I must have his utter confidence. But I promise to tell you everything I find as early as I possibly can."

This was unfortunate, but not unexpected. She huffed, but agreed.

"Where are his rooms? Can I meet you afterwards?"

"Better, I shall come to you. You have my word as a heathen." He gave her a cheeky grin and she laughed freely, all thoughts of annoyance now vanished. The driver turned his head to see the source of the noise, leading Alexander to laughter as well. In such a way, they covered the last mile of the trip, until they drew near their destination.

"Now here we are arrived. Let me see you inside," he said as he cleared his throat from such indecorous chuckles.

The hired carriage came to a halt and Alexander leapt to the ground, then helped Mary out. He grabbed at both bags—hers and his own—and after paying the fare, sent the driver on his way.

"Do you hope to be offered a room for the night?" Mary teased as he walked her up the stairs and knocked at the door. "My aunt might have a bed for you in the nursery, or the servants' hall."

He laughed at her. "I shall find another hack soon enough. For now, I merely wish to see you safely back in the embrace of your aunt and uncle."

Aunt Gardiner herself came to the door and dragged Mary and Alexander inside. A flurry of questions ensued, answered by an equal flurry of responses, and soon Alexander was invited to stay to dine, which he accepted with a smile and very civil manners.

Marianne, when she entered the front parlour, looked much improved for her short respite from Mrs. Jennings' house. Her smile came easily, and she joked with Mrs. Gardiner and the eldest two children, who were downstairs. She greeted Mary with a hug and Alexander with a warm smile, and seemed quite recovered from the terror that had overtaken her.

Being accustomed to early hours for the sake of the children, the family ate soon after Mary and Alexander arrived, and afterwards sat down for conversation when the younger two went up to the nursery. Marianne asked about the trip to Deer Park and Uncle Gardiner had some amusing anecdotes to tell of his time in those parts while he was delivering some goods there in his younger days.

They talked for a while until Mary recalled the envelope entrusted to her for delivery.

"Marianne," she drew the younger woman aside, "this arrived for you whilst we were gone. I do not wish to distress you, but thought you should have it. If you prefer to throw it unread into the flames, I shall not blame you."

She held out the package of folded paper. The writing on the direction was something she had seen before, in her momentary glance at the note Marianne had received several days before: the very note that initiated her terrible distress.

Marianne extended a tentative arm to take the letter, then dropped it as if she had been burned.

"Miss Dashwood?" Alexander was at Mary's side in a moment. "How may I be of assistance?"

"It is from him!" Marianne choked. "I know it! I know his handwriting and his seal. I have seen them so often… Oh, why cannot he leave me alone?"

Alexander lowered his voice so Mrs. Gardiner and the two older children could not overhear. "What is it, Miss Dashwood? Can you tell me? I truly might be able to help. It is my business to find solutions to people's problems, after all. Will you trust me?"

Marianne looked from Mary to Alexander and back to Mary. Mary nodded three times and gave what she hoped was a reassuring smile. With tear-damp eyes, Marianne bit her bottom lip and sniffled. "Yes. Very well. I cannot stay here forever, and when I return, he will find me then. I cannot live in such fear. Yes. Where can we talk?"

After ample pleading and explaining and a promise to keep the door open, Mary's aunt permitted the three of them to use the dining room for their conversation. "Three of you together ought to be respectable enough," she said, but fixed Alexander with a fierce glare that commanded him to behave as a gentleman.

Mary all but laughed at this. From what she had seen in her one-and-twenty years was that many men born to the rank had nothing gentlemanly about their behaviour at all, but that Alexander, born into the middle class and with the accent and garb to match, was more of a gentleman in his actions than most of them put together. Still, she kept her thoughts silent and thanked her aunt for the privilege.

When they were seated around the table, the door to the room wide open as promised, Marianne finally explained herself. She spoke almost in a whisper, her words dissolving into sobs, and more than once Mary thought the girl might swoon, as much for effect as from distress, but the story came out at last.

The original note was, indeed, from Mr. Willoughby.

He claimed, so Marianne told them, that he had loved her all the time; that his apparent devotion to her when first they met in Devonshire was genuine, and that he had hoped to offer for her. But his aunt, upon whom his hopes depended, had discovered an indiscretion in his past and in disgust had sent him from her home, separating him from the inheritance he assumed would be his.

How like Edward's circumstance this seemed to Mary! Edward's sin was to engage himself to the wrong woman, whilst Willoughby's seemed more serious (although Marianne did not know what exactly he had done), and both men had been cast from their homes and disinherited. But whereas Edward had accepted his fate with grace, Willoughby, it seemed, was made of baser stuff. Seeing no hope of wealth from his relation, he took himself immediately to London, where he preyed amongst the wealthy young women during the season and, as soon as he could manage it, had engaged himself to the richest of them.

Miss Grey, now Mrs. Willoughby, brought with her a fortune of fifty thousand pounds. This, at last, was the wealth Willoughby had sought. But it did not make him happy. Not even fifty thousand pounds could turn his wife into Marianne. And so, wishing for one woman and clawing onto the other's fortune, he hoped to have both at once.

"He... he was coercing me into a tryst!" Marianne sobbed. "He offered to set me up in a house and dote upon me if only I would... Oh, it is too horrible! After the dreadful way he treated me, after how he is acting towards his wife, to think that I would ever agree to talk to him again, let alone become his mistress... How low does he think I have fallen?"

There ensued a new bout of weeping which required one of Alexander's handkerchief's and two of Mary's to sop up.

"Why were you so afraid, Miss Dashwood? What did he threaten?"

She blinked at Alexander with big and red eyes. "He promised that if I did not agree, he would find a way to force my hand. I thought... I thought he might come and take me from the house against my will. How despicable a man he is! I cannot believe I ever liked him."

"Why did you not tell anybody? You are not without friends."

The girl seemed about to float away once more in a river of tears. "I was too ashamed. And I was so very frightened of what he might do." The last words were more sobs than anything, but her meaning was clear.

"And yet," Mary offered gently, "he made no approach to the house whilst we were away, according to the housekeeper, and only sent that one letter. Will you read it?"

Marianne blinked back her tears and found her voice. "No! No, I could not bear it! Mr. Lyons, will you read it? You need not tell me what it says. I can hardly stand to look at it!"

By his tight jaw, Mary could see that Alexander was growing tired of the young woman's overly emotional sensibilities, but he merely gave her a serious look and agreed. He took the letter and broke the seal, then scanned the contents.

As he read, Mary watched his face betray his reactions. His jaw grew tighter still and his shoulders stiffened beneath his coat.

"You will not like what he has to say, Miss Dashwood. I shall not read it all unless you wish it, but he is trying to blackmail you."

"Blackmail? Whatever is that?"

"A word we use in the north for a form of extortion. It is a vile practice," the investigator replied, "whereby an evildoer attempts to extort money or some action by means of a threat, usually that of exposure or scandal. In this instance, Willoughby claims he holds some letters you wrote to him whilst in Devonshire, and then immediately after he left, before he met and engaged himself to Miss Grey."

Marianne's face went white. "Oh no! He couldn't! Oh, I am ruined!"

Chapter Fourteen

The Wills

Alexander had learned nothing new from Marianne Dashwood. At the mention of her letters to John Willoughby, Marianne had dissolved into a flood of tears from which she could not be relieved, and at last Mary offered simply to take the girl up to her bed. Alexander found Mrs. and Mr. Gardiner, explained the unfortunate turn of events, thanked them for the delicious dinner and their hospitality, and set off for his rooms.

The evening was pleasant and his travel roll not heavy, so he chose to walk the two miles back to his corner of town. After two days in a carriage, no matter how comfortable, and several hours spent at the Gardiners' gracious home, he was more than pleased to move his limbs. He slung his bag across his back with the long strap he had requested be sewn into it and began his march.

He had rounded the corner at Drury Lane and Russell Street when he heard his name called out. It was close enough to his rooms that he wondered if some client had been lurking in the area awaiting his return. He looked about him and the flash of brass buttons caught his eye.

"Colonel Brandon!" He hurried his steps to meet the gentleman. "A pleasure to see you, sir. Were you here to find me?"

"Lyons," the colonel reached out to shake his hand. "Yes, I was indeed. Mrs. Jennings said you had returned and accompanied Miss Bennet to her relations. I wished to speak to you and thought to take a stroll through this amusing part of town."

"Amusing... yes, one might call it that!" The two men shared a quick laugh before reaching Alexander's laneway. They turned at the bakery at the corner and continued the few steps to his door, whereupon they climbed the stairs to his office.

"Please, sit and I shall attend you in a moment." He shrugged the travel case off his back and let it fall with a dull thud onto the floor by the bookshelf. The bag was not heavy, but it was nonetheless a relief to have it no longer weighing his steps. He rolled his shoulders to relieve them of the knots that had formed and then sat down in his chair. There was a fresh sheet of paper in front of him, as he had left it before his departure, and a pencil sharp and ready. For the moment, he ignored the short pile of letters strewn on the floor by the door, where his landlady had pushed them during his absence.

"Now, how may I help you?"

Colonel Brandon sat forward in his chair and leaned his forearms on the large desk. "It is Miss Marianne," he started.

Wordlessly, Alexander bid him continue.

"I know she is somewhere safe, but I cannot help but fret about her. What can you tell me?"

Alexander considered the man across from him. How much could he be trusted? He had not promised to keep Marianne's situation confidential, but neither had he obtained her permission to divulge what he knew.

"You are trying to decide what to relate to me." The colonel had seen his indecision and divined its cause. "Permit me to tell you something and then reconsider. What I offer you may change your mind. You see," he leaned even closer across the desk, "I am and have long been in love with Marianne Dashwood. I said nothing when she began her strange courtship with Willoughby, for at the time, he seemed to make her happy and her happiness was everything to me. I will not hurt her now."

"You trust me with a most intimate confession." Alexander still had not picked up his pencil. He suspected that this particular interview would remain unrecorded.

Brandon leaned against the back of his chair. "You are a friend of Fitzwilliam's. That alone speaks more highly of you than anything else I can imagine. But you have a fine reputation about town for discretion and honour and I am counting on that now." He leaned forward once more, a note of desperation colouring his voice. "Please, I must at least know that she is well. What can you tell me?"

It was the anguish in the man's eyes rather than his words that convinced Alexander to speak. "Very well. I can tell you that she is safe and in good health, and for the most part, not unhappy."

"Not unhappy... That, sir, does not put me much at ease. Mrs. Jennings told me about the new letter. Am I to assume that this has distressed her anew?"

"Sadly, yes. The letter was from—"

"Willoughby. I could not doubt it. What did it say?"

It was but a moment's decision. If Brandon truly did have the young woman's best interests at heart, he might be able to protect her. For she could not spend the rest of her days living with the Gardiners, no matter that they were excellent people.

"Willoughby is attempting to force Miss Marianne into an irregular arrangement," he started.

"The man wants to set her up as his mistress!" He then let out an epithet that almost made Alexander blush.

"At the very least, he wants a tryst. It seems our man is not so happy with the lady he has chosen as his wife and wishes to dally elsewhere. At first, he attempted to lure Miss Marianne with coaxing words, but this most recent letter was more coercive."

Brandon's face flushed red with anger. "What does he have? What does he claim to possess to sway her? Has somebody seen them together? Such a man can be paid to lie and need not be heard! A lock of hair? Who is to tell one woman's hair from another?"

"He writes that he has her letters."

The red face now blanched. "What do they say? What did the foolish girl write?"

Alexander shrugged. "I am afraid I cannot say. She would not tell us, only that she was surely ruined."

Brandon shot to his feet. "Thank you, sir," he stated in clipped tones. "I shall know how to act. Willoughby has injured me more than you or he can imagine. No, not only this. There are other... other matters as well. I have called him out before. This time I shall be satisfied." And with that alarming statement, he strode out the door, all but slamming it closed in his wake.

Ice ran through Alexander's veins. Was this man, this taciturn, solemn man, serious in his threats against Willoughby? It could not be, and yet that feral glint in his eye as he had mentioned these 'other matters' brooked no argument. The ice ran colder.

Alexander stared at the door that seemed still to shake in its frame until Brandon's heavy footsteps could no longer be heard on the stairs. He took a deep breath, hoping the inrush of air would calm his own mind, and searched for a course of action. There could be no good ending if the colonel's intentions came to fruition.

After several long minutes, his thoughts ordered at last, Alexander pulled out his notebook and began to record what had most recently occurred in his investigation. Following his pages about the trip to Norfolk and his extensive notes on the evidence they had discovered with regard to Mrs. Ferrars' death, he started a new sheet:

Attempted blaming of Edward for mother's death - why?
Evidence not intended to be found yet - what purpose?

And then he wrote:

Attempted Blackmail - John Willoughby against Marianne Dashwood

He jotted down all the particulars he could recall, including what little he knew of the first letter and the entirety of the text of the second, for he had that in his possession. He had not Mary's uncanny ability to recall verbatim what she had heard or read, and thus he was pleased that Marianne had not asked for the missive back. He recorded his impressions and Mary's responses. But he did not make any mention of Colonel Brandon's confession or threat against the miscreant. Some matters were best left private.

When he had finished, he retrieved the pile of letters from the floor and sorted through them. There were the usual assortment of bills and letters of account, which he would discharge the next morning. Since that first encounter he had with Darcy three years past, when he helped to find the gentleman's missing sister, his time had not been idle. And after the case of the slain clergyman, when first he had met Mary and worked with her to acquit her sister of charges of murder, his expertise had been much in demand by the most discerning of the *ton*. On the rare occasion, he considered taking larger rooms in a more fashionable part of town, but just as quickly discarded those thoughts. He was happy here. He knew and liked the neighbourhood, colourful though it might be, and he was pleased to be saving a good amount of money for when he would one day marry and set up a home with his wife. With Mary. If ever they could find a way past the differences that divided them.

He brushed those thoughts aside and considered the rest of his mail.

Here was a note from the Ferrars' solicitors, inviting him to call at their rooms at his convenience. He would do that early the next morning as well, as he had planned. And here was another from one of his associates. The man had discovered an expert on handwriting who would lend his skills to ascertain the legitimacy of Robert's signatures and the letters in his rooms. Alexander wrote a quick reply and ran down to find a messenger to send it off to this expert immediately, requesting him kindly to meet Alexander at Robert Ferrars' house the following afternoon. There would be a fee to be paid to the man, of course, but this was accounted for in the rates Alexander charged his clients.

The next note was from another of his colleagues, this one a chap who knew all the men who ran gaming houses and who always had the latest information about who owed what to whom. It was a long letter and Alexander put it aside to examine better the following morning after his meeting with Mr. Hollings.

The rest of the mail was an assortment of advertisements for new businesses in the neighbourhood, some invitations from friends to dine, and a reminder from his tailor that the new coat that his friend Darcy had bought for his birthday present some time ago was waiting for its final fitting. He resigned himself to some wasted hours at the tailor when this case was concluded and decided that after he received his compensation, he would avail himself of some of the curries from the Hindoostane Coffee House, which promised to bring the best of India's cuisine to one's very door. Mr. Mohamed was no longer the owner, but reports continued that the food was exceptional, and that there were plentiful vegetable dishes for his particular tastes. Did Mary enjoy currie, he wondered? Had she ever tasted it? Surely the Gardiners, with their cosmopolitan tastes and access to the best spices London had to offer, would have served up some dish to her. He must ask her. How much he would enjoy being the one to introduce her to this most delightful of foods.

With thoughts of Mary Bennet and fragrant Eastern dishes fighting for supremacy in his head, he tidied his office and locked the door before carrying his bag and the lamp up the stairs to where he dwelt, and there finally took to his bed.

As arranged, Alexander appeared at Mr. Hollings' chambers in the City early the next morning, where he was greeted by an efficient looking young assistant. He took a seat in the front office, as requested, and, after a short wait, was invited in to Mr. Hollings' private rooms. The solicitor had Mrs. Ferrars' will already out on the desk, and Robert's alongside it.

Alexander introduced himself and offered a hand to the solicitor. Hollings was a short and slight man with a high bald forehead and a long nose. He looked to be about forty years of age. His eyes were intelligent behind thick spectacles, and his face seemed inclined to good humour. If he held any reservations about speaking to Alexander, he did not betray them.

"This is unconventional," he stated without preamble. "It is not customary to exhibit such documents before somebody who is so little connected with the situation. But your reputation is excellent and I am further swayed by your credentials as a student of the law. I know you will read these documents properly. However, I must insist on being present when you examine the wills."

"Thank you for your confidence," Alexander returned. "I have no objection to your presence. I am hopeful, indeed, that you might help me as well. Shall we begin?"

The first item examined was Mrs. Ferrars' final will, in which she had stripped Edward of his inheritance and bestowed it upon Robert instead.

"I advised her strongly against this," Mr. Hollings stated, "but she would not be denied. She also insisted upon making the terms of this will irrevocable..."

Alexander looked up sharply from his perusal of the document.

"You are correct," the lawyer agreed. "Such a thing is not possible, or at least, not in my understanding of the law. I suggested to her that the best way to ensure that the terms of the will not be changed was for her not to change them, but she insisted upon something more official. I told her I would look into the matter and return to her with my findings."

"Then this will is not a final document? It is not complete?"

"Oh, no. It is final and binding. She insisted upon signing it forthwith and merely adding a codicil, or possibly having a second document drawn up to include the stipulation that it never be changed. But she died two days later at the Norfolk estate, and I took no more action. By her death, the will was now her final document and could not be changed. Any legal manoeuvring seemed quite unnecessary."

"Just so." How unusual to demand such a stipulation. The woman must have been quite set against her son Edward to insist upon such an unnecessary term.

Now Alexander put his attention into the will itself. Other than the decision to transfer her wealth to her younger rather than her older son upon her death, there was little unusual or of a surprising nature in it. It was well written and unambiguous. If Edward had chosen to contest it, he would have found very few grounds upon which to do so.

"Who knew about this will?" Alexander asked.

"The lady herself, of course, and me. I brought in my clerk as a witness, and the driver of my buggy. Yes, he is literate. I use him often in this capacity." Hollings rocked back on his chair in the manner of a much younger man. Then he sat forward again, bringing the front legs of the chair down onto the floor with a bang.

"And, of course, Robert Ferrars himself."

"Robert knew about this?"

The solicitor smiled. "Oh yes, without doubt. They both did. Their mother insisted upon summoning both sons to sit with us, so each might know exactly what he had lost—or gained. Edward did not attend: he had little incentive to attend to his mother's whims after all. How more could she punish him for his disobedience? He knew the general terms of the will and that was enough for him. But Robert was there. He heard every term and knew of the planned dispersal of every penny."

"Then if Robert knew of the terms of the will, he also knew that the will was not, indeed, irrevocable. That his mother might, at some time, when in better charity towards Edward, alter the document again to return to him some or all of his fortune."

"I do not like what you are saying, sir." Hollings' cheerful face now sported a rather forbidding frown.

"Furthermore, and I beg your indulgence, Mr. Hollings, if Robert had some action in mind that might disoblige his mother, he would be better to secure his inheritance by ridding himself of the lady and of the possibility that she might reconsider her actions."

"Sir!" Hollings leapt to his feet. "I must ask you to leave."

Alexander shook his head. "Forgive me, Mr. Hollings. I ought to have said this before. I already have ample evidence that Mr. Robert Ferrars engineered his mother's death. The tool was arsenic, and we have found the vials and have recorded the evidence of people who noted the poison in his possession. It is in the hands of the magistrate in Norfolk as we speak. I am sorry."

The solicitor glared at him but made no more attempts to eject him from the room.

"May I now examine Robert's will?" Alexander kept his tone as respectful as he could. Hollings seemed to soften a bit and handed it over in silence.

There was nothing remarkable in this document. It had been signed a little over a year earlier, upon his coming of age, and included nothing more than the usual comments about his worldly possessions—goods, chattel, credits and land—and all passing to his mother, and if deceased, then to his brother Edward, and if he should be deceased, to his sister Fanny and to his nieces and nephews of her line. There was nothing about Lucy or any wife, and nothing about a child.

"In a letter sent to Miss Steele, Robert made mention of making provisions for his unborn child. Did he ever make such arrangements with you? Here, I have recorded the words from this letter."

"Unborn... What?" The solicitor's head snapped up.

Alexander showed him the note.

Lucy,

I know that the elopement to Gretna did not meet your expectations. I shall visit with my solicitor soon to make provisions for our child.

Yrs,

RF

Hollings blinked in surprise.

"I knew, of course, that Robert's will is being challenged by this lady who claims to be his wife, and who claims her child is his. But until this moment, I had not known that he claimed the child as his own. Were they, indeed, married? For that, with this letter of acknowledgment, changes matters entirely."

Alexander could only shrug. "I do not know. I am seeking confirmation one way or another, and hope to have some answers before many more days have passed. But did you know that Robert wished to see to the child's welfare?"

"This is the first I knew of it," Hollings blew out a puff of air. "What question I now have is this: If Robert and Lucy were married in fact, why should Robert wish to make separate provisions for the child? Under every normal circumstance, such consideration would come automatically with the legitimate birth of said child."

"It is a pretty muddle, is it not? Every answer brings new questions."

Hollings had nothing to say to this, and Alexander continued. "Speaking of questions, I have one more. Miss Steele could not say where Robert kept the record of their marriage, assuming such took place and was legal. Did he, by any chance, commit them to your keeping? She claims the marriage took place in Scotland, and that there are, therefore, no lines in any church register."

Hollings shrugged. "I have seen nothing of these. If I had, and if I had proper evidence of the father of Miss Steele's child, there would be no question as to her rights to Robert's estate. But I cannot help you here."

"Whatever could he have done with them, then?"

"If, indeed," the solicitor commented, "they exist at all."

Chapter Fifteen

Colonel Brandon

The morning threatened to stretch interminably before Mary. She rose early, according to her habits, and slid out of her bed and into her clothing, keeping as quiet as possible. Marianne was still asleep in the bed across from hers, and she had no wish to wake the girl. She splashed some water from the jug onto her face and pinned her hair into a style not quite tidy and went downstairs to help her aunt prepare the children for their day.

An hour passed in a moment, but when the children had left with their nursemaid and Aunt Gardiner had departed to start her day at the family's place of business, Mary found herself alone and anxious for something to do.

She was unable to keep her attention on the edifying book she had taken from the circulating library to improve her mind and Christian morality, and likewise could not concentrate on the rather lurid novel she had borrowed from Mrs. Jennings' house. She had returned Elinor's copy of *Discipline* a while back, but there were a great many other books available for her pleasure there. Perhaps the pianoforte would afford her some amusement, but then she recalled Marianne still asleep just above and gave up that thought at once.

How she wished, not for the first time, that she were a man and could move about in the world as Alexander did. What freedom it would be to leave the house unaccompanied, to go about her affairs without an attending maid or footman, to walk hither and take a hack thither, and not to worry about who might see her in the wrong place. A man could act in the most scandalous ways, and society would wink and nod and secretly applaud him. But a woman could commit only the slightest faux pas and she would be ruined forever. She let out a most unladylike snort.

She contemplated Marianne's letters. Whatever had the girl written that could condemn her so? Or—Mary gasped at the thought—what had she done, the revelation of which could cast her out of good society? Had Willoughby.... Had she...?

No! That could never be, for otherwise nothing could explain Marianne's clear and deep distress at the man's insistence upon an arrangement.

Whatever it was, Mary was certain, it was something of that sort that would not so much as bruise a gentleman's good name. She snorted again in frustration at the unfairness of it all.

And then, there was the general disrespect with which society as a whole viewed women. Why could she not have accompanied Alexander to the solicitor's offices to examine the wills? Why should the man—any man—be disinclined to help merely because of her sex? What made men believe that women's brains were lesser than those of other men? Mary had known a great number of men and a greater number of women in her twenty-one years, and she knew without question that a woman was capable of just as much intelligent thought, if not more, than any man. It was only that men were afforded the education to expand upon their natural abilities that marked the real difference between them. How unfair!

It was in the midst of these musings that there came a knock at the door. The maid answered it and a moment later, stepped into the parlour where Mary sat to ask if she was home to Colonel Brandon.

"Yes, of course. Please show him in."

What would Aunt Gardiner think of her entertaining a man with no chaperone? Yet another thing a man could do that a woman could not! Still, she must ask the maid to stay in the room. A lady's reputation was too easily damaged and it would reflect poorly upon her aunt and younger sisters.

"Miss Bennet." The colonel stepped into the room with a click of his heels and bowed to her.

"Colonel, come in. It is a great surprise to see you here. Do you know my aunt and uncle? Please, do sit." She glanced at the maid, who understood her, and took a chair in the corner of the room near the door.

Colonel Brandon asked one or two questions about her health and that of her family, before giving up on all attempts at small talk. "Forgive my rudeness, Miss Bennet. I must ask after Miss Dashwood. I learned of her whereabouts from Mr. Lyons. Or, rather, I deduced it from what he would not say. I was desperate to hear news of her. I surmised much of the cause of her distress, and Mr. Lyons confirmed my suspicions. Do not be angry at him for telling me. I pleaded with him, and he did not part with his secrets easily. But I had to know. I had to find some way to be useful."

And indeed, the colonel did not look well at all. His eyes were heavy, as if he had not slept, and his face was pale. He sat perfectly still in his chair, with the exception of his thumb and forefinger, which he rubbed ceaselessly against each other. In an instant, Mary took great pity upon him. "I will help you as I can," she told him simply.

The colonel looked at her with world-weary eyes. "Are we alone? The maid..."

"Susie, would you please bring us some tea, and any buns or sweet breads that might be available?" The maid bobbed a curtsey and scuttled off.

"I have a sorry tale to tell you," Colonel Brandon sighed. "I alluded once to a lady I knew in my youth, much like your friend Marianne. There is a resemblance between them—the same warmth of heart, the same eagerness of fancy and spirits. I cannot remember the time I did not love Eliza. But at seventeen she was lost to me forever when she was married against her inclination to my brother. Her fortune was large and our family estate encumbered. We were within a few hours of eloping together for Scotland... the treachery of my cousin's maid betrayed us. I was banished, and she was allowed no liberty till my father's point was gained.

"My brother had no regard for her, and from the first he treated her unkindly. And I was with my regiment in the East Indies. The shock of her marriage was of trifling weight to what I felt when I heard, about two years afterwards, of her divorce."

He sank into the chair in a deep gloom.

"I am most sorry, sir. I had not known..."

"No. Very few do. It is a weight I carry with me in silence. But it grows worse.

"It was nearly three years later that I returned to England. I sought her, but the search was as fruitless as it was melancholy. I could not trace her beyond her first seducer. At last, after I had been in England six months, I did find her, in a spunging house where she was confined for debt. So altered—so faded—worn down by acute suffering of every kind! I placed her in comfortable lodgings; I visited her every day during the rest of her short life."

He rose from his chair and began to pace the room, finding comfort nowhere, his eyes looking into the past.

"Eliza left to my care her only child, a little girl, who was then about three years old. Having no home of my own, I placed little Eliza at school. I saw her whenever I could, and after the death of my brother five years ago, which left to me the family property, she frequently visited me at Delaford. Three years ago, when she had just reached her fourteenth year, I removed her from school to place her under the care of a respectable woman in Dorsetshire. For two years I had every reason to be pleased with her situation, but last February—a year and some past—she suddenly disappeared.

"Oh, how I wish I had known then of Mr. Lyons, for I now know of his great expertise at finding missing people. But such was not my—or Eliza's—fortune."

He fell silent for a moment in sad recollection.

"The first news that reached me of her came in a letter from herself last October. She had been destroyed, and by none other than Willoughby! That same soulless cur who spent all last autumn romancing sweet Marianne and making her fall in love with him, all while Eliza was carrying his child! For he had left my young ward, whose youth and innocence he had seduced, in a situation of the utmost distress, with no creditable home, no hope, no friends. He had promised to return, but no. He had left her and made love to Marianne Dashwood instead.

"Upon receiving that letter from Eliza, I made at once for London. I found her near to her delivery and as soon as she recovered from her lying in, I removed her and babe to the country where they now remain. They, at least, are safe. As for Willoughby..."

His fists clenched at his sides. "One encounter was unavoidable. We met by appointment, and both returned unwounded. But now I see I ought to have pressed harder. This time, he shall not prevail. I might be ten years older, but mine is the sword of a soldier; his is the feather of a dilettante. I am meeting him tomorrow at dawn, and I shall either retrieve Miss Marianne's letters, or—God forgive me—kill him in the trying."

"What? You will fight him? For me?"

Marianne's voice sounded from the doorway, bringing both Mary's and the colonel's heads snapping around. She stood there, looking very young, her eyes wide open and her cheeks flushed. She was only seventeen years old, Mary considered. Younger even than her sister Lydia, whom she considered too young to be out in society. How much of this tale had she heard? Would it break her heart to hear how the man she had loved in that first bloom of youth's passion possessed so low a character?

But the girl's eyes shone as she looked at Colonel Brandon.

"Miss Dashwood! I had no idea… I had not intended you to hear that. This tale, this sad tale, was not for such sensitive ears."

Mary felt a moment of pride that the colonel deemed her made of strong enough stuff to hear it, brushing aside any implied aspersions as to her own delicacy of constitution.

"I confess I have not been here long, but I believe I heard enough." She entered the room fully now and approached Colonel Brandon with as warm a look as Mary had ever seen from her. "Is it true? He was coming around to Barton Cottage and giving me gifts whilst Eliza—your ward—was abandoned by him and with his child?" Tears filled her large brown eyes. "I can hardly credit it. Had I not seen his treachery—his abandonment of me, his quick engagement to Miss Grey, and his indecent proposals—I should not believe it even now. I am sorely ashamed that I ever liked him at all."

"I am most sorry, Miss Dashwood."

"And you would fight him for me? Please, do not get hurt! I could never live with myself were you to be hurt!"

Mary did not quite know what to say. That Brandon was in love with Marianne was something she had long since divined. And now, it seemed, Marianne was on the way to caring for him too. Perhaps there was something left of the Romantic in the serious and dour Colonel Brandon, after all.

But a duel? What could she say to stop this? Her words would not sway the colonel, not now that Marianne had seen this side of him. Perhaps Alexander's would hold more weight.

Once more, she longed to see him, to hear of his discoveries, and to tell him of her own.

After a short visit, Colonel Brandon left. Marianne smiled wistfully after him and entreated him to take great care when he met with Willoughby. Her tender heart was lost once more, and this time, Mary considered, to a far superior man than had been her first choice.

Marianne soon begged Mary's pardon and disappeared into the back room to play the Gardiners' pianoforte, and once again Mary was left by herself to find what amusement she could. But her books still held no interest, and she could hardly commit her current thoughts to paper in a letter for Lizzy. To her pleasure, therefore, her quiet reveries were soon interrupted by another knock at the door.

"Alexander! Have you just now come from the solicitor's office? Is it nearby? What news do you have? What can you tell me? I have been aching to know what you have learned."

"Easy, now, Mary! Yes, I know you are eager to hear it, and I am here to relieve your curiosity. Yes, Mr. Hollings has his rooms only a short distance from here, near St. Dunstan's. I have not been back to my office, but came immediately to talk to you. Shall we sit here? Or take some sun and walk in the square?"

Soon they were strolling along in the park, Mary's hand resting too comfortably on Alexander's forearm. It would not be much for her hand to slide along his arm to find his, and from there, another moment for his hand to clasp hers. She envisioned them walking somewhere far from London, hand in hand, skin touching skin, in some world where they could be together.

"Do you wish to know what I learned?" His question jarred her from her thoughts.

"Yes. Very much." She also yearned to know what he thought, if his deeds would match his words, how he hoped to bridge the gulf between them. But now was no time to ask.

"I learned that Mrs. Ferrars wished for some way to make her will irrevocable, which she inadvertently achieved by dying, and that Robert knew every term of the will, including the fact that it would be possible to change it, after all."

"Then he might have feared that, if he did something to garner her disapproval, she might have had a new will drawn up, transferring her wealth back to Edward."

"Aye. That is something I have considered."

"And if she knew of his gambling debts..."

"She might not have been too well inclined to see the family's fortune spent at Brookes or at some other gaming table. Edward," he said after a pause, "might have incurred his mother's wrath for now, but she knew him to be sober and not profligate."

"And with the understanding that his status as heir might be short lived, Robert undertook to ensure the finality of her will by killing her."

"That all fits very well with my own thinking, and it explains his motives exactly."

"Then what of the evidence he hid pointing to Edward?"

"I believe," Alexander stared straight ahead, his eyes fixed on some distant point, "that if something went amiss, if there seemed to be some reason or cause to call the legitimacy or authority of the will into question, he must have a way to remove his brother as well. A man cannot gain from a will by means of murder. Accusing Edward would both remove him as the potential heir and would see him out of Robert's life permanently."

"Then he hid the false evidence because he had no need for it... or at least, not yet."

"Just so."

Mary shook her head at the horror of it all. A man, willing to kill his mother and see his brother hang, all for a relatively small inheritance, was a monster to her. Perhaps, in some dire way, Robert had met a just end.

"Did you learn anything else?" she asked.

"Only that Robert did not entrust his marriage documents to Mr. Hollings, nor did he make any mention to him of providing for Lucy's child. Her only hopes now lie upon finding some proof of this supposed marriage. For if she cannot prove it, she and the bairn will have nothing at all.

"And that is a very sad place in which to find oneself. Here, this is what I learned this morning, about another woman and babe in dire circumstances," whereupon she related what she had discovered from Colonel Brandon.

What dreadful creatures men could be. How lucky she was to be in the company of a good one!

Chapter Sixteen

Into Seven Dials

Alexander wished he could spend longer walking with Mary, but her circumstances and his obligations forbade it. He accompanied her back to her relations' house, pressed a kiss to the back of her hand, all the while wishing it were her lips that he might caress instead. Then, reluctantly, he turned and walked back to his rooms.

There he was to meet with the handwriting expert, a Mr. Redfern, before joining Atkins at Robert's house on Park Street again. He had produced several documents undeniably written by Robert—a letter here, a witnessed note at the club there—and wished to know for certain that the diary and letter to Hollings were made by Robert himself and not somebody in possession of a good counterfeit hand.

He bought a cheese and spinach pie and an ale at the bakery at his corner, and took his meal up to his office, there to wait for his associate. In the meantime, he proposed to examine the note about Robert Ferrars' debts and creditors that had arrived during his absence in Norfolk.

He read through the long list of names, many of which he knew, some of which he did not, and did some quick arithmetic. This tallied with what he had already learned from Atkins: Robert Ferrars was in debt to a great many men, and for a great deal of money.

John Yates, Francis Weston Churchill, William Lucas—these were all men with whom Alexander had some prior dealings. None of the debts to these men was excessive, although the amounts were more than pennies. He read on. George Tybern, Robert Hodges, Captain Frederick Tilney, Christopher de Bourgh... again, some names he knew, and some he did not.

Alexander pulled out the papers from Robert's rooms upon which he had marked down the initials, dates, and values of his debts and compared them with the list before him. With one or two exceptions, they matched exactly. Other than the great fortune he owed, there was little to surprise him in this direction.

But there was another comment at the bottom of the note. As well as owing a great amount of money, it seems Robert was not always unlucky at cards and was owed some debts as well. For the most part, the amounts were middling, and the men—at least, those whom Alexander knew by face or reputation—could easily afford the expense.

Ah—but what was this? Here was a name that Alexander had grown to know all too well: John Willoughby. And Willoughby owed Robert Ferrars a staggering amount of money, a full two thousand pounds! He did some more quick arithmetic in his head. If rumours were accurate and Miss Grey came with fifty thousand pounds, this debt to Robert would account for a full year's income, or close to it. And if the further rumours about Miss Grey's—now Mrs. Willoughby's—continued control over her fortune and unpleasant disposition were correct, Willoughby was in a great deal of trouble.

By ridding himself of Robert, Willoughby would also rid himself of a cause of significant strife, maybe even debtor's prison. All of a sudden, Alexander considered a new and most interesting suspect in the murder of Robert Ferrars!

The sound of boots on the stairs alerted Alexander to someone's arrival, and in a moment, Mr. Redfern entered. The two had not previously met, and a few moments of greetings and introductions occurred before they set about their business. Alexander showed Redfern the certain examples he had of Robert's handwriting and the man took some time to examine them before stating he was ready to depart for Park Street. "Bring these along, if you please, sir. I shall have need of them there as well."

Atkins met them at Robert's house as they had arranged. He knew of Redfern and introductions were quickly dispensed with, after which they went up to the man's room. Redfern spent a great deal of time poring over the diary and letter about Edward, and comparing them with the samples of Robert's writing. Lucy still had the note from Robert; should matters progress, she would have to produce that for examination as well. In the meantime, Alexander searched again through the shelves and desk drawers in hopes of finding something he had previously missed. No such document came to light.

Eventually, the handwriting expert sat up straight and clucked his tongue. "I cannot say there is no chance that these are forgeries, but I seriously doubt that to be the case. In every respect, the writing matches exactly with these samples. Sorry, gentlemen, but that is all I can do. Would you like a written record on my findings?

The pressure of the pen, the angle of the nib, how it becomes worn in a particular pattern, the nature of the upstrokes and flourishes? Yes? Very well. Allow me a few minutes to make my notes and I shall send the report to you forthwith."

"Bring it with your statement of fees," Alexander offered, "and I shall discharge that obligation at once."

On these amicable terms, the expert took his leave and departed the house.

"Before we also leave," Alexander said, "I would like another look through the study. Robert seems not to have taken possession of that room, but in the event that he was slowly moving his papers, I would appreciate one more examination."

"Be my guest," Atkins laughed. "Or, rather, be Edward's! I must be off to my other duties, but here is the key. Lock the house and return it to the headquarters later."

Bow Street was a minute's walk from his rooms; this was deemed more than suitable. After seeing Atkins out and locking the door behind him, Alexander returned to the study. There was nothing of interest in the drawers, nor in the ledgers of accounts that filled some of the shelves. An escritoire revealed a sizable stack of very fine paper, two new bottles of ink, and a supply of unsharpened quills. Alexander was about to concede failure when he noticed a slim volume hiding on the bookshelves against the very edge, tucked behind a large atlas. It was an odd place to put such an item, and he pulled it from its place.

It was another diary of a sort, this one filled not with an accounting of Robert's days, but of the games he had attempted, with which cards, which he had won and lost, and to whom he owed money. Again, this was nothing new, for Alexander had seen something similar in the man's private rooms. But at the bottom of the second page was the draught of a rather unpleasant letter to somebody who owed him a great deal of money. There was no name, but from what else Alexander had learned, the intended recipient had to be Willoughby. Robert demanded full payment of the debt and threatened the other with exposure. Exposure of what, Robert had not written, but the intent was clear. The man's good standing in the *ton* would be thoroughly destroyed if he did not discharge his obligation at once.

Here, therefore, was a grand motive for Willoughby to have wished Robert Ferrars dead, grander even than the size of the debt and his wife's great displeasure. Robert had information that could destroy the man and was prepared to use it to gain his advantage. Was it news of Eliza Williams, Brandon's ward, about whom Mary had only today told him? Or was it something else, something even more dire? In a way, it mattered little. Willoughby had every reason to wish Robert Ferrars dead.

The clock on the mantel chimed. Four o'clock. There was still a great deal of time left in the day, and a great deal to do. The evidence against Edward Ferrars for Robert's murder still seemed damning, but there were too many new questions for Alexander not to pursue.

It was now clear that Robert had worked to point at Edward as the culprit behind their mother's death. It seemed more than likely that somebody was now working to point at Edward for Robert's. But who? Surely not Robert!

The first place to seek answers to that question was in St. Giles, where the two ruffians who had actually done the deed had lived. It was still bright daylight and busy in the streets. Later, when the sky was darker, the area became more dangerous. This, therefore, was the time to go.

He made his notes and gathered his belongings and walked back to Covent Garden. Atkins was not in the Bow Street offices, but Alexander left the key for him in the care of the secretary, and turned northward towards Seven Dials.

"Alexander! I have been waiting for you!"

Once again, his feet were stilled by the sound of his name.

"Mary! What in blazes are you doing here? Who is with you?"

She grinned at him with a look of impish disobedience that he never would have imagined when first they met. Then, she had been this serious and self-important chit more interested in spouting moral judgments than in flouting convention. But here she was, in flagrant defiance of society's strictures, and seeming to enjoy every moment of it. How she had grown!

"I told my aunt that I was visiting Elinor. She believes my maid to be with me. But I could not spend another minute waiting for news. I had to know for myself what had happened. I came across Mr. Atkins and he told me about the key, so I decided to wait here. There is nowhere in London safer than in front of the Bow Street Courthouse, after all!"

He ought to be angry, but he was really glad to see her. Still...

"I am for St. Giles. That is no place for a lady."

She stopped in front of him and planted her hands on her hips. The defiant stance, in contrast with her pretty face under her demure bonnet, nearly made him laugh.

"Very well. I see I shall not convince you otherwise. But St. Giles is dangerous. Seven Dials, in the centre of the area, is a place where even I do not go willingly in the day, and certainly not at night. There are gin shops, old shops selling older items for the third and fourth time, unfed children, vermin, men better suited to asylums than the streets, harlots, terrible people..."

"I know what it has to offer. The church where my aunt and uncle attend sends charity there weekly. I have not gone myself, but I hear the others talk. I am not afraid."

"Have you a reticule? Just a small one? Good. Put it in your pocket and keep it safe. Put your necklace under your collar. You still look far too genteel. We must find you an old shawl or duster.

Do not leave my sight! Nay, do not stray further from me than the length of my arm. I will not have you come to harm."

She beamed up at him. "That is what Colonel Brandon said about Marianne." She did not elaborate upon her comment, but took his arm and walked with him into one of the most poverty-stricken parts of London.

She walked with a pace that matched his and he explained his mission as they went. It was mere moments before they were winding their way through a mesh of filthy and stinking alleyways between crumbling tenements, lined with piles of rotting rubbish and rodent carcasses, overhung with threadbare laundry on precarious lines strung between windows, and traced with open sewers. A thousand eyes turned on them as they crept further into the territory: hungry cats and dogs, weary mothers, drunken men and barefoot, starving children. None dared approach them—yet. Alexander had a pocket full of pennies should he need them, but he knew well that at the glint of the first coin, they would be quite overrun by the local denizens.

At last, they reached an open space between the crowded buildings. He could see the shadows of men—and maybe women—in the doorways, and already there were hoots beckoning from under the awnings offering Alexander some personal entertainment...and Mary too!. "Stay close," he whispered again.

"Oi there!" he called out into the stinking gloom. "I'm looking for Nan Thicket. No harm will come to her. I only have a question or two. I may send a lad later with some bread and pies."

"Whatcha want wif Nan?" Was that a man's voice coming from a window? Or a woman's, deep from drink and abuse?

"Only some questions. I have no wish to bring her any trouble."

"Jest yer bein' here is trouble enough," came another voice.

The din around them grew as the people wondered what his business could be, and then died down to a hush as a woman of about thirty years slid out of a doorway with a young girl of twelve or thirteen right behind her.

"I'm Nan," the woman said. Her eyes were cautious and with every motion she betrayed fear. "Whatcha want wif me?"

"You are Fred's sister? The one that disappeared with his mate, Gus?"

"And if I am?" Her expression dared him to challenge her. But he must. From the corner of his eye, he noticed Mary start to engage the young girl in quiet conversation. What a bleak life that child had ahead of her. She was a pretty enough thing, now that he took in her appearance, but scrawny and ill-used. He hoped that her future would not be spent entertaining men under cover of darkness and wished he had the means to somehow rescue her from such a fate.

"Your sister?" he asked her when she followed his eyes.

"My daughter. And don't you think me some lightskirt! 'Er father up and left us, 'e did. But she can read and write and knows how to sew, like I do. I take in mending. I lift my skirts for no man!" She stood tall and defiant before him.

"I meant no such thing. But I do need to know about Fred." Here was one of the few places in London where his Scots accent would be a help and not a hindrance. He was not one of them, but neither was he one of the toffs. Nan scrutinised him from top to bottom, then turned her appraisal to Mary, and then glared at Alexander once more. At last, she gave a curt nod.

"Fine. But just a short word."

They stood in the centre of this dingy widening in the alleyway, surrounded by people. "Is there somewhere quiet we may talk? Inside or out. Miss Bennet will join us. I merely have some questions about Fred."

She squinted at him and crooked her head to bid them follow her down the alleyways until they came to the square in front of St.

Paul's church, a small red brick building beside Covent Garden. "Go ahead. Ask your questions." She sat on a bench and Alexander sat beside her. Mary and the girl took the bench a few steps further along.

"Tell me again about the night Fred vanished, and anything unusual you noticed around that time."

"I've gone done this with that Runner already," she complained more than once. "Why do you need it again?"

"I might hear something he did not hear, even if you repeat yourself exactly."

She scowled. "And what about my Cassie? What will that lady do to her?"

"She is as safe with Miss Bennet as with anybody in London. I trust her with my life."

With another leery look, Nan settled onto the bench and told her story.

It was nothing more than Alexander had already heard. For two or three days before Robert's death, Fred Thicket and his mate Gus had been parading around the Old Nichol like kings, flashing a coin here and a sneer there. He had a new pair of shoes and a set of clothes that had only seen one previous owner. When asked about it, he crowed that he had taken a job and would be all the richer for it soon. In retrospect, Nan explained, it was clear that her brother had planned to vanish from the area. He had given away some of his oldest clothes and packed up his few belongings and told some of his mates he was unlikely to see them again soon. He knew he was involved in something dire and did not wish to be found. Alexander imagined the cutthroat was half-way to America by now with his ill-gotten gains and whatever he and Gus had managed to take from Robert's body.

He took his careful notes and noticed Nan watching his hand as he wrote. If her daughter could read and write, it was likely that

Nan was the one who taught her and he wondered where she had learned herself.

"I have another question," he said when the woman seemed ready to stand. "A gentleman often came with the charity workers from his church, so he told us. About twenty-four years old, quiet..."

"Oi, that sounds like Mr. Edward." There was a glimmer of a smile in her voice.

"You know him?"

"The other Runner asked about him, but I know him. He's a quiet one, but good. Never treats us like dirt, but gives us respect like we was proper people to him. Talks to us, asks after our families. Like we matter. Yessir, I know him."

"Tell me more." His pencil danced over the paper in his notebook.

"He isn't always in London, but when he is, he comes bringing food and goods. Those folks from the church think so high of themselves, coming to give us the dribs and drabs that they don't need, thinking it will get them faster into heaven. But the truth is, when you're as poor as us, you can't say no. We need what they give us and we're grateful for it. Sometimes when one of the nobs knows someone as needs workers, they'll ask one of our lads. Isn't always much pay, but something's better'n nuffin'. One of the lads—Bessie Hart's son—is a tall pretty-faced boy, got a position as a footman at someone's estate, even! So proud she is of him, is Bessie! All our lads hope to make it like he did."

She tucked a strand of loose hair behind an ear, her eyes still narrow with suspicion. She looked old, not from any roughness of feature, but from the hard expression she wore like armour.

"And Mr. Ferrars... Mr. Edward?" He turned his hand palm up, hoping to draw forth words like a conjurer pulls items from supposedly empty boxes.

"Yeh, Mr. Edward came often. Talked a lot wi' Fred; I think he was trying to convince Fred to change his ways, give up the drink, take an honest job. But Fred weren't interested in that. He was more for the quick take. We were never close, Fred and me, but I'm sorry he got tangled in this bad business. If you find him, tell him Nan loves him."

There was little else Nan had to say that Alexander did not already know. She could recall no new or unknown man who came by with the church group, or separately, and did not recognise any of the names he offered. There certainly had not been anybody she knew about asking after Fred or Gus. Still, he listened to her every word and made exquisite notes, as much to impress upon her the value of her words as for his own *aide-mémoire*.

He rose and thanked her for her time. "May we escort you back to your home?"

She gaped at him and then doubled up in laughter. "Wot's this, treating us like ladies. No, sir. It's a hop, skip, and a jump from here, and it's getting too late for the likes of you in a place the likes of that. We'll just be off."

He pressed another coin into her hand. "Take good care, Nan. You have been helpful."

And he walked across to Mary as they watched the two disappear again into the nightmare that was St. Giles.

Chapter Seventeen

The Handkerchief

As Alexander spoke to Nan, Mary had been sitting with the woman's daughter on a nearby bench, trying to draw her out. Watching Nan make her cautious way out of the building they must call home and seeing the woman's threadbare garments and worn-out shoes, Mary felt, for the first time, every bit of the privilege to which she had been born. Now she understood some of Alexander's contempt for the idle classes. That half-ruined structure before which they had waited seemed to stand through will alone. The bricks were crumbling and the mortar between them looked more missing than present. A shallow awning above the black maw where the door stood open was held up by two planks of wood that themselves looked to be refuse from some other edifice.

Nan, when she had emerged from that pile of incipient rubble, was not at all what Mary had expected. What, exactly, that might be, Mary could not say, but it was not this slight woman barely older than her sister Jane, with her proud bearing and untrusting dark eyes. She wore a skirt and shirt that had never been in fashion, but that were likely easy to make with old fabric, and her hair was stuffed into a boy's cap with some strands and tendrils escaping here and there. They had been mere steps from the bright gas lights and fashionable theatres around Covent Garden where she had attended so many times with her sisters or aunt and uncle, but there, in that dank place, Mary felt she was on the other side of the world.

But it was not Nan who had captured most of Mary's attention. Rather, it was the slip of a girl who walked behind her. Where Nan looked to be about thirty, this child could hardly have been more than twelve. She was painfully thin and her dress was far too short for her height. Long wispy blonde hair hung down her back, tied up with some old string. At one glance from her world-weary eyes, Mary's heart broke.

It sounded like Alexander wished to go somewhere quieter to speak to Nan; Mary and the girl would have to follow. She wondered why the girl did not stay in her room. She was certainly old enough. Perhaps she could ask. But first she had to befriend the girl.

Here was a challenge! Mary knew well that she was no virtuoso of the salon. She had not her sister Lizzy's gift of saying something witty at any moment, or Alexander's easy friendliness. No, in truth, Mary was more like her brother-in-law Darcy, who kept to the fringes until such time as he felt comfortable with his company. But this girl, so young and vulnerable, stirred her mettle and she resolved to make a great effort.

"I am Mary." She offered her hand to shake, but the girl looked at it like it was laced with poison. Her eyes darted to the side and Mary followed her glance. Oh.

"He will not hurt her, you know. His name is Alexander, and he's Scottish. Does he not have the funniest colour hair you have ever seen? He talks very strangely, too. But she is in no danger. He is the best man I have met."

The girl stared at him, where he was talking to the woman. She still looked wary, but not quite as anxious. Mary tried again.

"He is terribly clever. I know he speaks at least three languages, and he knows a lot about medicine because his father was a doctor. But he is a lawyer! Can you imagine that? But I have never seen him do a cruel thing in all the time I have known him." Even that first awful encounter, when he had castigated her and recused himself from all gentlemanly behaviour, had not been done in cruelty. Rather, he had been injured and in pain. And he had offered a pretty apology as soon as he had been able to move again. "He only wishes to speak to her."

The girl's stance eased a bit more.

"Nor does he mean you harm." Was she worried about the sort of low creature who preyed upon girls so young they were all but children? "He is not that sort of a man."

"There's lots of that sort of a man around these streets." The girl spoke for the first time. Again, Mary followed her glance to the building from which they had emerged. Oh. There was somebody in there with whom she wished not to be alone. How terrifying for the girl not to feel safe even in her own home.

"I am sorry to hear that. What is your name?"

"Cassie." It was just one word, but it broke down a wall between them. She smiled, and Cassie smiled, and they began to talk. Alexander was now following the other woman down the alleyways towards the broader streets near Covent Garden itself, and she and Cassie followed close on their heels. As they walked, Mary asked about inconsequential matters and when at last they found some benches in a pretty churchyard, a sort of rapport had developed between them.

A gust of wind picked up and flung some dust towards them and Cassie sneezed. She reached through the fabric of her too-small and threadbare skirt into a pocket to find a handkerchief. The piece of cloth itself was ancient and grey and it had never been square—part of a ripped cravat, perhaps, bought from a rag man?—but the stitching at the edge was bright and new and very prettily done.

"Is that your work?" Mary had to ask. It seemed unlikely that such a scrap of cloth would be a gift.

Cassie gave a shy smile. "Me mum bought the thread with some of her own mending money. I sew. I help her where I can."

"It's very pretty. Where did you learn to embroider?"

"Aye. I watched some of the old ladies who used to sew and learned what I could from them. See, here's a flower design, and here is my name." She turned the cloth around so Mary could see.

It really was beautiful needle work.

"And your name here—who showed you the letters?"

Again, the girl flushed red. "Me mum taught me my letters. One of the ladies that come round sometimes with the toffs from the church, she showed me a pretty cloth she did. 'Twas very plain, though, just the letters and nothing else, and I said I'd show her some flower patterns. She said I could get work in a shop, but that I'd have to know to read and write. I can, too, read and write!" The girl sounded outraged. "She didn't believe me at all! I even have a book that Mum found, even if it's missing half the back."

A place in a shop! That was a grand idea. Perhaps she might find a position for this girl at her uncle's fabric warehouse, or at one of the dressmakers they worked with.

"How old are you, Cassie?"

"Thirteen last May." The girl was so thin, she might almost have been ten. Mary had to find some way to help. There were, she knew, scores—nay hundreds or thousands—of similar children in the rookeries who had no such hope, but if Mary could assist just this one, she would feel herself to have some value in this world.

"You have a great deal of talent. If you wish, I shall inquire after honest and respectable work for you."

Cassie's eyes widened. "For pay and not scraps?"

"For real pay. May I? Perhaps I can bring you some fabric and thread so you can make some samples for me to show to people."

"Ooooh!"

That was all the answer Mary needed.

Soon Alexander had concluded his questions and he and Mary were walking back towards his offices. "It is getting dark soon. Your aunt and uncle will be worried about you." He put his hand over hers where it rested upon his arm.

"They believe me to be with Elinor." How unlike her this was, deceiving her aunt, running about the city like a hoyden. How she loved it!

Alexander's expression was not entirely approving.

"And Elinor?"

"Oh, she believes me with my aunt and uncle. And if Marianne should talk, well, the damage will already be done."

"I see. And what do you propose to do until you return safely to Gracechurch Street?"

"Why, help you with the investigation, of course! What are we to do next? And we must dine. I have a small amount of money that should see us to some respectable food."

Did Alexander roll his eyes at her? Ah, it was no better than she deserved! She, who had sermonised over the delicate nature of a woman's reputation, she who had castigated her sisters on their shameful behaviour around men, was now enjoying an evening in the vastness of London, quite unchaperoned, with the one man who made her heart beat faster. She ought to be horrified at her own actions, and yet she was not. This sort of freedom was a little frightening, but it was also too exhilarating. She giggled at the impossibility of it all and followed him down the lane to wherever it was he was leading her.

"Here is the bakery where I often get my meals." He gestured to a small establishment at an unprepossessing corner. Any other day she would have walked past it without a thought, but now her feet slowed. The aromas emanating from within were enticing, and whilst she was certain that anything purchased there would not match Mr. Darcy's table in elegance, she was equally certain that the food would be quite tasty.

They made their selections to take for their meal: a chicken tart for Mary and a vegetable tart for Alexander. Next door they purchased a jug of lemonade, and a few doors further along, some cherries for pudding. The lot they carried with them up a narrow staircase to the space Alexander informed her was his office.

As Alexander placed their purchases on his large desk, Mary stared around the room. So this was where he did his work!

"Ach, you never have been here before! I had not realised it. Welcome, Mary."

He walked around the desk, which took up most of the space, and threw open the window. The sounds and smells of London wafted in, but the air was cooler than that inside, and she welcomed it. He then found a cloth and some plates in a drawer in the corner, which he used to set the desk to form a table upon which to dine.

"I usually eat in my rooms upstairs," he pointed upward with his eyes, "but even I cannot see myself to inviting a lady there alone. Perhaps..."

She finished his sentence in her mind. Perhaps one day it would not be scandalous to walk up that further flight of stairs and see his private rooms herself. Perhaps one day she might enter them as his wife! Then it crashed down upon her. She was accustomed to a manor house on an estate that brought in two thousand a year, more than most people earned in a lifetime. Here in London she stayed with her wealthy uncle whose house, while not in fashionable Mayfair, would not be out of place there. Would this man ever feel it possible to ask her to give all of that up, to live as mistress to two rooms above a bake house? The chasm between them was so very vast!

This reminded her of her offer. "Here," she retrieved her reticule from her pockets. "I promised to pay. This should be sufficient. I was tallying the cost at each establishment." She placed some coins on the desk. Alexander's glance was fierce.

"What is the matter? Is this not enough?"

"Mary..."

Her head tilted to the side as she peered at him.

"I do not need your charity."

This was confusing. "Charity? What charity? I offered earlier to put my coin to our dinner, and I am meeting my debts. As Mr. Ferrars did not."

"These are pennies, Mary. I do not need you to pay for my food. I am quite capable of meeting my own obligations."

She huffed. "Oh, really, Alexander! It was my suggestion, and I happen to have more coin now than... well, than you likely have at your disposal. Lizzy and Mr. Darcy sent me a large purse before my stay here, and I shall never spend it all." She pushed the coins towards him.

"And I say again that I have a perfectly adequate balance at my bank and do not need your charity."

"Pshaw Alexander! This is not charity. Charity is what the missions do, or what the churches do when they send people to, well, to St. Giles to feed and clothe the poor. Buying my friend a pie is not charity."

He looked about to argue further, but instead, he gave a nod. "Then, I thank you, and hope to return the gesture at some time." He pinched his lips and let out a sigh. "It is hard to think of St. Giles, and all those people there who cannot afford to say no to the offer of a pie. It is not a part of town I visit often, for all that it lies five minutes from my door. I am chastised and ought to make more of an effort to offer assistance there. Perhaps my community—" he stopped short.

"Edward is said to go often on behalf of his church. He surely has to be a good person if he offers food and clothing to the poor, does he not?"

"Aye, every gesture of alms must be welcome. But are mere clothes and some scraps of bread enough? Surely better charity would be to find a way to take them out of that gateway to hell and help them move upwards in the world. If one can take a man, a family, out of those depths, how much good that would do."

Mary was not certain how to respond to this. It was a fair point, and she, herself, had been moved to find a way for Nan and Cassie to move out of the cesspool that was St. Giles. But it seemed not enough. "One can help one or two people that way. Taking food feeds scores, hundreds, even. Without food, what good is the prospect of bettering themselves at some future time?"

"Your point is excellent, I admit, and feeding the poor is essential. But it leaves them little way to feed themselves when the ladies and gentlemen from the church are no longer there."

She pondered him for a moment. "What do your people know of charity? I see churches offering succour often, but I do not even know where you worship, what you do. Is charity an important aspect of your faith?"

"It is vital. As vital as life. As vital as in your own faith. We are all commanded to help those in need. We are not so different, you and I."

She considered this for a moment. "Yes. I believe you are right. Sometime, I would like to know more. And I can tell you of the work my church in Meryton does."

"I would enjoy that." He took a bite of his vegetable pie and the scent filled the small office. "Why were you asking so many questions?"

Mary sighed. "I was thinking of poor Nan and Cassie. Nan is her mother, although she looks like her sister. She cannot be more than thirty."

"Nan is twenty-seven."

Mary gaped. "Cassie is thirteen. Then Nan was only fourteen when Cassie was born! I know that is the lot for so many of their class, but I cannot be happy with it. I wish so much to do something for them. For Cassie. She is a child, and she has a gift. Merely bringing them food will not help, not really. I wish to do something more." She stopped for a moment. "I see now what you were saying before. Perhaps both aspects of aid are necessary. Poor Cassie."

"Do you want me to help?"

"Oh!" Mary's fingers toyed with the edge of the pie she had not yet tasted. "I had not thought of it, but yes, if you can. I shall ask my uncle as well. The child embroiders with skill far beyond her years. She would be an asset to a dressmaker."

He smiled at her then and waited in silence whilst she partook of her food. They poured the lemonade into two pewter mugs that Alexander drew from a shelf, and then ate the cherries. Mary found herself licking the red juice off her fingers, and once again was shocked at herself for such appalling manners, ignoring how much she was enjoying herself.

The sun was starting to dip in the sky now. She really must be going back, or her aunt would send a servant to Mrs. Jennings' house and then her ruse would be discovered. Alexander seemed to realise the same thing.

"We should find you a hackney." He began to clear the cloth of the debris and set the mugs aside to be washed. "Here…" he reached over to where Mary was collecting cherry stems and their hands touched. She did not move. Neither did he. Then he clasped her hand in his and walked the extra step needed to bring him immediately before her.

"Kiss me, Mary."

She did not need to answer, for her lips were already against his. Oh, the scandal of it all! But perhaps losing one's good name was a lot more enjoyable than she had ever thought.

Chapter Eighteen

The Duel

Alexander rose very early the next morning after a night of very little sleep. Every time he closed his eyes, there was Mary, laughing, teasing him, challenging him. Being in all the places she was not supposed to be: St. Giles, his office, his head! What in the name of Heaven had she been thinking? What had become of the demure and moralistic virago who had been so offended by his comments just three years past? She had turned almost brazen!

Nor had she shrunk from that kiss. He had issued the invitation, and she had accepted with enthusiasm. She had closed those last few inches between them and placed her hand on his cheek, and made him forget about all of London. This was becoming a habit, one which he could come to rely upon far too much. Mary Bennet had become a part of him, and he never wanted her to leave.

He lay in bed for longer than he ought, dreading the morning ahead and wanting to retreat into his all-too-pleasant dreams, but then twisted himself out from under the thin blankets. His room, on the second storey of this narrow building, was still warm from the sultry summer evening, but he threw on his coat, nonetheless. Had he only been walking down the flight of stairs to his office, he might have carried it with him, but he had an appointment at this unseemly hour.

The sun's fingers were gilding the city in their pale gold embrace when he found one of the few hacks around and climbed aboard. The driver looked at him askance when he gave the direction. That field, only a short way out of town, and at such a time as this—not even a quarter past five in the morning—could mean only one thing.

"Not you, sir?" the driver asked.

"No indeed. I am trying to stop it."

"Very well then." And the hack started on its way.

Colonel Brandon and Willoughby were already at the field when he arrived. Their seconds were conferring by one of the nearby carriages, their backs to Alexander, although he heard the murmur of their voices. He thanked the driver and paid his fare; he would get a ride back to London with Brandon, or the doctor if need be.

"Lyons!" Colonel Brandon called from the field. "What the devil are you doing here? You have no need to witness this. Go back to Town." The man looked fierce, almost feral, in his sporting wear. He swung a sword about in his hand as if it were a twig and his practice feints and lunges appeared, to Alexander's eyes, deadly.

To Willoughby's too, if the man's face was any indication. He strutted about at the far end of the field in an attempt at nonchalance, but his ashen skin and rapid breathing, noticeable even at this distance, suggested the truth was otherwise. His one hand dandled a sword; the other moved up to mop sweat from his forehead every few seconds. Perhaps Willoughby was an unacknowledged master of swordplay, but if Alexander were a betting man, he would place his wagers on Brandon.

"What can I do to stop this?" Alexander called out as he crossed the field towards Brandon.

"Nothing our seconds have not already tried. I want those letters, and I want this cur out of London for good. But first, I want my drop of his blood."

Willoughby looked up at these words and turned, if possible, an even paler shade of grey.

"He is terrified, Colonel. He can hardly walk in a straight line. Are you so cruel?"

Brandon bored into him with his eyes. "The cur ought to have been less cruel when he seduced and abandoned my ward, Eliza. He ought to have been less cruel when he dallied with Marianne. He ought to have been less cruel when, after marrying for money alone, he sought to coerce sweet Marianne into an illicit tryst, against her will and against her nature. No, Lyons, I am not the one who is cruel. Willoughby made his bed. Now let him lie in it."

There must be some way to reason with him. "You cannot wish to do this. You will be a murderer; you risk hanging, unless you flee England. What good will you be to Eliza then? How will you be of use to Marianne?"

"I shall not be swayed, Lyons. Now leave me."

Brandon turned his back and resumed his stretching with some deep lunges in the other direction.

At this moment, the seconds and doctor emerged from where they had been conferring at the carriages. One of those men was familiar. Alexander walked over and greeted his friend with a grim handshake.

"Colonel Fitzwilliam! What are you doing, embroiled in this nonsense?"

Fitzwilliam was Darcy's cousin, and the two had met some years before in the course of a case. Fitzwilliam had not Darcy's handsome visage and great fortune, but he had the advantage over his cousin in being the son of an earl. To his own merit, however, he was a friendly and gentlemanly fellow and was always excellent company.

"I wondered if I would see you here, Lyons. In any other place, I would be delighted. No, Brandon here asked me to be his second. I was as surprised as any man. We are friendly, indeed, but not intimate friends. I think, perhaps, he wished for as impartial a pair of eyes as he might procure for this ill-advised event. I have spoken long with Haversham there," he gestured to a thin young man who must be Willoughby's second, "but the men will not be swayed. Brandon wants justice and Willoughby is too cocksure to allow him his satisfaction. They have met before, so I believe..."

"And both men walked away unharmed. I fear we shall not be so fortunate today. Willoughby has brought much suffering to Brandon and those he loves."

The colonel grimaced. "I am not of such a bent as this, but I too should be tempted to call a man out for such insults."

Willoughby's second walked over, his watch in his hand. "Time," was all he said. Fitzwilliam nodded curtly and went over to the field to summon the two combatants to come forward. The doctor strode over to stand with Alexander but did not introduce himself, and the two stood as silent and unwilling witnesses to what Alexander hoped would not be carnage.

At the call of *en garde*, the opponents took their positions, weapons held before them. Swords touched at the call of *prêt*, and at *allez*, the fight began. At first, nothing happened. The two men stood facing each other, swords intersected in a mockery of St. Andrew's cross. Willoughby leapt backwards, his sword held out before him, beyond Brandon's reach, and for a moment Alexander thought he might turn and run. But he held his position. Both men shifted on their feet, tiny motions that betrayed the tensions in their muscles, their stances adjusting and adapting to each shuffle. Then, without warning, Willoughby lunged. The swords met with a great clang, and Brandon deflected the attack as if he were swatting a fly. Willoughby leapt back and the brittle silence began again.

Alexander's breath stopped in his throat. In the stillness of the early morning field, every blade of grass, every chirp of distant birds, came into the sharpest of relief, until the entire universe was focused upon that spot, not so many yards distant, where the two duellers faced each other. Silent, still...

Then, with a shout, Brandon leapt forward and darted to the side as Willoughby tried to block the attack. Metal struck metal, and the din flooded the area, punctuated by shouts and grunts as the two waged their personal war. It seemed to last for a year and a moment.

Now Brandon hung back, catching his breath. Was he wounded? Was he less fit than he thought? Willoughby advanced with careful steps, the tip of his blade circling in the direction of Brandon's heart.

Closer, closer...

And Brandon lunged again.

Willoughby let out a great cry and dropped his sword, then sank to his knees. Alexander stared in horror; the doctor edged forward.

"He has no need for you yet," Brandon yelled. "'Tis only his hand! Look!"

Willoughby held out his appendage. The palm was covered in blood, but when he wiped it on his white shirt, Alexander could see a thin welt running across the surface. It might need stitches; it might heal on its own. What would Brandon do next? Would he really run a wounded man through, or would he seek to wound until his opponent could no longer wield a weapon? Surely, he had not insisted on a duel *à l'outrance*, to the death. Had he?

"What shall it be, Willoughby?" the colonel taunted. "I have my first blood. Agree to my terms and there need be no more. I do not wish for your death, only justice for others. Give me the letters and I will grant you your life."

"Do it, man!" Haversham urged. Even here, Alexander could hear his whispered plea.

"I encourage you to listen," Fitzwilliam echoed. "Your pride is not worth the cost of your life. The letters..."

"Are in my carrying case," Willoughby all but sobbed. He was on the ground, holding his scored hand in his other, trying to push the edges of broken flesh together. "A bandage! Help!"

The doctor now dashed forward and knelt on the ground beside the injured man to wrap a piece of white cloth around the bleeding wound. Brandon picked up Willoughby's discarded sword and then spat on the earth by Willoughby's feet. Then he turned his back on him and walked away.

Fitzwilliam was already at the carriages and leapt aboard Willoughby's. "I have them," he called after a moment, his voice echoing from the interior of the large coach. He jumped out a second later and handed the package to Brandon.

"You need not look at me like that, Lyons," Brandon wiped his head. It was damp with perspiration, whether from the physical exertion or latent worry, Alexander did not know. Perhaps Brandon had not been quite so sanguine after all. But he continued, "I never had any notion of killing the man. He is not worth it. You were quite correct earlier in that I would never throw my own life away over a rat like him. But he had to believe me serious. He had to know fear. And now he knows that I have the mettle to complete the task if ever he wrongs me again."

Alexander's opinion of the officer both grew and shrank upon hearing this, but he was relieved beyond measure that the man who had engaged him was not as ruthless a killer as the person he was now trying to find.

"I am comforted to hear that, Colonel. I am also pleased that Willoughby will live to see tomorrow, for I have some questions for him relating to Robert Ferrars' death."

Brandon turned to face him, brows high on his forehead. "Oh yes?"

"I have uncovered a reason he might wish Ferrars dead. We know he is a man not afraid of violence, but also the sort who would prefer not to be present when it happens." He recalled Willoughby's ashen face before the duel. "I do not say he is guilty, but he has become more interesting to me."

Alexander paused. How could he make this request? Perhaps the bold way forward was the best. "To that end, in the hopes of learning everything I can about this man, may I read that stack of letters? I give my absolute oath that I will use nothing in them against Miss Marianne, and that I shall return them to her as soon as I have finished my examination."

"You must ask Miss Marianne herself."

"Time, I fear, is of the essence in a case such as this. You have my word that I will use only what I need for the investigation."

Brandon's face took on that same black and fierce look he had worn when first Alexander appeared this morning.

"Your life depends upon it." He held out the package, almost withdrew it, and then at last committed it to Alexander's hand.

"I shall not disappoint you."

As he had hoped, Alexander rode back to London with Colonel Brandon and his entourage. He would need to interview Willoughby soon, but now, with his injury so fresh, was not the best time for it. Later today would suffice, after he had read the letters.

Conversation in the carriage was stilted. Brandon did not seem inclined to talk, so Alexander and Fitzwilliam exchanged some polite inquiries into each other's affairs and then lapsed into silence. He wished he could start to peruse the package of letters that he could feel crying to him from his pocket, but that, too, would have to wait. Soon enough, he would be back in his office with a cup of coffee and one of Mr. Jacob's hot breakfast rolls before him, and then he could read in peace.

My Dear Willoughby,

For dear you are, although we have known each other for so short a time. It is a week—seven days—since you rescued me like a hero from a romantic novel, and I feel I have known you all my life! For indeed, it is not time or opportunity that is to determine intimacy; it is disposition alone. Seven years would be insufficient to make some people acquainted with each other, and seven days are more than enough for others...

Thus the first letter began. It was by all accounts a perfectly ordinary love letter, perhaps enough to raise an eyebrow, but certainly nothing of the sort to ruin a lady's reputation. Of course, the very existence of the letters between an unmarried lady and a gentleman was scandalous enough, although this was an everyday sort of scandal, one which all the demure young things of the *ton* entered into. But the content was innocuous enough. This was no reason for such histrionics on the part of the writer. He must keep reading.

The second letter was similar in tone.

Dear Willoughby,
How fine you sounded when you joined me in song last night. Your love of music matches my own exactly; your likes and dislikes are mine. How this pleases me, for I could not be happy with a friend whose taste did not in every point coincide with my own. Such a friend must enter in all my feelings; the same books, the same music must charm us both. Such a friend I have found in you...

Again, the words betrayed a very young and immoderate heart, but offered nothing to feed scandal. But the package contained several more letters.

Marianne wrote of poetry and her love of dancing and the splendours of the countryside, all innocent diversions. And then the letters changed. Suddenly she began to make allusions to some goings on in "the great house," which Alexander eventually discovered was Allenham, an ancient and very grand pile, about a mile and a half from the cottage where the Dashwoods lived in Devonshire. Some of the references were innocent, but even these led Alexander to the realisation that the girl expected a declaration.

How I liked that pretty sitting room upstairs; fitted up with modern furniture, it would be delightful, one of the pleasantest summer-rooms in England.

It was evident that Marianne pictured herself as the one to refit the house as its mistress.

Other comments, though, alluded to activities that the couple ought not to have entered into.

When you kissed me in that way in the upstairs bedroom, oh, that scandalous way, I felt a power rush through me that I had never felt before. It started at my toes and suffused all of me up to the very spot on my face where you placed your hand. Of other sensations, I dare not even write.

Well! This was more concerning. This could certainly damage a girl's reputation. No wonder she had been desperate to retrieve the letters. Alexander had no prurient desire to pry into Marianne's most private thoughts, but the need to learn something that might be of use about Willoughby was tantamount. He swallowed his repugnance for the job and kept reading.

Willoughby, it turned out, was every bit the cad he had been led to believe. Willoughby had never uttered the words but had convinced Marianne that he would soon offer her marriage, and had taken such liberties as only an affianced or married man ought to take. He had not quite relieved the lass of her virginity, thank heavens, but had introduced her to some of the more private interactions between a man and a woman. This was a relief, for Willoughby clearly had not stopped in his seduction of young Eliza Williams. For a moment, Alexander wondered if Colonel Brandon had any notion what the letters contained, what Willoughby had done. He suspected not, for surely, had this been the case, Willoughby would not have walked off that field with only a scratched hand.

Sometimes the letters grew more playful, or more set on the future. Allenham, Alexander learned, was Willoughby's expected inheritance. Nowhere did Marianne say exactly what it was worth, but it seemed much more valuable than Willoughby's own estate. Alexander consulted his notes: his sources had indicated that Combe Magna brought in a moderate income of about seven hundred a year, beyond Willoughby's personal wealth. One of

Marianne's letters suggested that Allenham would provide at least twice as much again.

> *Two thousand a year is a very moderate income, but one on which a family can be maintained. I am sure I am not extravagant in my tastes. A proper establishment of servants, a carriage, perhaps two, and hunters cannot be supported on less.*

This sounded far beyond what Combe Magna could support. Why Willoughby could not have been happy with his seven hundred—an amount of money that seemed as far beyond Alexander's expectations as was flying to the moon—Alexander could not fathom. But the man had a taste for the gaming tables, and in all likelihood for the horses, and seven hundred pounds could vanish quite quickly in such circumstances. Hence the need for a second estate, or a very wealthy wife. And when the first was denied him, he sought the second. Yet none of this brought any new insight into Willoughby's character.

Alexander continued his examination of the letters.

Now here was something interesting.

> *Mama refuses to allow me to keep Queen Mab, that lovely pony you gave me. It is quite unfair of her, with which I am certain you will agree. She must talk about money and how much things cost, where other more important considerations ought to prevail. A young woman must have her own means of conveyance, must she not? She sounds more and more like Elinor every day.*
>
> *Why, just yesterday Elinor made the most alarming comment: that she has no notion of greatness as being necessary for a happy life, nor even wealth, but only a competence to be able to live without fear of deprivation. She is becoming just like Edward. Have you met him? I believe not. He is our sister-in-law's brother,*

and has no great appeal to me. His eyes want that spirit, that fire, which announce virtue and intelligence. Moreover, he has no ambition! His mother has him for a military career or as a great politician, and he wishes for—can you believe this?—for the church! I heard him once say with his very own mouth that he had no wish for the prestige and splendour of Town at all.

This hardly exonerated Edward, but it did continue to paint the man as unlikely to kill for his inheritance. Alexander copied down the relevant passages. He would have to beg Marianne not to burn the letters, or to allow him to keep the ones he needed.

But you, my dear Willoughby, are destined for far greater things. Parliament! Your passion for politics enthrals me. You shall be a great statesman! When you speak of your ambitions, I know the fire of the gods burn in you. Oh, it frightens me a little when you talk, in your quiet moments, of the men you know in London who can make unpleasant things happen to other people, but what great man of public life can forge his career without such means of clearing up inconveniences. When Allenham is yours and you come into your full fortune, what greatness shall lie at your feet!

The pencil danced, tracing these words, so innocently written by a thoughtless, love-entranced child, but so damning. Did she know of what she wrote? Did she know the sorts of men these people must be? He wondered if Willoughby knew what she had written, if he had remembered these lines? For had Alexander been in those shoes, he would never have allowed such admissions to be aired, but would have burned the message containing them at once.

There was one more passage of note. Alexander read it twice before committing the passage to his notebook.

How fascinated I was to hear of your intimacy with the great poet Lord Byron. A man of his eminence and deep feelings must only have met with perfect accord from your own sensibilities. To have been a part of that world, to have engaged with him with his closest friends and intimate circle—oh, this is something of which I can only dream!

But is it true? Is it true, dear Willoughby, that the poet is engaged in affairs d'amour with his very own sister? What a scandal! One might well be tainted by association. I understand well why, with your great political aspirations, you must find a way to keep silent forever that young man RF (oh, how I long to know his true name!) who you said saw you at a certain place. Such would most grievously interfere with your plans. But you say you are in no danger, and I must believe you.

What was this? Some young fellow with the convenient initials RF had knowledge of Willoughby that could destroy his political aspirations? And Willoughby had means to some ruffians who could remove any impediments to his career? This only reinforced the previous information about Willoughby's great gambling debt to Robert Ferrars. He must talk to Atkins at once, for Edward's position as the main suspect in the case was in great jeopardy. Willoughby was becoming of greater and greater interest!

The rest of the letters contained more along these lines. There were heartfelt admissions of love, descriptions of passion, and references to Willoughby's ambitions. By the time Alexander had finished reading the lot and copying out the important lines, he felt filthy and in need of a bath. For a moment he wished he were still in his home village in Scotland near Glasgow, where on a hot summer's day he might walk to the river and wash off the day's grime therein. Here in his rooms in London he had only a hip bath and sponge with which to clean himself. He steeled himself for the toil of carrying his bucket downstairs to the water pump at the back of his building and then carrying that same bucket up two long flights of stairs.

He sighed again. He could not marry Mary, not now. Mary deserved better than a room with a small hip bath and a wash basin! She should have a house with servants and a bathing room and all the luxuries that the modern age afforded. He had a good amount of money saved; he would need to save a lot more before he could offer for her and give her the life she deserved. He sighed, put away the letters, and went to find the bucket.

Chapter Nineteen

The Aftermath

The knock at the door came shortly after Mary and Marianne had finished their breakfast. As was her habit, Mary had risen early and had completed her morning routine, but kept her young friend company whilst she took her repast. Marianne's pallor and distraction betrayed her agitation, and Mary had spent some time coaxing the girl to take some cocoa and a piece of toast.

Both ladies looked up when the maid showed Alexander into the comfortable room, with delight on Mary's part and a stricken look on Marianne's.

"Mr. Lyons!" she cried out as he entered. "What has happened? I must know." She leapt from her chair and all but threw herself at him in supplication, begging for news.

"Be calm, Marianne," Mary breathed. "He will tell us in good time. Alexander, please sit and I shall find you some tea and toast."

He accepted with words of gratitude and then turned his attention to Marianne.

"Miss Dashwood, I do, indeed, have information to relay of the unfortunate event—"

"That dreadful duel!! I have been quite beside myself all morning, wondering what had happened. Was there much bloodshed? Did both parties survive? What of Colonel Brandon? I had hoped to see him, and am more than concerned that he has not appeared!"

The young girl's eyes were wide and her face pale.

"Be easy, Marianne!" Mary encouraged her. "By Mr. Lyons' calm demeanour, I am certain the news is good. Had there been something dire to report, he would surely have been here earlier."

She saw Alexander's head bob up and down. "Colonel Brandon was triumphant, and no grave injury was received by either man. Do you wish to hear the account from me, or from the colonel when he arrives later?"

"Can you assure me he is well and that the matter is ended?"

This Alexander did and Mary saw her friend visibly relax.

"Then I shall hear of his victory from him. I would not have his glory diminished by a second telling of it."

"Very well, Miss Dashwood. Now, I have business I must discuss with you. The colonel entrusted me with these letters to return to you." He placed the package on the table, too far from Marianne for her to reach at once. Mary could see there was not one pile, but two. Had Alexander been separating the letters into groups somehow? Marianne reached out a tremulous hand, but Alexander cautioned her, "I would beg your indulgence not to burn these, at least not for now. I'm afraid I had to read them—"

She let out a cry of dismay, and he hurried forward, "—not to learn anything of detriment to you, but to see if I could learn anything of Willoughby."

"Was that necessary, Alexander?" Mary felt for the poor young woman whose most intimate words had been laid bare for unknown men to read.

His eyes lowered. "It is not something I do out of pleasure, but out of necessity. The colonel was most reluctant to hand them to me until I promised him several times I would use nothing of their contents to trouble you in any way. I shall honour that promise. I have no wish or need to see you embroiled in a scandal. Your reputation is safe with me."

Mary scowled, but nodded her assurance to Marianne at last. "He is, indeed, the most honourable man I know," she whispered. "He will never divulge your secrets."

Marianne screwed her eyes closed. "Yes, very well. I wrote so many things, so many ill-advised things... How foolish I was! But they are there in ink and I cannot undo them."

He kept his eyes on her, his face a serious study. "May I keep them? At least the ones I might need? For I did, indeed, learn some things that might help forward my investigation. I promise to return these to you as soon as I no longer need them—although I may require them if this ever comes to a trial. Only the relevant parts, I assure you!"

Marianne looked defeated, but agreed. "Yes. I suppose I must. I would not see justice denied because of my shame."

Mary reached over and hugged the girl. "All will be well." Her voice was low, but she knew Alexander could hear her. He picked up one of the piles of letters, tied with a thin string, and passed it across the table.

"Colonel Brandon will surely come to pay his respects later. I believe you are now perfectly safe from Mr. Willoughby, should you wish to return to Upper Berkeley Street. The danger is over." Then he took his bows and left the room. Mary dashed after him.

"What happened? You can tell me. I have no need to revel in the colonel's glory by his own account."

In a few words, Alexander did exactly this, recounting Colonel Brandon's quick victory and Willoughby's injury.

"Was it really that simple? Did he truly call Willoughby out and draw him to a field in the countryside merely to scratch his hand?"

Alexander's face was blank. "I cannot say what he truly intended. He certainly looked fierce enough when he faced his opponent, and when I tried to dissuade him from pursuing the duel, he brushed me off like an unwanted insect. I would not have been surprised to see only one of them return alive. Perhaps it was the sight of Willoughby's blood that changed his mind, or the simple fact that Willoughby, despite his bravado, is a coward. And to an officer's sense of honour, killing a coward would make him a coward himself. Regardless, this was the best possible ending to an ugly affair."

"And Willoughby just gave up the package like a discarded piece of ribbon?"

A nod was all the answer she was to receive.

"He is a man of little principle and fortitude, less, even, than what I had imagined from accounts of him. Then it is over and done?"

"So we all hope!"

He found his hat and kissed Mary's hand before taking his leave. Even after the door closed behind him, Mary felt the pressure of his lips on the back of her hand and wished he might have kissed her lips instead. With a sigh, she returned to the breakfast room where Marianne was still sitting perfectly still. She held the package of letters against her breast as if they were a rope thrown to a drowning man. Perhaps, in her eyes, they were.

"Will you keep them?" Mary's curiosity was stronger than her resolution not to intrude upon the younger woman's intentions.

"I... I do not know. For now, I expect I shall. There is nothing left of that love that once I felt for him. He was handsome and dashing and everything I dreamed of in a man, but my eyes have been opened. I believe I shall keep these for a little time, to remind myself what a fool I was, and as a sign that some men are made of far better stuff. And, when my heart is wholly healed, then I believe I shall burn them all and dance around the fire."

"And so you shall, my friend, so you shall!"

It was an hour later that Colonel Brandon appeared at the house. He was everything polite and civil, but Mary could see he wished only to speak in private to Marianne. She made her excuses to leave, and was granted such permission after hearing the colonel's account of the duel.

"You might have killed him, but you ceded him his life! Oh, how very brave and gallant!" Marianne gushed her admiration as Mary crept out of the room in search of her sewing or a book. She must reappear soon, but a few moments would not cause any further damage to Marianne's good name.

The colonel had been most concerned about Marianne's health and soundness of spirits. He had knelt beside her as he assured her once more that he had suffered not the slightest harm, and told her that he at no time really intended to cause serious injury to Willoughby. His only desire was to scare the man into ceding the letters and removing himself from society. As he spoke, Marianne gazed at him with wide adoring eyes.

What was it like to be loved to such a degree that a man would be willing to commit murder for you? Mary stopped still as she considered this. It was, on the surface, a romantic thought, to be the object of such passion. But it was a frightening thing, too. The sort of passion that could spur a man to a duel to the death might, in other circumstances, spur him to other rash acts as well that might cause equal harm to other people. Mary even knew of some ladies whose well-bred husbands beat them! Oh, one never spoke of such matters, not even to one's most intimate friends, but there were signs if you were observant. A cautious way of moving, a hairstyle that might cover a bruise, a scared glance towards a doorway... Mary saw these things far too often for her liking.

Fortunately for Marianne, Brandon did not seem the sort to inflict violence upon a woman. This was what had infuriated him, after all, what had led him to call Willoughby out. And his restraint at the duel spoke to some degree of self-regulation. But nonetheless, the notion was unsettling.

Would Alexander ever engage in so rash an act for her? Would she want him to? She pictured him as she sometimes did, hair long and wild and tossed by the wind, tartan kilt whipping about his bare knees as he wielded a claymore against an unseen enemy, sweat dripping off his high forehead. But no, this was no more her Alexander than was the cold determination of the honour-bound soldier bringing a man to his knees with a sabre.

Alexander would fight for her, that she did not doubt, but he would do it with cunning and intellect and with the weight of the law behind him. He was, in his way, as beholden to morality and the precedence of good over evil as she was, and she would have him no other way. That was why she loved him, after all.

She sighed. What good was it to love a man who wished only for an occasional kiss? That he loved her too, she did not doubt. But love was not quite enough, not when the lovers seemed fated never to be together. What would bring him finally to offer a formal courtship, or a proposal of marriage?

Marianne seemed fated for Colonel Brandon, and once freed from the accusations that lay over him, Edward would almost certainly ask for Elinor's hand. But once more, Mary and Alexander would remain as they were, joined in their souls but too far apart in too many ways.

She found her book and remained in the library for a few moments before rejoining the lovers in the front parlour. There they talked of general matters until, not long after, the colonel took his leave.

Marianne now sent a note to Mrs. Jennings and Elinor, and a reply soon arrived, welcoming Marianne back to their fold. It took but a few moments to pack up Marianne's belongings and call for the carriage, and soon Mary and her friend were riding through the crowded streets of London on their way back to Upper Berkeley Street. Marianne, relieved of her worry and animated by the thrill of an ardent suitor, talked without pause until they arrived. How vile was Willoughby, how unappealing that glint in his eye, but how dashing and mature was Brandon, and what an air those years of experience had given him!

Mary hoped the young woman's ardent passion would blossom into an abiding love when the first blush of gratefulness and enthusiastic infatuation had passed.

Soon they were arrived and Marianne was bustled into the house by her sister and Mrs. Jennings. Her bags were sent up to her room with a servant and she was pulled into the parlour to recount every moment of her time at Gracechurch Street. Mary, too, was summoned to attend, which she did for a short time before announcing her need to ride with the carriage back to her relations.

"You really must stay, Miss Bennet!" Mrs. Jennings cajoled her. "Miss Marianne has had the pleasure of your company for some days, but I have not. Why, I have not seen you since we returned from Norfolk!" She spoke as if that event were years in the past rather than only two days before. "Look at the clock: it has not yet struck two! Some of the *ton* have not even had their breakfast yet! What can your aunt need with you now, when there is so much pleasant society here? Let me send the carriage back with a note, and you can remain."

Mary had to refuse. She thanked Mrs. Jennings and reiterated her pleasure at accepting an invitation to dine, which was to arrive shortly, but she did have obligations towards her aunt. "The children are quite relying on me. They wish to put on a play with their puppets and need me to sew the toys' outfits."

"Puppets! How amusing! Faith, when the children have their play ready to perform, you must invite me over so I may enjoy it and tell them how wonderful they are. Puppets indeed! What a grand entertainment!"

After asking once more after Marianne's health and promising to see Elinor the next day, Mary took herself out of the house to regain her uncle's carriage. To her surprise, Alexander was leaning against the conveyance, talking companionably with the driver.

"I knew this coach from down the street, and then I recognised Gordon here," he smiled at the driver, "and hoped that if I waited long enough, I might see you. I was walking along after visiting the gaming house where Robert dealt his last cards. No joy to be had. And next, I am for Willoughby. I have a great deal of interest in hearing his account of some matters."

"To Willoughby? Is he sufficiently recovered for company?"

Alexander laughed. "This is no social call. I shall praise his bravery and make a great deal of his grievous wound and then commend him for his stoic suffering. And then I shall ask my questions."

"And I shall take notes for you. Oh, do not scowl at me like that, Alexander! I can write as well as any man, and Willoughby knows me well enough that he will not refuse to talk if I am present."

"The things I must ask about—"

"—are things I am strong enough to hear. Come, let us set on our way. Perhaps Gordon can drive us that far and then continue home in case Uncle needs him later. My cousins' puppets can wait. Will you, Gordon? Good. Here is the direction on Bond Street."

She climbed into the carriage and pulled Alexander after her.

But Willoughby had little to tell them. He had not been pleased at their intrusion into his home, and almost refused to speak when he saw Mary, but eventually he capitulated. He reclined on a long settee in an overly ornate salon with a huge white bandage on his right hand and his arm in a sling. Alexander did not roll his eyes, but Mary could all but see the effort he exerted upon himself to prevent this action. After the requisite inquiries about his wellbeing and expressions of sympathy over his injury, she took a chair in the corner and opened Alexander's notebook to write down what she could.

"Yes, I admit that I owed Robert Ferrars a great deal of money. I am not proud of this, but neither am I ashamed of it. It is no uncommon thing to wager a penny or two at cards." His handsome face dared them to object.

"And yet," Alexander countered, "we have a draught of a letter indicating that Mr. Ferrars was keen to receive his winnings. The message threatening, even."

Again, Willoughby looked down his elegant nose. "It was a grand sum, and the letter of which you speak was received. But the debt was also discharged. I win as well as lose, sir, and paid the man in full the day after he sent that unpleasant missive."

"May I ask at your bank to confirm this?"

Willoughby laughed. "Of course not! Do you think I would leave such matters to the banks? Not I, not with my wife's eyes on every transaction! No, I had other ways of discharging my debt that left no trace. Gold, sir, is heavy but carries no second set of eyes." He yawned and looked down at his swaddled hand. "Are you finished with your questions? My wife will be home soon and I would rather she not see you."

"I have another question, Mr. Willoughby. Are you at all acquainted with any men who might help resolve certain issues through violence, threatened or real? I am talking of people who would injure or kill for a fee."

Willoughby had the good sense to look offended. "I say! What insult is this? What do you take me for? Can you believe that I would be party to murder?"

"I know you are the sort of man to seduce a young woman barely old enough to merit the term and leave her expecting your child, with no way to find you and with no hope for support to raise that infant. If a man can condemn a child to a life of shame and poverty, I could not immediately think him unable to commit other immoral acts."

"I do not need to listen to this! And in my own house." He reached for the small bell on the table beside him and rang for a servant.

"Mr. Lyons and Miss Bennet are leaving. Please see them out."

And within moments, Mary and Alexander were standing on the street once more.

Chapter Twenty

Another Conference

I t was now four o'clock and the heat of the day still lay heavily in the air. After the cool air in the Willoughbys' shaded rear parlour, the sun beat strongly on Mary's back, and she was thankful for her bonnet. It would never do for a lady to perspire freely, and the bonnet would hide evidence of the same, even if it could not prevent it.

"Shall I find a hack?" Alexander asked. "I will see you home." The Gardiners' carriage was long gone, having been sent back when they alighted in front of Willoughby's house. Alexander had no notion of how long their interview would be. Would they even be admitted to the house? Or invited to dine? As it was, their half hour inside had been more than long enough for them to require other transportation. It was too warm to walk in any comfort.

The carriage they found was the open sort, which precluded a lingering kiss or two, but which was adequate for conversation. Mary stared at the passing buildings for a moment, but then needed to talk through her thoughts.

"I cannot make sense of this at all," she complained. "Something is eluding me, and I cannot discern what it is." Her companion nodded, and she continued. "It seems like a jumble of unconnected pieces, all hinting at something, but ultimately not connecting to each other at all. Or, rather, they must connect, like one of the dissected maps children use to learn geography. But if you do not know where your map is, the individual pieces seem destined never to fit."

"Speak on," Alexander raised his voice above the clop of the horse's hooves over London's noisy streets. "I get your meaning and agree all too well."

Mary sighed. "The first piece is Mrs. Ferrars' sudden death. It was made to seem Edward's doing, but after our visit to Norfolk, we now know it was perpetrated by his brother Robert."

"Who is now, himself, dead."

"Just so!" Mary stopped. When had she started using Alexander's favourite expression? She must take better care of her speech! She quite ignored the amused glint in her friend's eye.

"Which brings us to the second piece: Robert's murder. This is most perplexing, for it was at first made to look like a violent robbery ended in tragedy, and so it might have been designated. But somebody went to great lengths to implicate Edward as the instigator of the vile act."

"But he was too eager," Alexander said. "He laid out too many pieces of your puzzle map, and the bits and pieces are lying askew. There is too much evidence pointing at Edward. Just too much for my liking. There is the man dressed as a gentleman who happened to be on the scene, and who happened to drop a handkerchief with

Edward's initials." Mary nodded her agreement. "There is the fight between the brothers the night Robert died. We must go and speak to the servants there to see if anything else can be learned. There are the two cutthroats from St. Giles who were known to Edward. And there is Edward's pressing motive, to regain the fortune and estate he had so recently lost to his brother. These, all together, present so convincing a case against him it is almost like a present, all tied up with a bow."

A dog ran out into the street in front of them and the horse jigged to the side, throwing Mary against Alexander's side. She did not move back and did not object when he slid his fingers between hers. He gave her a private smile, and she answered in kind. When would he step forward and declare himself? For they were clearly so much more than passing acquaintances, or even friends.

"Soon, Mary," he whispered. Could he read her thoughts? They sat in silence for a few minutes as the bustle of London unfolded around them.

Mary's mind could not leave the case, however. She must have made a sound because Alexander asked her if all was well.

"I am still thinking about our mixed-up clues. Because now it seems Willoughby is involved. He is piece number three, I think. Can we believe him when he says he had paid his debt to Robert? If there is no record of it at his bank, how can we know? Might Robert have a record of it at his?"

"This is a very good question. There was no mention of it in the books I found, which seem to have been updated almost to the day Robert died. Still, if Willoughby insisted upon there being no documentation, Robert might have agreed."

"It was a great deal of blunt, though. More than twice Willoughby's income from his estate, if what Colonel Brandon says is correct."

Alexander found his notebook. "My sources state that Combe Magna provides about seven hundred a year. Willoughby was playing with money not his own."

"Is it true that his wife still maintains control over her fortune? I should like to know how!"

"I would very much like to see that marriage settlement!" he agreed. "But it is not unfitting that a woman should maintain such control. I have seen too many wealthy brides laid poor by their husband's profligacy."

"If that is so, and if Willoughby was lying about discharging his debt, he would have been left with very empty pockets, all while trying to make his mark amongst the *ton*. I heard rumours that he had an interest in politics!"

Now Alexander sat up straight and turned to face her. "Mary! Did I not tell you? No, I do not believe I did. There is more. Listen!" And he recounted what he had read in Marianne's letter, both about the ruffians and about Willoughby's involvement in some sort of scandal.

"Oh heavens! If Willoughby did have such aspirations, and if Robert did possess information which could bring a great scandal upon him, then this is even more of a reason to wish Robert dead. What was the scandal, I wonder?"

"Oh, with Lord Byron involved, it might be anything. He has rather the wild reputation..."

"I know a little of what he is supposed to have done. He really is said to be quite wicked. Is it true that he engaged in an amorous relationship with his own half-sister?"

The look of horror on Alexander's face confirmed her words.

"You may tell me these things, you know. It shan't break me or destroy my morals to know about it."

He cleared his throat and turned red, but said nothing.

"Being associated with that sort of behaviour would not do well to further Willoughby's aims, would it? I read my father's newspaper and my uncle's when I am in London. I know more of the ways of the world than many might think. I know that the wrong word in the wrong ear would be enough to destroy a far greater man than Willoughby. If Robert had threatened to reveal some news of him being at a certain gathering, or associating with certain groups of people, or engaging in certain activities, his dreams of prominence would be at an end before they even began."

Alexander replied. "I was hoping to talk to him about this at our interview. I shall have to try again, but I now doubt he will talk to me again. I should have been more temperate with my accusations, but the man, quite frankly, annoys me beyond reason. Still, his attitude and refusal to speak alone cast a pall of blame on him. It seems our young friend might have a lot to conceal.

By now the carriage was rumbling into the City, soon to reach Gracechurch Street where she would alight. This was accomplished in a moment, and she reached into her reticule to find a coin to pay the driver. Alexander stopped her. "I do well enough to pay the fare; I am saving what I can, Mary... But this I can afford." He asked the driver to wait, and accompanied her up the stairs and saw her into the safe welcome of her aunt's home.

He was saving! Those words set her heart afire, for they surely meant only one thing. There was so much meaning in them, so much said and unsaid, that she hardly grasped what she had heard. How he had looked at her as he said them, the cast to his head and the eloquence of his eyes! Dare she think... dare she believe...? She could, and she must. This was not the first intimation he had given that he had serious intentions toward her.

She blushed as she recalled their passionate kisses. They were all but lovers, two people who had found their perfect complement in each other. But their situations were so different... *They* were so different. Could he have something in mind? He was saving...

"Mary, are you woolgathering again? Do come in, dear!" Her aunt tugged her into the entrance hall and helped her with her bonnet. "I trust Miss Dashwood is in good spirits. It was good of you to send the carriage home when you were invited to tea with Mrs. Jennings. How is that lady?"

Time now passed in a flurry of familial activity. Mary greeted her young cousins with all the affection that was due between them and quickly became engrossed in tales of their day at the parks with a gathering of friends. She read to the younger ones and practised arithmetic with the older, and listened to their ideas for the puppet show.

Then it was time for dinner, where Uncle Gardiner talked about a new shipment of spices that had arrived this very day, and then, at last, she found a chair in the parlour by the light that still filtered through the window to do some of the sewing she had promised the children.

As her fingers worked, her mind grew busy again, and she began to mull once more over the strange case of Robert and Edward Ferrars.

If only they could find the two ruffians from St. Giles. They were the only people who could say for certain who engaged them to commit the crime, but they had most conveniently disappeared from the neighbourhood. Mary wondered if they would ever be found. More likely, they were both on their way to the Americas now, with their pockets full of Robert's gold.

This brought Mary to mind of young Cassie and her skill with an embroidery needle. She had quite forgotten to talk to her uncle about employing the girl. The light was fading, so she laid down her sewing and walked over to where her aunt and uncle were playing at cards and told them what she had seen.

"Thirteen, you say?" her uncle quizzed her. "That is young for such a position, but talent is talent. I have no need for someone with those skills, but the people who buy my textiles, they well might. Let me ask."

"The poor thing is living in those crumbling buildings, afraid of the men who prey on young girls? How terrible!" Her aunt's concern was evident. "What of her mother?"

Mary spoke of Nan and her insistence that she and her daughter not become so much merchandise in a part of town that thrived on the sale of human flesh. "She survives by taking in sewing; Cassie sews too, and does the most beautiful embroidery. She showed me a scrap of linen that must have seen five owners, but with such delicate edging and filigree along the sides I could scarcely believe my eyes. I can only imagine what she might do with a fine and new handkerchief..."

Aunt Gardiner started to talk, and Mary's ears captured some sounds that might have been "demonstration" and "talk to me," but her mind was elsewhere.

A handkerchief... She now recalled Cassie talking about a very plain handkerchief, one that she thought needed better ornamentation, but that had only two initials. And then she thought of another handkerchief that had only two very simple and unadorned initials that she had recently seen.

Could it be? No, surely that was impossible! But what if...? Her mind was racing.

"Mary? Mary, are you listening to me?"

She blinked and shook herself as her aunt's words penetrated through her thoughts.

"I apologise, Aunt. I had a notion..."

Her aunt's eyes crinkled at the corners. "Did you find the solution to that mystery you and Mr. Lyons are trying to unfold?"

"I cannot say for certain, but I do know I have some more questions I have to ask!"

The sun had dipped behind the buildings and night would soon be upon them. It was too late to travel across town in search of Alexander. She had no idea, even, where he might be. Would he be taking his dinner at his office desk, alone with his notebook and a small flagon of ale? Or did he choose to dine at one of the coffee houses where he might get a hot stew and some company? Or, perhaps, with some friend or colleague he had not told her about. A man must have friends, after all.

He did not belong to a club, although he had accompanied his high-born friends to theirs on an occasion, so he told her. Or—she shuddered at the thought—perhaps he had descended into some gaming hell to ask more of his questions or even (Heaven forbid!) partake of the activities.

It mattered not. She could hardly go traipsing through London alone, looking for one person in some unknown place. Even were she a man, with access to a waiting and biddable horse and no fear of what might be lurking behind every doorway, the impossibility of finding him was paramount. She put away her sewing and her book and took herself to bed. Tomorrow would be a very early day.

Chapter Twenty-One

Cassie

Aunt Gardiner was not well pleased at Mary's request to embark upon her pursuits the next morning. It was unbecoming for a lady to be out alone, she insisted, and especially at such an early hour. Mary must think of her reputation! Furthermore, she was concerned that it was simply not safe. After a great deal of discussion, Mary's aunt relented, with the condition that Mary take Gordon, the driver, with her.

The Gardiner children really needed very little supervision and assistance, and it was therefore only a few minutes later that Mary was able to leave the house. Her first destination was Alexander's office.

The laneway was far too narrow for the carriage; Mary must make the last few steps by foot, a matter which pleased her. Enticing aromas were emanating from the bakery at the corner, and she purchased a small package of buns and tarts, some of which she gave to the driver to eat whilst he waited for her, and some of which she took with her. She hoped Alexander would enjoy her morning offering.

His office door was locked, and no sound from inside answered her knock. It was very early, she now reckoned - not yet seven o'clock. Working men and women in the city were up and active at this hour, so unlike the members of the first circles, but perhaps this was too early.

She knew that Alexander had his personal rooms above his office. It would be most improper for her to intrude on his private space. A young lady simply did not visit a man's bedroom! Her reputation—nay, her very virtue—was at stake. And as she well appreciated, loss of virtue in a woman is irreparable! And yet...

And yet Alexander would never harm her. She knew this with absolute certainty. And she was alone. Who would denounce her? Even if she was seen, who would even know her? The driver was sitting down on the main street at the corner with his bag of warm and fragrant buns and a flask of tea. He believed her to be in Alexander's office, and she would not correct him.

Should she? Dare she?

With a deep breath, she squared her shoulders and strode up the stairs, more confidence in her steps than in her heart.

There were two doors. Which to choose? Walking in on Alexander was immodest enough! To disturb a stranger in his own rooms was unthinkable. She stared at the doors, wondering how to determine the right one.

But wait—what was that? There was a small box, about the size of her middle finger, about two-thirds up the one door jamb. She stepped closer to peer at it, and was surprised to see a painted character on it that looked like one of the Hebrew letters she had seen in a book in Papa's library. Papa did not know how to read the language, but for him, possession of a book was its own reward, and she had glanced through the volume with interested eyes. She still did not know what this symbol on the box meant, but it was enough to give her the confidence to tap on that door.

There was a shuffling sound from within, and then the door opened a crack.

"Good God, Mary! What in blazes are you doing here, and at such an hour? We must get you back home before your aunt learns you are out."

The door swung open a little and Mary could see him in his shirt sleeves and with his waistcoat unbuttoned. The sight of him so incompletely dressed sent unwelcome—or were they very welcome?—sensations through her limbs. He stepped back and opened the door completely. "You had better come in for now. You cannot be found loitering out there." He reached for her hand and pulled her into his room.

Mary gazed about the space. She had never been in a man's private room before, and was not quite certain what to expect. Would there be some secret altar to manhood along one wall, or some mysterious paraphernalia whose purpose she, as a mere woman, never could guess? She had glimpsed her father's shaving equipment once, which had sent her to her mother with a great many questions, the answers to which were rather uninteresting. What she did see was both intriguing and disappointing.

There were two small rooms; through the open doorway, she could see the bedroom, with a bed, a washstand, and a wardrobe. If there was something else outside of her field of view, she could not discover it. She could not keep her eyes from the bed. From this distance, it looked neatly made and with good linens, all very respectable. But that was where he slept... there he dreamed, pondered late into the night... maybe thought about her! Those sheets had touched his naked flesh... With a physical shake, she pulled her thoughts away from such improper directions and forced herself to take in the front area where she now stood.

Here she saw a small table, where Alexander must take his meals, and two chairs, and another armchair by the fireplace. An overladen bookcase leaned against one wall and a smaller cabinet stacked high with neat piles of paper stood against another. There was little space to move about, but the whole was tidy and not unpleasant.

"'Tis not what you are accustomed to, I'll wager. I have no fine furniture or great works of art for my walls. It is basic and suits my needs for now. Are you disappointed?"

"Disappointed? No. I had no idea what to expect, and it is rather smaller than anywhere I have lived or stayed, but no, I am not disappointed. I cannot imagine my sisters' rooms to have been this tidy, and that is with the assistance of our servants. You are ordered in your belongings as well as in your thoughts." She paused. "I... I brought breakfast. I had something I wished to discuss with you and hoped to find you before your day began. I need to go back to St. Giles."

"St. Giles?" He frowned. She sat in the chair he held out for her and placed the small bag of baked treats onto the table. "That is not where I would wish to be at any time of the day. What do you seek there?" He sniffed the air; the scent of the cinnamon-infused buns wafted through the modest room. "I have coffee on the fire. I know you prefer tea."

Mary now noticed the small cup balanced at the other end of the table beside a book. She had tasted her father's coffee and found the flavour bitter, but did not wish to disappoint her host. "A small amount, please. I shall endeavour to like it."

He found a second cup in a squat cupboard beside the fire and put it on the table. "Here, add a spoon of sugar. It is one of my indulgences." He chipped a good amount of the sweet substance from a block into the cup and then poured in the thick black liquid. "Stir it well and let it sit a moment. Good. It will do nicely with whatever it is I smell in that bag you carried."

Soon they were sitting with their breakfast of coffee and buns as Mary explained her idea. "It was the handkerchief, you see. If I am correct, the handkerchief Cassie saw was Edward's. And if Edward is telling the truth, the last time he saw it was on the morning of his mother's funeral, three months ago, and then it went missing. It seems reasonable that Robert was the one who took it, possibly as part of his ploy to implicate Edward somehow in their mother's death.

"But that same handkerchief was found at the scene of Robert's murder. Robert could hardly have left it there himself to blame his brother for his own death. But I can think of several reasons why it was there at the site. It might have been on Robert's person and was dropped or deemed of no value by the thieves who stripped him of his belongings. Robert might, for some reason, have given it to the men, or it might have been left in St. Giles and one of the attackers picked it up then, and let it fall by accident.

"Or, there is another possible reason, and one that places one more person we know into the midst of St. Giles, where the two ruffians were from."

"And you wish to confirm the identity of that person."

She smiled at him and took another sip. Coffee, suitably sweetened, was not unpleasant when one grew accustomed to the taste. "Will you come with me? I hope it will not take long."

"I can hardly allow you to wander there alone!"

She turned her eyes to him and changed the subject. "I saw the box on your door. What does it mean?"

He looked at her in surprise.

"I nearly did not notice it. It is the same colour as the door frame, and quite small. But then I noticed the image on it and knew this had to be your set of rooms."

He did not speak for a moment. He must have been considering what to say. "It merely contains some lines of scripture," he replied at last.

"Does it bring luck? Or ward off demons?" This was quite intriguing. Alexander did not seem to her a man given over to superstition, but the box did bring so many questions to mind.

"No, it is not magic. Some people believe it has protective powers, but not I. I am a man of science and the modern age, after all. It is more a reminder to myself of who I am. The text is nothing mysterious, merely a passage from Deuteronomy. You have surely read it many times yourself. I would show you, but the only Bible I have here is not in English."

"How interesting!" She kept forgetting that this unusual man read several languages. With his flaming hair and broad Scottish accent, he had surprised more than one person of her acquaintance with his knowledge of Latin, and she knew he spoke creditable French; he probably also read Greek. It should not amaze her that he read Hebrew as well. "May I see it?"

He shrugged and walked over to the crowded bookshelf. He reached for a volume with the practised ease of one who knew exactly where to find what he wanted and handed her the volume. It was an ordinary sized tome, perhaps thinner than her family's Bible, and bound in dark red leather. The spine was well worn, as is common in a book that is opened often. She turned the cover and was confronted with a blank page.

"Hebrew is read the other direction." He guided her hands to what ought to be the back, and helped her to open that cover. Once more, the touch of his bare hands upon her own sent frissons through her body that seemed quite inappropriate for one holding so holy a book.

She stared at the unfamiliar shapes as if exposure would render them comprehensible to her. "One day, can you teach me to read this? I would like to know more."

To her surprise, these were not mere words. She really was interested. It was not for the sake of making an argument or trying to disprove something, but instead, it was simple interest and curiosity.

"Let us resolve this case, and then all the time I have in the world is yours." He grinned at her and she grinned back and the sun shone a little brighter as they finished their breakfast.

Nan was not pleased to see them when they came calling at her crumbling building. "I've nothing more to say to you, and I'd best be on with my work. My sewing might bring in only pennies, but they're all the pennies I've got."

It was only the promise of a shiny coin and two more of Mary's cinnamon-scented buns that convinced her to call Cassie out to speak to them.

"I've spoken to my uncle," Mary told the girl, "and he will ask of his customers if anybody has need of an embroiderer. If I bring you some cloth and thread, can you make me some samples so I can show people what you do? Yes? I am pleased to hear that! I shall return as soon as I can, if your mother permits it. But I have one or two quick questions for you about that handkerchief you mentioned yesterday."

Cassie looked up with scared eyes at her mother.

"It's alright, child. But perhaps something to eat first? And I don't want everyone and his dog hearing us. Can we go back to those benches?" Nan's gaze flitted from window to window. "Don't need the neighbours thinking we be telling tales to the toffs."

Neither, Mary thought, did she wish for the neighbours to think she was bestowing other favours on Alexander... or coaching her daughter to do so. Alexander was a handsome man and many a female eye turned his way as he passed. As if reading her thoughts, Cassie turned a deep shade of red and looked resolutely at the ground before her.

Alexander merely bowed to Nan. "Of course, let us reclaim those benches. And then, if you wish, you may partake of the buns Miss Bennet has brought with her."

They walked the short distance. London was awake and noisy, but the churchyard was still peaceful, an island of calm in the ocean of bustle. Once settled in her seat with a sticky bun half eaten in her hands, Cassie relented to speak.

"There were two ladies," she whispered, "sisters, they were, I thinks, who came with Mr Edward and the church group. One seemed very fond of him."

Alexander moved to the bench where Cassie was sitting and asked if he might join her. Nan rose and shifted immediately to stand at her daughter's side. It seemed that even now, here in this public place, she was inordinately protective of her daughter and unwilling to trust Alexander. Mary admired her for this; sometimes she wished her own father was more solicitous of his children's wellbeing. But his first passion was his library, and now that Lizzy was gone to Derbyshire, little could draw him from his books.

As Nan hovered about them, Alexander asked in the gentlest voice Mary had heard, "Please, Miss Cassie, tell me everything you know. Would you like another bun? I smell something fragrant in the air."

Cassie's first bun had disappeared into her mouth and her sticky fingers wiped at the paper wrapper as if hoping for some more of the sweet pastry. The girl nodded, despite Nan's quick exclamation of refusal.

"Mary," Alexander reached into a pocket, "there is a bakery just there on the corner. See if you can find us some sweet buns. If they have more like this Chelsea bun we have enjoyed, I should like another as well." He handed her a coin, and held out two others for Nan and Cassie to take. Cassie took hers; Nan refused.

"Not another word till Miss Mary gets back," Nan admonished her daughter. "If he wants news, I'll not have him taking advantage."

"Very well," Alexander leaned back and smiled. "We shall wait."

Mary's task was accomplished in a moment, and she returned with four sticky Chelsea buns wrapped in paper. She let Nan and Cassie select theirs first, then took one and gave the last to Alexander.

"I shan't eat my dinner!" he complained, but took a large bite with a smile.

Cassie broke off a tiny piece and put it into her mouth, then licked sticky fingers and began her recitation. "She didn't come often, but it was often enough that we knew her, to look at if not her name. She seemed to be Mr. Edward's friend, 'cause she talked to him more than to the others. I don't think she really wanted to come to help us, only to show to Mr. Edward how good she was."

"You never heard her name?"

The girl shook her head. "But I know what she looked like." She proceeded to provide a rather accurate description of Lucy Steele. "I even remember her asking after my embroidery and saying how she made him a set of handkerchiefs once and that he lost them all but one. I thought she was going to pay me to make him some more, and I asked her if she would. But she just laughed and said she had no need for them anymore."

Mary glanced up and her eyes met Alexander's own gaze. Was this significant?

"How often did the church group come?" he asked.

"Oh, that was once a week, sir. Most often on Mondays, sometimes other days." Cassie looked to her mother again for approval, and Nan nodded but remained silent.

"And this lady?"

"Mebbe every three or four times. Not every week, to be sure. But enough that we knew her."

"And can you recall when you saw her last?"

"Oh, yes, sir. That was the week before Uncle Fred gone disappeared. She talked with him when she was handing out the bread they brought, and then after her sister and her went with the church group, he followed them. He come back happy and he smiled all the rest of that night. I thought she had asked him... Well, I'm not supposed to know about that."

"Is that so?" Alexander's pencil moved across his notebook once more. "That is very interesting, young lady. You're a right smart girl, you are. Here's another penny for your trouble." Cassie grabbed the coin, and it disappeared into some pocket under her skirts that Mary could not see.

"I saw her again." Nan's words brought Mary's head up with a snap.

"You did?"

Alexander blinked as well. He was equally interested, it seemed, in what Nan had to say.

"Aye, that I did. 'Twas three weeks ago or thereabouts. I didn't think much of it at the time. Thought she only wanted some mending done, but she brought a small pile of handkerchiefs and wanted them embroidered with some initials. Said they were for a gift. I didn't bother you," she spoke to Cassie, "because I knew you were busy and I can sew as pretty a trim as you can. It was some extra coin to pay for our dinner."

"Did you now?" Alexander remarked. "What can you recall about these pretty pieces of cloth?"

Nan described the work she had done to the best of her ability, and Alexander scribbled down notes on the pad he carried.

The woman finished her account. "I hadn't thought she would be the one to come back, though, and definitely not alone. But we're all surprising each other all the time, aren't we?"

Nan began to shift about and said something to Cassie, but Mary hardly noticed. Something was bothering her about this revelation.

Could it be? No, surely not. Some of the pieces of the picture were starting to come together, but as of yet, they did not form a clear image. But... But what? She was still uncertain. Hopefully, Alexander would be able to make more sense of her thoughts.

She must have made a sudden movement, for at that moment he looked up at her with questions in his eyes, but he said nothing of it. Instead, he turned back to the woman from St. Giles.

"You may have helped us a great deal, Nan!" He shook her hand like a colleague and assisted Cassie up from the bench, and bid them well with such pretty words that even Nan smiled.

"What did you think of all of that?" Alexander asked a short while later as they walked back towards his office. "They both had quite a story to tell."

"Yes. It seemed so inconsequential, but it might have been the piece of knowledge we needed. I am," she enunciated her words carefully, "starting to see the picture of who instigated Robert Ferrars' murder. But I need more information, and I still do not quite understand why. I can hardly make that out, unless..."

"Unless?" he raised his eyebrows in question.

"I believe," she stated, "I need to make one last call."

Chapter Twenty-Two

Lucy Once More

Mary waited for Elinor to alight from the Gardiner's carriage before she climbed down. They were on the street in Holborn where the Miss Steeles were staying with their cousins. Gordon, the driver, knew of a stable a few hundred yards away and he proposed to take the carriage there, and then ask if he might wait in the kitchens below whilst the ladies were visiting.

It had been Alexander's suggestion to include Elinor in this visit; If Mary had arrived alone, any engagement would have the aura of an interrogation, for she and Lucy Steele were not friends. But Elinor and Lucy had a long-standing acquaintance and her presence gave this meeting the air of a normal social call.

Therefore, Mary had parted from Alexander with a promise to talk to him later and had made her way back to Marylebone to speak to Elinor and include her in the plans.

Mrs. Jennings was of a cheerful and trusting enough disposition to ask no questions as to the ladies' wish to visit. She declared herself quite happy to sit with Miss Marianne, who was greatly improved and who was expecting a call herself from Colonel Brandon.

"The colonel will be sad to have missed you," the lady of the house declaimed, "but his true goal is elsewhere." She winked in a rather vulgar but amusing manner and hustled Mary and Elinor out the door.

Now they stood in front of the house where Lucy and her sister Nancy were staying. Mary surveyed the house, sandwiched as it was between two others exactly like it on this small street in Holborn. She knew this style of building from her outings with her aunt. There would be a narrow mews at the back giving access to the servants' rooms and the kitchens below, where delivery boys might come with their wagons of milk and buckets of coal, and where servants might empty out the household's refuse without fouling the streets. There, she was certain, Gordon would find his way to the kitchens, where he would ask for a chair and maybe a cup of water until they were ready to leave.

With a smile at Elinor, Mary marched up the three stairs and knocked at the door.

"Miss Bennet and Miss Dashwood to visit with Miss Lucy Steele," she announced to the maid.

This time, Lucy was at home to visitors. This was a great relief; Mary needed to speak to her, and there was little time for delay. She smiled at the servant and followed her into the house.

They were shown in and led to a sunny parlour at the back. The room was not large and betrayed more common tastes than what she was accustomed to, but it was not an unpleasant space. After a short wait, Lucy entered. She looked pale but smug, with a decided tilt to her head and an aura of satisfaction. Mary wondered what she was thinking.

She had spent a long time trying to determine how to make her way into Lucy's good graces. Lizzy was the one with such natural talent; even Jane, whom everybody liked so well, was too genuine and honest to encourage intimacies for some ulterior purpose. And Mary herself—well, there was a reason her best friends as a child had been her books. She could comport herself well enough in the salon when necessary, but she always felt like a lumbering oaf when she attempted any sort of subtlety. Perhaps that was one reason she liked—loved—Alexander so well. With him, she need never dissemble. With him, she could be Mary, plain and unimproved, and he liked her anyway.

But for now, she must somehow befriend Lucy. She had eventually confided in Elinor, who was as sensible as she, but who had more of those natural sociable abilities that Mary so admired. And Elinor had a suggestion. Mary had liked the idea and vowed to use it as advantageously as possible. Now was the time to determine how effective she would be as an investigator!

The two friends greeted Lucy and made the appropriate how-d'ye-dos before setting down for a cose.

"I am so pleased you are feeling better," Elinor cooed as soon as the women were alone. "I was so troubled to hear that you were indisposed the last time I came around. I was honoured by our intimacy in Devonshire at Barton when you trusted me with the secret of your engagement to Mr. Ferrars." How cunning was Mary's friend, not to mention which Mr. Ferrars was implied. "Now, knowing of your marriage and your tragic loss, I could do nothing but pay you a condolence call. I know it is nigh on two weeks since he died, but I wished to give you time to mourn in private." Across from them, Lucy dabbed at her eyes, although Mary had not seen the mist of tears in them.

Elinor made the appropriate sympathetic but meaningless noises, then continued. "I do hope you will excuse me for bringing Miss Bennet on this call. She has been a great solace to me, and I hoped that her kindheartedness would be of comfort to you as well."

Lucy dabbed at her eyes again. She really had a pretty face, but the coldness and calculating nature of her expression prevented her from being truly lovely. "I thank you, Miss Bennet. It was kind of you to come. So few people have come... so few know. It is hard... I wish now that I had not listened to Robert's urgings. I ought, perhaps, to have made our marriage known immediately upon returning to London, but Robert insisted." She gave an exaggerated sigh. "He said we must keep it a secret until his year of mourning was complete. I know men are not held by the same strictures as we women, but he thought it more proper. And now..." she sobbed artfully into her handkerchief.

"I am most terribly sorry for your loss," Mary moved close and put a gloved hand on Lucy's arm. "So tragic! And he was so young too, with so much to look forward to. I... Oh, what a beautiful handkerchief." She allowed her eyes to fall onto the piece of embroidered linen that Lucy was using to mop her eyes. "It has your initials on it, too. LF. What a precious memento of a too-short marriage."

"My sister Nancy ordered a set for me as a wedding present. She was the one person I told in advance, and they were waiting when I returned as Mrs. Ferrars. Nancy is not always the first to understand, but she is monstrous kind and thoughtful. She discovered a lady to do the needlework, and are these not the best leaves and flowers at the corners? She will not tell me where she bought them. I believe she does not wish me to know how much she spent."

"I can well understand that." Mary let her head bob up and down as she spoke. "Excellent embroidery is a most elegant accoutrement. Why, my acquaintance Colonel Fitzwilliam—oh, you must know of him, for his father is the Earl of Matlock—he has the finest set of handkerchiefs that ever I saw, most tastefully and elegantly done by his very sister. So beautiful, and yet so suited to a man of his elevated rank and station."

Lucy sat a little straighter. "You are acquainted with the Earl of Matlock?"

"Oh, intimately!" Mary lied baldly, and hoped God would forgive her. It was all being done in the interest of good, after all. "I have dined with the family often—" well, she had dined with the colonel twice, although Alexander knew him far better, "—and I am a favourite of his relations." Those relations would be her sister Lizzy and brother-in-law Darcy, but Lucy did not need to know that!

"La! How very interesting! Is the family in Town? Surely not in the summer! They must, rather, be at their country seat. What grand people to know! So sophisticated and elegant, I am certain!"

"Yes, they are indeed! But you are so correct, they are at their estate for the summer. Only the colonel himself is in the neighbourhood, and he is busy with his military duties. I do look forward to seeing them again. They were so very kind and generous at my sister's wedding, welcoming Elizabeth into the family as if she were born to her rank. But alas, her husband is merely a gentleman, no matter that he is wealthier than many a titled nobleman. Her wedding was so very lovely. It was everything tasteful and of the finest quality... La! Forgive me. We are not here to talk about my sister. Please, Mrs. Ferrars, I would so love to hear about your own wedding. If the recollection does not cause you too much pain, of course! I thought the telling of it might bring some happier recollections to mind."

"Yes, it well may, but..." Lucy began.

Mary placed her hand once more upon Lucy's forearm. "I must know," she lowered her voice, "however you managed to wed without calling the banns! Did Mr. Ferrars purchase a licence? Even then, I thought you must marry in your own parish. Or am I mistaken? I know so very little about these things, and I have hopes, but dare not say more at the moment." She looked down at her lap in what she hoped was a coy gesture.

Lucy's eyelids flickered up and down. Mary could all but hear the thoughts rushing through the other woman's head as she decided what to say. Once more her hand brought the handkerchief to the pretty eyes.

"That was of no matter, Miss Bennet, for we did not marry in England at all."

"What? You eloped? To Scotland?" Mary waited for the affirmative nod. "Faith! How unspeakably romantic! To run away like that, and with the man you love to be married where none can stop you. Oh, how marvellous! Tell me every detail."

Lucy seemed to be enjoying her audience. She looked about to ensure that no servants were in attendance and beckoned both Mary and Elinor to come closer. "It was everything of my dreams," she gushed. "Robert was so attentive from the moment we left London. He had made his excuses to visit his estate, and I claimed an invitation from new friends to their country house, but in truth, we made for the north. Robert had arranged for rooms at every inn, and the best they had, and dined so well you might never believe we were not in some fine house with a French chef. We were three whole nights on the road and we did not achieve Scotland until the very last evening."

"Why, that is even further than my brother Darcy's estate in Derbyshire! Do tell—did you go to Gretna Green? Everybody goes to Gretna Green, I hear!"

"Oh no! No indeed. Robert did not wish to be known, so we went to Canonbie. And so romantic it was, let me tell you!"

"And what of the wedding itself? I do love a wedding! I must hear all about yours."

Now Lucy's blush was genuine, but Mary thought it more from embarrassment than from recollection.

"It was not a fine affair, to be certain. We had no time to prepare a great event or an elaborate wedding breakfast. But it was everything perfect in its simplicity."

"Oh, yes, of course! Was the ceremony lovely? Was it particularly special?"

Lucy nodded. The ringlets about her face bounced up and down with the motion. "It was indeed the most wonderful rite ever. The parson, Mr. Craig, read the words—la, I know they are the same words that are spoken everywhere—but for us, they seemed perfectly chosen, as if they were set down for Robert and myself alone. There were, of course, so few people with us, merely the parson's wife and brother, and the local squire upon whose land the church stands, and his wife. I felt that God Himself was present with us, blessing our union. How unfortunate that such a prospect of perfect felicity should be so overcome by the cruel hand of fate."

"So very, very sad." Mary gave a sympathetic shake of her head. "But please, I must hear of the wedding breakfast. I have a great appreciation for simple beauty; it is so much more pleasing than ostentation and overdone display, is it not? There is nothing like quiet elegance. Who was present? I long to hear all."

"We had only a small gathering, as you must understand. The innkeeper was in attendance, of course. That was Mr. Rummage, for I recall it being so odd a name. Robert had written to him the previous day requesting a special breakfast, and he set his cook to work, especially for us. Mrs. Rummage was a most genteel lady, and the squire, Mr. Malloch and his wife, and their children, who are just now out in society. The parson and his wife were present as well, and three or four of the other first families of the neighbourhood. And such a selection of dainty cakes and finely cured meats and soft breads you never have seen! It must have been the finest such event the village had known in many a year."

So much for simple and elegant. "And what did you wear? Was it something especially purchased for the occasion, or your best dress? Brides always look so beautiful, no matter what they choose for their wedding clothes."

From the corner of her eye, Mary could see Elinor trying not to smile. She kept her eyes on Lucy, hoping her own mirth would not be discovered.

"Oh la! My dress! It was merely one of my best gowns. We had not the time to purchase new clothing, as you surely understand, nor would my cousins have understood the reason for it. But Nancy always tells me how fine I look in my blue silk..." and on she spoke with great animation.

"It must have been most trying to return to London," Elinor now added, "and to have to act as if nothing had happened."

"So very true!" Mary inserted herself. "Had I just returned from a most romantic elopement with the man I adored, I should feel like the queen herself. And then to keep everything a secret! How trying, and yet... how mysterious and charming." She sighed and hoped it sounded genuine.

"But it was! It was so terribly romantic, Miss Bennet. Having my husband so very close and yet unable to tell the world that we were wed, well, I felt like a character in some great novel, sacrificing her happiness for the good of the realm. But I was happy! I was in raptures at being united with Robert. I can hardly account that nobody guessed it, for I felt my smile must shout my secret."

At last it was time for Mary and Elinor to take their leave. A maid informed Mary that yes, her driver was in the kitchens and would meet her out at the carriage. The ladies exited the house and climbed aboard the vehicle, but before it began to move, Mary leapt out.

"We shall await you at the mews," Elinor called out for all to hear, and Mary slipped around the corner to where the small alleyway let out onto the side street.

Her knock at the kitchen door brought a rather shocked and red-faced matron to greet her.

"What's here, Miss?" The woman—a cook by her apron—looked almost offended at her appearance. "Door's around front. Beth will see you in and take you to the Miss Steeles."

She moved to close the door again, but Mary stopped her.

"No, no, I am not here to pay a call. I was just here moments ago with Miss Dashwood. Our driver lost a button, and the mistress gets most upset when brass goes missing. Miss Dashwood is in the carriage and Gordon is attending her. We did not wish to inconvenience Miss Steele again. She was looking rather tired. I am merely here to ask after the button. Please, may I come in?"

The cook cocked her head and looked through the corner of her eye. "I cannot rightly say so. Go around the front and I shall inform the misses."

"Please, do not trouble them. I left Miss Lucy only moments ago and I really do not wish to trouble her further. She has been through a most trying time of late..."

The cook's eye softened. "Aye, that she has, poor lass. She has been most unhappy and tired. You do kindly to think of her health. A button you say? Brass? Very well. Come in and sit and I'll ask after it."

Mary followed the cook into the house. "You sit here." She pointed to a chair by a large wooden table, part of which was covered with flour, part of which held a pile of vegetables ready for chopping for the evening's meal. Along one wall a fire blazed in the hearth, over which sat a large pot of something fragrant and beside which a rack of pies were baking. The family did not aspire to the first circles of society, but they seemed to enjoy a fine table.

The cook bustled off to inquire about the button, leaving Mary alone with one young kitchen maid who was at work peeling a pile of carrots. Mary sat very still for a moment and waited for the young maid to become more at ease.

"I hope I am not disturbing you," she said after a moment.

"Oh, no, Miss. Not at all."

"I had hoped my appearance here would not cause too much bother. Does Mrs. Richardson venture into the kitchens much?"

"Oh, no, Miss. Cook meets with her upstairs."

"And the Miss Steeles? Surely such healthy young women must wish for a piece of something to eat every so often. I am a frequent visitor to my own family's kitchens. I quite enjoy taking a cup of tea with our cook, where I may just be Mary and not some fine lady."

"Oh, no, Miss. The older Miss Steele eats all but nothing. Well, the younger Miss Steele comes now and again. She is not one to eat much, but often asks after a piece of dry toast or ginger tea."

"Does she now? I quite enjoy a piece of dry toast myself on occasion. Has this long been her habit?"

"Oh, no, Miss. Just since the last month or two. Shortly after she got back from her visit to her friends up north, that is. I thought it was something she learned there, which is why I remember it."

Mary gave a reassuring smile. "I am certain that is so. One often discovers new treats and foods when one visits. Miss Steele must have been very happy after her visit. London is a grand place, but it can be a relief to be out of the city in the summer."

"Oh, no, Miss!" This time, the maid's eyes were wide. "Not at all. Poor creature came down here so often we thought she was taking a position in the scullery!" The young girl laughed at her own joke. "In truth, Miss, she was most distressed. Cook will not talk of it at all, but I'm thinking she wished for a place to be away from Mrs. Richardson and her sister, where they wouldn't pry, don't you think?"

"Absolutely! A woman always needs a place away from prying relations. Was there something amiss that she wished not to talk about?"

"I couldn't say, Miss. But she was most unhappy when she got home, she was. Moping about and floating in and out of rooms like a ghost. I thought she was taken ill, and even asked Cook, but she told me never to mind anyone else's business. Still, it was mighty strange, Miss Steele before being such a lively creature."

"How unfortunate. But she seems much recovered now." Mary watched the young maid very carefully.

"Aye, Miss. This past week or thereabouts, she has been like a different creature. I do not see her so much now, but she seems like one who just won a great prize and cannot tell anyone of her fortune. Oi... here comes Cook. I must be back at my carrots."

A moment later, Cook reappeared. There was a frown upon her face, but she held something in her hand. "Beth found the button. It was under a pile of rags behind the stairs. Cannot imagine how it got there, for the man was seated here in the kitchen all the time he was here. Well, fairies must keep their hands busy. As long as they don't upset my pies. Here it is. You'll be off now, I gather."

It was a command. Mary stood and thanked the cook most gratefully for her efforts. Then, with a smile at the young maid peeling carrots, she took her leave and slid out the door.

Chapter Twenty-Three

Deliberations

Alexander had been waiting for about half an hour when Mary returned to the Gardiners' house. He sat on a bench in the small park across the narrow street, reading through his notes but looking up every time he heard the clop of horses' hooves and the squeak of carriage wheels. At last, he saw a vehicle he knew and waved as the carriage approached. He could see the moment she noticed him, for her eyes locked upon his through the window and she smiled. The vehicle came to a halt in front of the Gardiners' front door, and Mary urged the driver on. "You need not wait to see me inside," Alexander heard her say. "I will sit in the park a moment before going into the house." As soon as the conveyance disappeared around the corner, Mary dashed across the quiet street to greet him.

"Do you have a moment to talk, or are you needed inside?" he asked when she drew close enough for conversation. "I would present myself at the door like a gentleman," he alluded to their first meeting when he was anything but gentlemanlike, "but wished to speak without your well-meaning aunt in attendance."

"She is most attentive to my reputation." Mary rolled her eyes; he affected not to notice. "Come, there is a place past that monument where we may sit for a while. There might even be shade, and I would prefer to be out of the sun."

They found the spot, a small bench in the dappled shade of three young trees that would one day grow mighty. A slight breeze prevented the air from becoming stifling, and after his half hour in bright and warm sunshine, Alexander was pleased for the shade.

"What news?" he asked when Mary was seated.

"No, sir. I would hear from you first. Where did you go when we parted?"

"I paid an obligatory call upon Robert's bank. The clerk was not pleased to speak to me, but the letters I have from Colonel Brandon and from Edward convinced him to let me see Robert's accounts. As we suspected, there is nothing unusual in there. The expected deposits and withdrawals, some larger and some smaller, depending on the cost of the toothpick case or the size of the debt. But there was no record of any payment from our friend John Willoughby."

"Then he did not discharge his obligation after all, despite his protestations?"

Alexander shrugged. "We cannot know. As Willoughby said, there are ways of satisfying such an obligation that do not involve the bankers. He might have given Robert a piece of gold, as he joked, or might have made some arrangement to transfer to him a piece of land or a winning racing horse. A painting could well have changed hands, or perhaps a membership in some grand club was paid for the next decade or two."

Mary said nothing, but looked at him with sad eyes.

"And what of your news, Mary? Did you learn anything of use today from Lucy Steele?"

She stared off somewhere into the distance. "Can you please remind me of your interview with her? I know it is several days past, but I must be sure that everything I am thinking accords with your notes."

This was unusual. Mary had the most uncanny memory for every detail. What might she have forgotten, what nuance might be blurred? But, he reminded himself, she had not been there when he had spoken to Lucy, and he might have missed one or two minor particulars in his telling of it.

"You insist on challenging my skills at recollection!" he teased. "Very well. Here is my notebook. Let me see..." He turned to the right page and scanned what he had written. "She was not pleased to speak to me, but relented when I told her I would send messengers off at first light on the morrow to verify her claims. She provided me with several names..."

"Craig, Rummage and Malloch. Am I correct?"

"Aye, Mary, you are never wrong." How proud he was of this young woman. What a fine memory she had. He had to record all of his information in his notebooks; she merely needed to search her mind. It was a God-given talent, to be sure.

"I heard these names only today. They are fresh in my mind."

"I informed her I would send messengers the very next morning, and she then related her yarn to me."

"Am I to presume that you sent off your rider within minutes of leaving her house? You might have told her they would not leave until morning, but I know you too well, Mr. Lyons. If I were one to wager, I would bet the man was halfway to Stamford before Lucy could find a pen to write letters of her own. That must be why she could not see us that same afternoon. Your messages certainly reached Canonbie before hers."

"Ah, so you discovered that, did you, Miss Bennet?"

"So I did, Mr. Lyons, and some more besides. Shall I tell you?"

"Of course, silly thing! That is why we are sitting here, after all." He grinned at her and she grinned back and for a moment he thought there was nothing better in the world than sitting and chewing over a case with Mary. There was still so much to discuss, so many concerns to work on, but nothing else under heaven would do for him.

Mary glanced around and then snaked her hand along the bench to find his. She grabbed it for a moment and gave it a squeeze and did not let go until some voices began to approach them. Then she let go and told some of her tale.

"It seems that Lucy was most distressed upon her return from her supposed visit to her friends. This visit, you must know, was the excuse given for her absence from London. The Richardsons cannot be very attentive guardians."

"Lucy would benefit from your own aunt's prodigious care."

"Really, Alexander! Do let me continue."

He smiled again.

"According to Lucy herself, she returned to London a triumphant bride, bursting with joy and hard-pressed to refrain from shouting her happy new situation from every doorway. But not so, according to the maid I spoke to. That girl insisted that Lucy was most troubled and sought refuge from her sister and cousin Mrs. Richardson in the kitchens."

"The bride was not so glowing?"

"If she was, I believe there was another cause. Expectant mothers are also said to glow."

"Really, Mary! Young ladies are not supposed to know about such things!"

She gave him a playful punch in the arm. "You disappoint me, Alexander! You know I am no ordinary young lady. Besides which, I am a country girl. One does not grow up surrounded by farms and animals without being exposed to some of those lessons ladies are not supposed to learn. I know more than I ought, perhaps, about such things.

"And Lucy's delicate condition is no secret, after all. She has not made a grand public announcement of it, but it is the basis of her claim on Robert's estate, is it not?"

Wherever did she learn of these things? "Do you know the law?"

She shook her head. "No, not well. But I heard you speaking. If there is no new written will, a man's previous will is deemed to be made void upon marriage and the birth of children, but it must be both. Am I correct?" She looked up at him. "It cannot be one or the other. A marriage without issue is not sufficient cause to revoke a will, nor is the birth of an illegitimate child."

"You would have made an excellent lawyer. You are mostly correct. It used to be as you said: the *birth* of a child. But the law changes and adapts over time, and now an unborn child is considered the equivalent of a living child for these purposes."

"Then Lucy being enceinte negates his prior will."

"Ah, but there is one more proviso. The father must know about the child, for it is deemed that *this* is when he would have it in mind to change his will to provide for his offspring."

Mary looked disappointed.

"Never fear, Mary. That letter we discovered shows that Robert did know about the babe. In that respect, the law is satisfied. Let me look for my notes..."

"I shall visit with my solicitor soon to make provisions for our child," Mary quoted.

He let out a snort of air. "I do not know why I bother with my notepad. Yes, you have it verbatim. *Our child*. He knew about the babe."

"I thought as much, but I was not certain whether the child had to be born at the time of the father's death or not."

He searched his memory for a moment. "*Lancashire and Lancashire, 1792*. That relates to a posthumous child."

"Your memory is every bit as good as mine!" She gave him another playful punch in the upper arm. "Then, as I understand it, this part of the requirements is satisfied, but there is another that I fear is not. For I am quite certain, after my visit today, that Lucy Steele is not married."

"What makes you think that? I am still awaiting a reply to my inquiries in Scotland. I had expected it some days ago."

She cocked her head. The angle of the sun was such that a few brave rays crept below the brim of her bonnet and illuminated her eyes, making them glow like topaz. "I had wondered about that. What can be the matter that a response is taking so long?"

All he could do was shrug. "But please, I would hear your reasons for this conclusion."

He reclined on the bench and let Mary tell him of her observations. The air was warm and her voice so soothing and pleasant it would be easy to drift into that dreamlike state between wakefulness and sleep. Only the import of her thoughts kept him alert.

"She told a very grand story of her wedding day," she explained. "But her account of the wedding does not match anything I have heard from others, nor from what I have read."

"Your romances and novels are not likely to paint too accurate a portrait of the Scottish rites."

"Perhaps. But here, you are a lawyer and a Scot! You must know this. Please tell me what such a wedding might have entailed."

Now he allowed his eyelids to drift closed. "There is very little involved, really. All one requires to be married in Scotland is to assert such a wish in front of witnesses. As long as both parties are of age—there it being fifteen and not twenty-one—and neither closely related nor already married to another, the marriage is legal."

"Is there a rite or a ceremony?" Her voice filtered through the tendrils of thought that caressed his mind.

"One is often contrived, of a sort. It might be something like, 'Are ye of legal age to wed?' And if the answer is in the affirmative, 'Are ye already wed to another?' If that response is correct, the anvil priest will declare, 'Then you are married.' And often he will strike the anvil with his hammer to punctuate his pronouncement, but it is all for effect. The declaration of a will to be married is sufficient for the law."

Mary was silent for a moment, and he coaxed his eyes open to look at her. "This is not what Lucy told you. What did she describe?"

"From her recollections, it sounded exactly like a Church of England service... That is when the parson reads from the *Book of Common Prayer*..."

"I know the rite, Mary. I might even be able to recite it from memory, even if mine is not as flawless as yours."

She flushed red. "I am sorry. I ought to have known better. But there was no anvil, no blacksmith... this is half of the romance of eloping, is it not? A Church of England ceremony could have been as easily arranged here in London, for all that Lucy is three-and-twenty and required no one's permission."

"Hmmm..."

"What else did that letter from Robert say? Have you written it down?"

Alexander flipped through his notebook once more and found the appropriate page.

"I know..."

"*...that the elopement to Gretna did not meet your expectations.*" Mary finished for him. "This hardly accords with her account of a beautiful and very romantic wedding."

He sat back for a moment, feeling the hard metal of the bench press into his spine. He allowed his eyes to drift closed once more, but now in thought and not in the haze of drowsiness. "What we have, then, is an unwed young woman who is expecting a child..."

"And desperate for the respectability and financial security of the married state."

"And if these were not hers in reality," he added, "then..."

"Then," Mary concluded, "we have a terrified person in a most precarious situation, willing to make some rather drastic decisions."

Alexander followed Mary into her aunt and uncle's house. She explained that they had met in the park, and if her aunt had suspicions she did not raise them, but welcomed him inside with a warm smile. The children were in the front parlour at their activities, ready to tell all listeners about their day, and when he was invited in for refreshment and perhaps to stay for dinner, he accepted at once. He had felt this sensation before, the feeling of being in a home. This was not a small set of rooms in an old building above an office, nor was it a grand showpiece of a palatial estate, but it was a home where real people lived and loved and carried on their lives.

It was the way he felt about Longbourn, Mary's home in Hertfordshire, with the working farm so close to the manor house, with five animated daughters disrupting their parents' lives, where friends and relations wandered in and out at will, and where the servants were as much family as were the squire and his offspring. It always brought him to mind of his own home, so far away and so long ago, before his father died and before the new laird decided he had no need for a Jewish doctor in the village. It brought back memories of the rich smells of baking bread and warm stew, of children running through the village streets and playing in the ponds, of the family gathered around at night to hear somebody read from a novel or to make up a story, of gently squabbling sisters and folk songs rendered out of tune and goodnight kisses at bedtime.

The Gardiners had such a home, and in his mind he congratulated their four young children for selecting such excellent parents.

He took the offered chair and listened happily for fifteen minutes as the oldest daughter, trying to be so very grown up, told him about the day's outing to the park with their friends, and then he got down onto the carpeted floor to help the youngest, a boy of five years, build a castle from a set of wooden blocks. Mrs. Gardiner smiled indulgently at him and Mary beamed. Was she imagining him with their own children someday? He would be a doting father, not one of those men who appear at the nursery door for five minutes every other day to ensure his progeny were all still accounted for.

His time was thus pleasantly spent for about half an hour until Mr. Gardiner appeared, home from his day at his place of work, and the invitation to dine was reiterated.

"When Mary rushed off this morning," Mrs. Gardiner smiled, "I imagined we might have company this evening, and I requested my cook to prepare several vegetable dishes. I know you do not eat meat."

His heart glowed at this welcome. Mary had clearly spoken of him warmly to her relations, and they were considerate enough to take his idiosyncrasies into account in their invitation. He accepted gladly and spent a most enjoyable evening amongst excellent people.

He was about to take his leave when a knock sounded at the door and the maid slid into the parlour.

"Begging your pardon, sir," she addressed herself to Alexander, "but there's a lad here for you with important news, he says. Will you see him?"

Mary's eyes were curious, and he beckoned her with his hand as he rose to see the lad, who was waiting at the front steps.

It was Tom, whom he often used to run errands for him in the neighbourhood. "Sorry to be bothering you, Mr. Lyons, but these came by express just now. Mr. Baker," he referred to the bookbinder whose offices stood beside his own in the building, "mentioned how you might be here, and I thought to come find you. If these come by express, they're important, I gather."

Alexander fished a coin from his trouser pocket. "And well you did so, lad. Did you ride? Is the beast cared for? 'Tis not so far across town. Treat him to some oats when you get back."

Then he looked at the small package of papers in his hand, all bound together in brown paper and tied securely with twine.

"Mary, love, I believe these are the answers we seek. Join me in the library?"

Chapter Twenty-Four

The Summons

The package of letters revealed nothing new, but confirmed everything Alexander had thought. He scanned through the contents with Mary, who nodded and hummed her satisfaction at what they said.

"They took so long to arrive," Alexander mused, "because the information we needed was not in Canonbie after all, nor at Gretna Green. Poor Jock's travels took him another fifty miles and more, in every direction, before he found what I asked. 'Tis a sad tale."

As he prepared to take his leave, there came another knock at the front door.

"Message for Miss Bennet, if you please," he heard through the library's open doorway.

The maid came in a moment later with a note, which she handed to Mary. Mary took the folded paper and scanned its contents. A frown formed on her forehead. "At this hour? That is unusual! I wonder what she wants?"

"Mary?" Alexander reached for the note. He had no claim on it, but hoped that his friend would allow him to read it, and she passed it to him without hesitation.

Mary,
Please come at once. It is quite important. I have sent the carriage.
Elinor

The words were unambiguous, but there was much to learn from what remained unwritten.

"And?" he asked. He did not need to elaborate. She could all but understand his thoughts, after all.

"It is not her handwriting. Somebody wishes me ill."

"It is easy enough to decline. Your aunt can provide a more than reasonable excuse."

She considered him for a moment. "But now we are forewarned. If I refuse, there will surely be another attempt, for which we will not be prepared. Can you help me?"

He went cold. This was not something he was willing to do! "Oh no! I shall not be party to this. You must refuse and then stay in the house until this is all concluded."

"We do not know when this will be concluded. Even after we catch the murderer, assuming that is who sent the messenger, the cutthroats will not necessarily cease their pursuit. This is the only way I can really be safe." She levelled her brown eyes on him, daring him to defy her.

He tried this argument, then that one, to convince her to refuse the note, but she would not be moved and eventually he had to give way. She would either agree now, when he could be there to help, or later, after he departed, when he could not. Some called her sister Elizabeth obstinate and headstrong, but Mary was more stubborn yet than her older sibling.

"Very well." He walked to the window, which looked over the street, and stood at the side, peering out the best he could without disturbing the curtains. There was a small town coach immediately before the house. It was not Mrs. Jennings', but that was of little surprise. He saw a driver on the box and the messenger outside the front door. They would expect Mary to take a maid, especially at this time of night, which meant there was likely another man in the carriage as well. One against three. The odds were not in their favour.

"Give me ten minutes," he said after he had thought the matter through, "and be sure to bring your maid. They will be expecting as much. We want them unaware of our plans."

He moved to the back door near the servants' quarters as he heard Mary inform the messenger that she would be ready shortly. He made his plans and crept out into the alleyway behind the house. Thankfully, Gordon was sitting in the kitchens, and Alexander pulled him along, explaining his scheme as they moved. The first destination was the workers' shed near the stable at the top of the mews. Alexander borrowed an unattended and rather threadbare coat and then searched for a weapon of sorts. There—that was perfect. He found a long metal pipe and grabbed it. He then slipped the pipe up his coat sleeve, so when he walked along, it looked like he was carrying only a short piece of rubbish he had discovered on his way. Then he followed the alley to where it met the cross street and began to amble down Gracechurch Street from the far end, as if he were a working man, just on his way from somewhere to somewhere else, quite unconcerned with anybody who lived in the neighbourhood.

"Fine vehicle that," he called out to the driver as he approached the Gardiners' house and the coach that stood before it. He dredged up his strongest Glaswegian tones and hoped to be clear enough that the Londoner would understand him.

The driver grunted and shooed him off with a wave of the hand.

He shuffled closer. "Ach, and look at the cattle," he moved toward the horses. "I recall such 'uns when I was a lad, up north. Hard to see in this light, mind ye. Beauties, are they? What colour their coats in the sunlight?"

The driver was still unimpressed. "Begone with you, Scottie. I ain't got no time for your meanderings. Waiting for a lady, I am, and when she arrives, we'll be right off. Shoo."

"Now, now, that's no way to treat your fellow man. Just admiring the horseflesh. Ain't nothing to get your knickers in a twist over. Aye, did you know that when I was a lad I worked with the laird's stable master. Saddled his nob's chargers, I did, when he went a-hunting. It were fifteen—no, nigh on twenty years ago. I was merely a young laddie then, but..."

He had no need to fabricate further, for whilst he had been engaging the driver's attention, Gordon had crept up on the other side of the carriage and now jumped aboard the box to incapacitate the coach's driver. By the time the driver felt the shift of the vehicle under Gordon's weight, it was too late for him, and within moments he was trussed up in ropes with a length of fabric between his teeth to prevent him from crying out.

"What's that?" came from inside the carriage. This was the other thug whose presence Alexander had anticipated.

"Nothing," Alexander called out in his best approximation of the tones from Seven Dials, where these men were assuredly from. "Horse got nervous nelly from that Scotsman came to talk. I sent him off. Hush now."

There was no more protestation from inside, so the ruse must have worked.

There was a noise from the Gardiners' doorway. Mary and her maid Annie were exiting the house. How Mary convinced her aunt to allow this, Alexander must discover! But later. For now, the ladies were followed by the messenger as they approached the carriage. Mary stood back to allow the young man to open the door for her, and as he stepped forward to do so, Alexander crept up behind him and cracked him over the head with the metal pipe in his hand. The man fell with an audible thud onto the street.

"What's that?" came once more from inside.

"Help!" Alexander cried in his St. Giles accent. "Tough out here is trying to do me!"

A lumbering figure all but tumbled out of the coach, fists raised to fight off whoever had beset his friend, but once more it was too late for him. The same metal pipe that had felled the first ruffian now connected with this man's head.

Alexander stood there, hardly a bead of sweat on him, holding the pipe like a claymore, and Mary gazed at him with a look upon her face that was half amusement and half adoration.

"I had long wondered what you might look like fighting in the highlands with a broadsword and a plaid kilt. Now I need only wonder what you look like in a kilt." She leaned in quickly and planted a kiss on his cheek before turning to her maid. "You did not see that, Annie, and I shall see you off in a moment if ever you breathe a word of it!"

Annie chuckled.

"That was a rather unexciting fight." Alexander shook his head. "I did not even breathe hard. It seems unfair, somehow. Gordon, have you more rope?" he called. "Let us secure these two as well, and I shall send off at once for Atkins."

"Can we question the driver as to who sent them? I would not have anybody else being attacked or—" She stopped as if turned to stone.

"Elinor!"

"Quick! Gordon, can you drive these creatures?" He gestured to the horses, still in harness. "Take us to Mrs. Jennings as quickly as the streets allow!" Alexander pushed the two fallen thugs into the coach and jumped in after them with some lengths of rope. He was not well pleased to see Mary crawl in after him, but there was no time to argue. Within seconds, the carriage jerked to a start, and they began their race through the narrow streets of London.

"Are we too late?" Mary breathed as she secured the knot around the one ruffian's feet. Her voice was tight with worry.

Alexander pulled his own rope tight against the other man's wrists. He would be mighty uncomfortable on the floor of the carriage, but such were the wages of sin, or something like that.

"I hope not. It is possible our adversary only employed this one set of bruisers and one carriage. In that case, since we are in the coach, she is in no danger..."

"Or has already been attacked." She echoed his thoughts.

"But it is equally likely that whoever hired these men sent a second set to waylay Miss Dashwood, to prevent either of you from somehow warning the other." He paused and gripped the side of the bench as the racing coach took a corner far too fast, almost leaning onto its side as it did so. It settled back solidly onto its wheels with a jolt, and Mary gasped.

"If we get there quickly enough..." He could not finish his sentence. If they arrived in time, they might be able to save Elinor. If not, there was no thinking about what might happen.

The four miles between Cheapside and Marylebone had never seemed so great. No matter the urgency with which Gordon spurred on the horses or the terrific speed with which they travelled, every second seemed an hour. Alexander wished he had taken a single horse instead. But the time it would have taken to find and saddle up such a beast would have been more time lost, and he was thankful for the coach. Here they could secure the men who had come for Mary, and hopefully—assuming a satisfactory ending to this adventure—equally truss up whoever might be intending ill towards Elinor.

At last they arrived at Upper Berkeley Street. Before he could advise her one way or another, Mary leapt from the still-rocking coach to run up the stairs to Mrs. Jennings' door. Her desperate knock was answered by a maid, and Alexander heard the girl's response to Mary's query.

"No, Ma'am. Miss Dashwood left a few minutes ago, nay, a minute even. She said she had a note from you... but seeing as you're here..."

"Which way did she go?" Mary's voice carried through the deepening night. The maid pointed, and Mary was back in the carriage in a moment. Thank heavens, they did not need to turn the conveyance around.

"Towards the Park!" Alexander yelled at Gordon, who spurred on the horses before the words were even out of his mouth.

As they began to move, a jolt hit the back of the coach. Alexander's heart, already racing from concern, now hammered in his chest and he had to fight to control his breath. That could only mean...

"Someone is on board!" he called, hoping his voice could be heard over the thunder of the horses' hooves. What new danger was this? Were the miscreants so certain that there would be pursuit that they had left another to ward off any who dared to catch their carriage? Was that man, even now, creeping up to the top of their own vehicle, ready to attack all those inside? His throat tightened.

"Who is it?" Mary whispered. Heavens, he could not lose her now. He would fight to his final breath to save her.

Perspiration-drenched hands fumbled to grasp the metal pipe which he still carried, barely aware of the two bound men who moaned from their positions curled about each other on the floor. Across from him, Mary's face went white in the darkness, and she reached out to grip his hand with an iron clasp. Who was it, indeed?

He steadied his grasp on the makeshift weapon and moved to the window. He dared not open it to look out in case this new assailant had a pistol, but perhaps he might see something in the lamplight. No, this man, whoever he was, must be at the back, clambering up from the boot or the small rumble. Was that another creak on the roof?

There was little he could do now, for the coach was flying along again at great speed, but the moment they came to a stop, he must be ready. Likewise, whoever had leapt aboard as they began to move must surely be holding on for dear life as well. This was no gentle parade through the city for a tiger to endure at the back of a landau, but a heart-quickening race at what must be ten whole miles an hour! To his relief, the sounds from the roof stopped; their attacker must be biding his time as well.

"There!" Gordon's voice filtered through the window. "I think I see 'em. A small coach, riding fast through the park. I'll catch 'em down!"

If it was possible, the horses made even more speed and the small carriage bounced roughly along the stone streets, and then, jolting up onto the lawn of the park, across open fields. Alexander wished he had brought his pistol, not to use but to threaten. He despised carrying the weapon, but knew there was a need in his line of business and he kept one locked away in his rooms. But there, unfortunately, it lay now. He could not use it to bring the other coach to a halt.

Gordon's coaxing quickly brought their own carriage alongside the one which they chased across the fields of the Park. Could Gordon bring down that other driver whilst managing his own team, or somehow wrest control of the horses? Alexander thought fast and hard about how best to stop the second vehicle. If he opened the door at just the right time, could he grab the reins? No, that seemed an impossible feat.

Mary must have followed the movement of his eyes, for her grasp on his hand grew tighter still. "You must not," she whispered, a sound barely audible in the dark space. But what else could he do?

Then, from outside, there came a great cry and a violent shudder, and the carriage shook again as it raced through the darkness. In the flicker of the lamps, Alexander saw the carriage beside them swerve and jerk, before a dull thud filtered through the creak of carriage wheels and the heavy breathing of the horses.

"There's another one up there," Gordon shouted. "Can you... no! Good God! He has them!" He called out to his horses and in a moment, the coach slowed almost to a stop.

Now was the time. Alexander gave Mary's hand a final squeeze and took a fortifying breath—hopefully not his last. The pipe was still there, thank heavens. He reached through the door's window to the handle and leapt out of the carriage even before it had stopped moving. He landed hard on his feet, the force of the impact rattling through his bones, but there was no time for self-pity. He must reach the other vehicle, and soon!

The distance felt infinite, his legs endlessly slow, but he put every ounce of power he had into his run and at last, he achieved his destination. There seemed to be a fight on the driver's box, two men grappling, a blur of indistinct arms and feet, but the horses— thank the heavens—were slowing rather than taking fright and speeding away. That way would lead to disaster.

What to do? Who was this other man? Surely not another of the gang, but was he friend or foe? And which was which? Whom should Alexander assist? No, better to make for the doorway and see who was inside.

But as Alexander watched, one of the figures swung back and landed a great punch on the other's face, dropping the man to the ground. The first man grabbed the reins and pulled the team to a full stop and then leapt down to fling open the door.

The driver lay groaning on the grass a few feet from where he had been flung down; he was lucky to be alive, let alone conscious. Hopefully, Gordon would secure him. But Alexander had to know what the other man was now up to.

Within moments, he was at the coach door. Yells and grunts came from within, the din of two men at fisticuffs within the confines of the tight space. Then there came the sickening thud of a foot connecting with a body and someone tumbled out of the space. It seemed, in this dim light, to be the man who had beset the driver. He was injured, that was clear, and he fell backwards onto the grass with a groan.

"Drive on!" came a yell from within. "What are you waiting for, man? I've got the chit; we need to get rid of her before they catch us!"

"Too late!" Alexander threw himself into the small coach. In the darkness, he could barely identify a shape that looked like a large man about to throw a punch, and a second shape that might be a woman with her hands bound. He did not wait for his vision to adjust, but he dived down as low as he could to avoid the fist that was now flying towards where his head had been and he grabbed at the man's legs, pulling him off balance. He swerved to the side as much as he could and positioned himself by the man's shoulder, at once straightening up and slamming the man's head into the wall of the coach above the second set of squabs. How he managed in such tight confines he never did understand, but he could not allow his adversary even a moment to recover himself, or all would be lost. While the man was still staggering from the crack. Alexander slid his metal pipe into his hand and brought it down squarely on his assailant's head. Down he fell with a heavy thud.

It was over.

He turned to the woman. His eyes had adjusted enough to the light that he could see her now. "Miss Dashwood!"

She was gagged, and as he thought, her hands were bound. He found his pocket knife and cut the cloth holding her hands together and then fumbled behind her head to release the gag in her mouth.

"Mr. Lyons!" she gasped. "I had given up all hope. But before you... I must see him! Where is he? Is he well?"

Together, they escaped the confining coach to the wide-open space of the grassy park. The figure still lay on the ground, but he was moving and complaining in colourful but coherent English. Then he looked up and his eyes fixed upon Elinor. In a moment she was beside him, down on her knees on the damp grass.

"Edward! You were so brave! I saw it all! You did that for me!" And she clasped him to her breast and smothered his hair in kisses.

"I believe," Mary's voice came from somewhere behind Alexander, "that they are irrevocably compromised." He turned to look at her and despite his ragged breath and thundering heartbeat, his smile matched her own. "I do hope to receive an invitation to that wedding."

He stumbled backwards, barely able to stay upright, until he was immediately at her side. She reached an arm around him and held him close for much, much longer than was proper.

Chapter Twenty-Five

The Gathering

By the time Alexander had taken care of all the bits and pieces following the attack, it was far later than he liked. He had to summon Atkins and tell his tale to the Runner before turning the miscreants over to his tender care. Then he needed to assure himself that Edward and Elinor were physically well and in no danger of swooning or otherwise suffering as a consequence of their adventure that evening. Edward was a bit worse off for his adventure, but his injuries were not serious and he would wear his wounds as a badge of honour for a few days.

Finally, Alexander had to see Mary back home. Gordon insisted that he could discharge that duty, but Alexander knew he would not rest until he knew that she was safe and in her aunt and uncle's house. He helped Gordon with the two coaches and led the horses to the edge of the Park, where the Runners had somebody to care for the animals and trace the provenance of the seemingly stolen vehicles, and then he found a hackney to take them all back across London to Cheapside.

When Mrs. Gardiner insisted that he stay for the night, he was too tired to argue. He had no desire to find another hack to carry him back to Covent Garden and was really pleased at the thought of a soft bed that he did not have to make himself in the morning. The bedroom on offer was a small space downstairs near the kitchen, but it was private and clean and comfortable, and most welcome. Before he took himself off to retire for the night, however, he begged some paper and leave to send off a few messages, for which permission was granted. Mary helped him copy out the notes, and when he finally lay his head on the stuffed pillow long after midnight, it was with the satisfaction of knowing this case would soon be at an end.

He slept later than his usual habit in the morning and took his breakfast with Mr. Gardiner, who ate early before leaving for his day at his place of business. With a cup of strong coffee and a steaming bowl of porridge before him, he did not even object to that gentleman's critique of his late-night adventures with Mary.

"Be glad you brought her back whole and unharmed." The older man's tone belied the severity of his words. "I do not envy the man who brings grief to my niece. She has, these last two or three years, grown into herself, and I have come to admire and respect the woman she has become. Should anything happen to her..."

"I would be the one to hunt down the perpetrator and bring him to justice, Mr. Gardiner." Gardiner's tone was half in jest, but Alexander's was deadly serious.

"I know you care greatly for her, lad. Just do not allow your adventures to put her at risk."

"Aye, sir. I will do all I can, for she is a determined young lady."

"She is determined to have you, I believe. What are your intentions? I know I have allowed you more liberties than I ought. She is, after all, not even my own child, and I am acting as her parent."

"With all due respect, she is of age and can make her own decisions." He was prepared to be ejected from the house for this rather bald statement. But instead of growing angry, Mr. Gardiner laughed.

"Right you are, lad. You are as determined as she, I believe. But I would like to know your intentions."

Alexander considered him over the top of his coffee cup. "Perhaps, sir, I ought to express them to the lady herself before I discuss them with her relations."

"That is a conversation to which I would enjoy being party myself."

Alexander's head snapped up. Mary stood at the door, an odd look on her face. How much had she heard? She must understand that he was waiting only until he could provide for her. And until they might find some way to bridge the chasm that lay so inconveniently between them. Their social positions, their ideas of wealth and comfort, their religion... How many times had he enumerated these obstacles in the past? And yet, with each accounting, they refused to disappear. Once more, he came to the conclusion that he did not quite know what to do.

He looked back at her with confusion in his eyes. "Mary... we shall talk, and soon. I have been waiting..." He spread out his hands in supplication.

"Yes, Alexander. So have I." But she seemed not angry, only disappointed and resigned.

With Mr. Gardiner still present, there was little more he could say. Would a mere glance be enough to assure her of his sincerity, of the depth of his feelings? Her eyes met his and perhaps something did pass, unspoken, in that shared look, for she graced him with a short smile.

"Later," she mouthed, and then aloud, asked if they had any news from last night's missives.

Alexander put his hand on a stack of messages that had arrived earlier that morning. "We have received replies from all. Mrs. Jennings has agreed, and everybody will attend."

"Even Willoughby?"

He nodded. "Even he. Although the reply is in a woman's hand. His wife's, I assume."

"Elinor's presence, and my own, will be an unhappy surprise to somebody. We ought, by that sad person's reckoning, to be dead."

"Our entertainment awaits us!"

At one o'clock exactly Alexander walked into Mrs. Jennings' front parlour. As was so often the case, the room was full of company. The Dashwood sisters sat on one sofa, almost but not quite touching each other's hands. To Marianne's side, Colonel Brandon sat still upon a tall wooden chair, and to Elinor's side sat Edward, his scraped hands fidgeting with the pleats on his trousers. He sported a scratch on one cheek and a rather magnificent black eye, and he looked very proud of himself.

John Willoughby squirmed in his large armchair, his wife, whom nobody had yet met, beside him. She must be there to ensure his good behaviour. Alexander wondered how much she had learned of her husband's recent attempt to coerce Marianne into a tryst. If his suppositions were correct, no wonder she wished to keep him on a very short chain. Willoughby would not have an easy life under her thumb.

Mrs. Jennings herself reigned over the room from her armchair by the cold fireplace, with Lucy and Nancy Steele flanking her on either side, the former looking rather smug, the latter confused. Did Lucy expect this meeting had been convened to announce the validity of her claims on Robert's estate? Well she might, from the expression on her face.

"Mr. Lyons, you have arrived," the matriarch of this little clan greeted him. "We are all in great anticipation over what you have assembled us to say. It must be something quite remarkable, I gather." Her words were echoed by the inquisitive looks of several sets of eyes.

"And I thank you, all, for attending." He moved to an empty space in the collection of chairs that formed an ill sort of a circle. He let his regard drift from person to person, seeing who was present and who was not, observing each guest's expression with deliberation. They were all here. He smiled. "I have a purpose which will be of interest to most of you, hopefully to all. I thought it best to tell the news once, hence my invitations."

The eyes that returned his regard were curious, tense, and perhaps a bit worried, but none displayed the panic of a trapped animal. That would come.

"Let me begin with the reason I was brought into this sad affair. I was engaged initially to investigate the contestation of Mr. Robert Ferrars' will. This document, which was dated some time ago upon Mr. Ferrars reaching his majority, made no provisions for a wife or child, and all of his estate was to pass to his brother, Edward. At the time of making this will, Robert had almost no wealth. When he died, however, Robert was a rich man due to the terms of his own mother's will. But I digress. What is important here is that Miss Lucy Steele protested that she was the lawful beneficiary of Robert's will, being his secret wife and the mother of his yet-unborn infant. Since I am a lawyer as well as an investigator, I was called to consult on this matter."

Lucy straightened in her chair, a smile touching the corners of her lips. This was the triumph she had been waiting for, but it would not come.

Alexander lowered his voice and spoke gently. "But your claims were not true, were they, Miss Steele?"

Lucy squeezed her eyes tight. The anticipatory glory drained from her features as she crumpled into her chair. Misery was etched on her face and she hugged her hands around her abdomen. She let out a whimper. "No, no, no," tumbled from her lips, the short words all but incoherent.

"We do not need to discuss it here, before all these people," he breathed. "It is enough that we know the truth. But do not fear for the bairn..."

"No!" Lucy all but shouted, as if struck by a bolt from Heaven. "It is not my sin, but another's. My shame is written heavily upon me! Let me confess it to everyone here, so they may see where the blame truly lies. If they are my friends, they will stand with me. If not, I shall have lost nothing by the telling."

Elinor extracted her hand from where Edward held it and walked over to Lucy's chair. She knelt down beside the weeping young woman, and Lucy seemed to take strength from that.

"He... he lied to me! He worked on me to break my engagement with Edward, and then worked on me further to marry him instead. At that time, it was an easy choice. I am not proud of my decision, but neither am I ashamed of it. Marriage is about security, not love, and Robert was suddenly rich." She sniffled in a rather unladylike manner and Mrs. Jennings handed her a handkerchief. She wiped her eyes and blew her nose and crumpled the piece of fine fabric into her hand.

"He said we should elope, that we should not tell anybody and keep it a great secret. He explained that it would be expected for him to mourn his mother for some time, and that such a hasty

269

marriage would be looked at askance, and I accepted this. It seemed reasonable... it seemed romantic, even. A secret marriage! That is the stuff that books are made of." She sniffled again, but kept on with her story.

"We were to go to Scotland. It would be quick there, with no need for a licence or calling the banns. It was the perfect way to keep our marriage a secret and we could be wed at once. And so we made our plans, and we took his carriage north. But... But I do not know the land as well as I might! I did not know how far we went. I thought it was Scotland, but it was not! He sent a rider ahead to the smithy. It was so near to the border, I thought we were there, but we were still in England and the marriage ceremony that the smith performed was nothing! It sounded like a wedding, with all the ceremony I expected, but it was only so many words! Robert tricked me, and I believed him, and then I let him take me as his wife..."

Now the weeping started in earnest and the handkerchief was soon wet from Lucy's tears.

"He told me on the way back that it was all a joke, that we had never been in Scotland, and that we were not married. But by then..." Her hands rubbed at her belly. "He told me all sorts of things, of horrible things he had done. He made them sound like more jokes, but they were not jokes at all. He told me how his mother thought of changing her will again to return some of Edward's inheritance, but that he killed her before she could act. And he told me how he made it look like Edward had done it! Oh, it was too awful! He laughed and said how grand it was to have somebody to whom to boast about his cleverness. He made me promise not to tell a soul, or else he would shout all over London how he had ruined me." The last words were almost lost in a torrent of weeping. "Nancy was the only one who knew. I had to tell somebody; I could not have borne it entirely alone, and she has always been the one person who looked out for me and cared about me entirely."

"That is why," Alexander spoke gently, "we could find no documentation amongst his papers. Because there was none to be found. I am sorry, Miss Steele. My agents in the north discovered this same thing, and reported back to me only last night. They were looking in Gretna Green and Canonbie—"

"That is where he said we were!"

"And discovered nothing. Only after asking for some of the people you mentioned did they find the true village near Longtown. My man thought to go northward, but really he found what he needed to the south instead." He paused for a moment to allow for some more weeping and another blow into Mrs. Jennings' handkerchief.

"Then we are lost. There is no hope." She all but collapsed into her chair, and on the other side of Mrs. Jennings, Nancy grew visibly alarmed. She leapt from her seat and went to cradle her younger sister in her arms.

"All is not lost, Miss Steele. For I have some good news for you as well." Lucy looked up through wet and red eyes. "Mr. Edward Ferrars is now the undisputed heir to his family's fortune, and he is quite a wealthy man. Despite some, er, unexpected activities recently, he has informed me of a most generous decision. Mr. Ferrars?" Alexander looked to Edward and invited him to make his announcement.

Elinor returned to her seat and Edward stood behind her now, one hand upon her shoulder. "Miss Steele, since the child seems to be my brother's, I cannot, as a Christian—nay, as a thinking and feeling person—allow that child to live in want. Miss Dashwood has agreed to be my wife, and together we agree that we shall provide for the babe. He or she will never starve and will be assured of a good start in life." Elinor turned her head to look up at him and beamed with pride.

"You... you will take care of us? It is so much more than we deserve!" Lucy gasped out as she dotted her handkerchief over her red eyes.

"Ah... your own fate is not quite decided, Miss Steele," Alexander interjected. "May I please continue?"

Panic danced across Lucy's face, but she sealed her mouth closed. Nancy remained at her side, her jaw tight and her hands white with tension.

"You see, the inquiry into Robert's will soon developed into an inquiry into Robert's death. It quickly became apparent that it was not merely a tragic end to a violent robbery, but that there was something more nefarious afoot as well. Robert was deliberately killed." He paused for a moment. "Murdered." There. He had said the word, and whilst it was news to nobody, every face in the room looked shocked. Was one set of eyes anxious as well? It was time to press on.

"Furthermore," he added as he surveyed his audience, "there was a great deal of evidence discovered that pointed the blame rather squarely at his brother Edward's feet." He turned to face one person. "What can you tell us about this, Miss Steele?"

She glared at him, not quite disguising the panic in her eyes behind a show of defiance.

"I know all. Would you prefer that I tell the tale?" His voice was still gentle, as one would speak to an unhappy child in need of coaxing.

Her gaze faltered, and she crumpled again against her sister's side.

"Very well," Alexander continued. "Some person made certain he was seen leaving the scene of the robbery. The person was dressed in gentleman's clothing, and more importantly, he dropped a handkerchief with the initials EF, which Edward Ferrars later claimed as his own."

"Robert gave it to me!" Lucy wailed. "He said he brought it back from Deer Park in Norfolk, and that I should keep it as safe as I possibly could in case he needed it. It went missing from my chest, but I do not know when. I only knew that when Robert died and I went to find it, the handkerchief was gone."

"Very well. We can return to the handkerchief later. Regardless, everything seemed to point to Edward. As well as the clue of the handkerchief, Edward had the great motive of wishing to regain his fortune, and he was heard in a loud argument with his brother the very night that Robert died. It seemed that they disagreed about Robert's new habit of visiting the gaming tables and losing vast amounts of money. This line of inquiry brought us to somebody else in the room. Mr. Willoughby?"

Willoughby had been lazing in his chair, affecting nonchalance to such a degree that he seemed almost asleep. Now his eyes snapped open, and by the sudden tension in his limbs, Alexander could see that he retained his lolling pose only by force of will.

"Who? I?" Willoughby yawned, though the gesture was forced. "It is no secret we were acquainted and that we occasionally owed each other gaming debts. What of it?" His hand was still wrapped in layers of white bandages, but his fingers moved easily.

His wife sat ramrod straight beside him, eyes narrow and hands clutching at her reticule. Alexander did not envy the man upon his return home.

"You have political aspirations, sir?"

"So do many."

"Your hopes might have been dashed by a scandal, the details of which Mr. Robert Ferrars knew. You are known to have mentioned threats against him should he breathe a word, and you are also known to have associated with the sorts of men who might, for a fee, rid you of a problem like Mr. Ferrars."

The casual loll was a little less easy now.

"We have spoken of this. I discharged my debts and had nothing to fear from Ferrars. There is no scandal attached to my name..."

"Other than Miss Williams, I suppose?" Colonel Brandon spoke for the first time, his voice colder than the steel in his sword. "As I suggested, sir, I would retire all thoughts of statesmanship and head for the country. I spared you once. I can destroy you thoroughly should I desire it, your name, your wealth, your body."

"John?" His wife's tone was not friendly.

"If, that is, the Runners do not find your role in Robert's death of interest." Alexander made his statement and stepped back to observe the look of horror on Willoughby's face.

"We shall be departing by Saturday." Willoughby flexed his injured hand and did not look at his wife at all, gazing instead at Marianne, who responded by moving closer to Colonel Brandon. Alexander was satisfied that the man would regret his choices every day of his life. He hoped beyond hope that his own fate would be a happier one.

A sea of eyes still looked to him. He must bring this farce to a conclusion.

"We had all but concluded who was the instigator behind the attack on Robert Ferrars when something occurred last night." The mood of the room changed, and somebody shifted in his or her chair. "There was an attack upon Miss Mary Bennet."

Every head swivelled, every eye swept across the room, as the gathered party realised severally and singly that Miss Bennet was not one of their number.

"My God, is she well? Was she gravely hurt?" Colonel Brandon all but leapt from his chair. Willoughby squirmed, and Mrs. Jennings cast a disapproving eye over her guests.

But it was Lucy to whom Alexander now looked. She was as white as the handkerchief she still held crunched in her hand, her face drained of all blood. She swayed in her chair and Alexander thought she might faint.

"Miss Bennet is well," he announced, "as is Miss Dashwood, who was likewise the intended victim of such an assault. Yes, Lucy, we discovered your men before they had a chance to carry out their instructions. Did you think that you would not be found out?" He looked up and called to the doorway, "Mary, you may come in now."

Mary strode in. There was nothing at all dainty or mincing about her steps, but rather, they were strong and determined. She would have made a great man, but she was a greater woman!

"Your ruffians talked, Lucy. When they were bound hand and foot and the Runners gave them some idea of what might be in store, they were pleased to share the blame. Why did you do it? What did you think to gain by my death? Or by Elinor's? She has been nothing but kind to you, even when that kindness was met with conceit and triumph."

"You knew!" Lucy's eyes narrowed, rendering her pretty face harsh. "By your questions, I knew you knew! It was all so well planned, it was all going so well, and then you came and you ruined everything! I had to stop you before—" She caught herself before saying more.

"Before what, Lucy?" Alexander's voice was gentle again. "Before she told somebody? Before we learned who the true perpetrator of Robert's death was? We know. It is too late. You did it to protect your sister, to protect Nancy."

Lucy let out a strangled squeak and beside her, Nancy crumpled to the floor.

The room fell deathly silent for a moment. Then, just as suddenly, everybody rushed forward from their chairs to help and the space was full of shouts and cries of alarm.

"Somebody help her!"

"Can anybody assist me?"

"We must move her to somewhere comfortable!"

Elinor and Marianne cleared space on their sofa, and soon the room was rearranged, with Nancy Steele's eyes fluttering as she roused herself from her swoon on that seat. Lucy stood protectively at her side; Alexander faced them both from across the low table in the centre of the room.

"Nancy was the one who engaged the two ruffians, Fred and Gus, to kill Robert. She has always protected you, always been your guardian. She was the one who looked out for you as a child, and who encouraged your engagement to Edward four years ago. She knew then that she was unlikely to marry but that you could make an advantageous match, and that Edward was in line to become quite wealthy.

"She was always hanging about in the background, looking in cupboards and listening in at doorways. She likely knew before you did that Robert had killed his own mother for the inheritance. She knew about your proposed elopement and acted to enable it, and she knew that this supposed marriage never happened."

Nancy was alert now and lay curled up on her side on the sofa, weeping. "Oh, Lucy," she choked out between sobs. "I'm so sorry. It was for you. I only did it for you. It was all for you."

From a doorway near the corner of the room, Mr. Atkins emerged and walked towards the ladies. "Come now, Miss Steele. I am certain Mr. Lyons knows a good lawyer. But I am afraid you must come with me now. There's a cart in the back. Let me help you up." There was great kindness in his tone, more, perhaps, than a murderer deserved.

"She cannot go without me!" Lucy asserted herself.

"Aye, Madam, that is true. For while you are not under arrest for murder, you are being charged with attempted murder for your engagement of those men who attacked Miss Bennet and Miss Dashwood last night. Rawlings?" Another man now entered the room, and they escorted the two sisters from the house.

"What will happen to them?" Elinor asked.

"I cannot say exactly," Alexander sighed. "If Miss Steele is fortunate to have a friendly judge and can convince him of a lack of mental acuity, she might escape the noose in favour of transportation. Lucy's fate will almost certainly not be decided until after the baby is born."

"We will raise the child, of course!" Edward asserted. Elinor's nod seconded that statement.

"There is little enough left for them in England. The colonies might be the best chance for them."

There was more silence.

"But how did you know it was Nancy?" Mrs. Jennings asked. "She is such an ineffectual thing. How can she possibly have perpetrated such evil?"

Alexander moved towards the fireplace and leaned against the heavy marble mantel piece. Mary moved next to him, her presence solid and assuring. "People will do great and terrible things to protect those they love, ma'am. Upon thoroughly examining the evidence, the person who instigated the attack on Robert had to be either Lucy or Nancy. The evidence against Edward was too obviously manufactured, and that against Mr. Willoughby circumstantial, with no real proof that he was at all involved. But Lucy knew the cutthroats through her visits to St. Giles with Edward, and was seen in the neighbourhood even when not with the church group. It was on a visit there, with the stated purpose of procuring embroidered handkerchiefs for Lucy, that she met with Gus and Fred and arranged the murder."

"I cannot gather why," the colonel grunted. "Surely Lucy's interests were best served with Robert being alive; he might still be persuaded to marry her as he had promised."

"I believe, although with no evidence, that he intimated exactly this to Lucy," Mary spoke. "Even after the failed elopement, he fluttered about Lucy, even as she danced attention on Edward. She must have believed him still willing to marry her."

"And," Alexander added, "when he learned of Lucy's condition, he was prepared to acknowledge the child and make suitable provisions. With this in mind, it was no stretch to think he might follow through on his promise."

"But what of Nancy? Why did she do this?" Marianne cried out. "How did you know it was her?"

"Nancy knew the whole story. Lucy might have thought Robert was still in love with her, but Nancy saw him flirting with Miss Bennet's sister Kitty. She must have decided that he was still toying with Lucy, only pretending to care about her respectability, and that he would never marry her. When Lucy discovered she was expecting, Nancy saw only one way to save her sister's name and ensure her future.

"She had discovered how Robert had tried to lay all the blame for Mrs. Ferrars' death on Edward, and to her mind, this was the perfect plan for arranging Robert's death as well. Now it seemed as though Edward was behind two deaths, and such things are not uncommon." He took a breath as the company absorbed his words.

"And I am most grateful for your diligence, Mr. Lyons," Edward breathed from his seat. "I would be in a hangman's noose by now if not for you, and Miss Bennet, of course. Words cannot express my relief and gratitude. But tell us once more how you knew it was Nancy behind my brother's death."

Alexander nodded. It had only recently become clear to him, and it would take time for the others to see all the details. "Nancy was the only one who knew the whole story from Lucy. It was she who had gone to the little embroiderer, Cassie, in St. Giles to have new monogrammed linens made for her sister after her elopement. It was Cassie's mother's story about Nancy coming to ask about the handkerchiefs that provided us with that last piece of evidence."

"But I still do not understand why! Why did she need to have Robert dead?" Mrs. Jennings seemed quite distressed at her young protegees being at all mixed up in something so sordid.

Mary stood forward. "It seemed simple to her, I believe. Lucy was with child and abandoned, and the man responsible had a great deal of wealth. By killing Robert and convincing the world that Lucy was, indeed, his wife, the baby would be heir to Robert's fortune and Lucy would be rich. It was all to save her sister."

Alexander leaned back to allow Mary her last words. "There was little sense in it to us, but to Nancy, it seemed the most sensible thing in the world to do."

Chapter Twenty-Six

A Quiet Stroll

"**M**ust you go back to Hertfordshire now? Can you not stay longer, even a week? Would your relations not have you for a few more days?"

Mary let Alexander's question wash over her as they walked through the shade in Hyde Park. They had both left Mrs. Jennings' residence as soon as they could, neither one wishing to be party to the inevitable lamentations that would come after the Steele sisters' guilt was made public. Elinor and Marianne and their betrotheds would wish to commiserate with Mrs. Jennings, and the Willoughbys would wish to leave the house—and the city—as quickly as possible. Nobody raised any objection when Mary slipped out of the room. She only heard Colonel Brandon call to Alexander that he would come by his office by the end of the day, before Alexander followed her out into the front hall.

The Park was a short distance away; after the tension of the recent confrontation, they were both pleased for some time in the serene tranquillity of some lesser-travelled paths and a breeze that, if not cool, was a relief from the stifling air of the sitting room.

They walked side by side, hand in hand. Nobody was around to see them or to chastise them. And if they were to be seen, no one would care, neither of them being known in these parts, or important enough in London's society to warrant a scandal over anything so insignificant.

"I must. I must go back home." Mary's voice was wistful. She both did and did not wish to return home. "My aunt and uncle have promised the children a holiday in the Lake District, and they are leaving on Monday. I have been in London for far longer than we first expected. I should have gone home in April."

"That is a while ago. Why did you stay?" His soft brogue was as welcome as the breeze, those tones that once sounded strange and harsh now as beautiful as music.

"I cannot say... Perhaps I wished, although I could not say it even to myself, to see you."

"I, for one, am very pleased that you stayed." He moved closer to her and tucked her arm under his so they were pressed together, side to side. It felt wonderful. "But I do wish you had let me know you were here. When I think of all the time we might have spent together, time not consumed by chasing killers, but going to a museum or seeing a performance somewhere, or walking in the park."

Should she be angry at him? No. She had been angry, and for little reason, and it had not helped her at all. It did not change how he acted, nor did it make her feel better.

"I did not know you wished me to do so. It is customary for the gentleman to pursue the lady, and not the other way."

"Aye, lassie, but we have long since established that I am no gentleman."

She punched him playfully on the arm.

"I wish I had known your thoughts. I wish we were not so bound by these foolish rules. Why can we not correspond? What evil is there in the exchange of letters, or of visits when one or the other of us is not otherwise occupied? But I had no window into your mind, and had no notion of your intentions. I was confused. Perhaps I still am."

"Here..." He pulled her into the shade of a small stand of shrubbery. It was not, perhaps, the most private place in London, but in this quiet section of the park, they would not be seen. He turned to face her and took her hands in his own.

"You must surely know this. My intentions are honourable. I would not dally with you, for you are worthy of so much more... so very much more. I would not dishonour any lady, and especially not you. After what we have seen recently—"

"You are speaking of Willoughby and Colonel Brandon's ward Eliza, and then Robert and Lucy?"

"Aye. Nobody deserves to be played with and discarded like that, and especially not you. Your worth is beyond rubies."

"That is from Proverbs." He knew his scripture. She should not be surprised, for she knew he read it in its original forms.

"Aye. But being of such worth, you are also worthy of so much more than I can give you right now. I am working hard, Mary. I am doing all I can to save enough to give you the home you deserve and that you can be proud of. But it will take more time. And we have other issues that might not be so easily resolved."

She understood him. They were one soul, but different faiths. As much as she had changed these past three years and extended her understanding of the world far beyond the pages of Fordyce's *Sermons to Young Women*, she was still devout in her adherence to the Church. She knew that some people chose to adopt their chosen love's faith, but she could not see her way to abandoning that which had sustained her for all her life. Nor, she imagined, would Alexander be eager to desert his own family and traditions to convert to her religion. He was not diligent in his practice, but it was nonetheless important to him—as vital as Mary's was to her. He was proud of who he was and she could not ask him to forsake this part of his identity.

And so she looked up at him with sad eyes and forced a smile onto her face.

"We shall find a way," he whispered. "I do not yet know how, but we shall! I know it."

She leaned into him and he wrapped his arms around her and pulled her close to his chest. It felt good. It felt right. It was meant to be.

"Yes," she replied as she raised her head and stretched up to meet his lips with her own. "We shall."

The End

Historical Notes

A Legal Note

The court cases and precedents mentioned in this novel are real. Alexander is a lawyer, after all, and he would not be the sort to make things up out of whole cloth!

The legal point at the centre of this mystery, that concerning inheritance laws and posthumous children, is an issue that has concerned jurists for centuries. Here is a very brief history of these cases, to the early nineteenth century.

The point of law at issue in these cases, and in my novel, is the question of when a written will is deemed to be revoked. In other words, what must happen for a will to no longer be in effect, other than writing a new one. The jurists, quite early on, decided that a material change in circumstance, such as having a child, would automatically negate a will because the person would necessarily intend to provide for his new family. The issue goes back to the time of the Romans and has been a key component of Civil Law since.

Cicero, in *de oratore*, stated,

pater credens filium suum esse mortuum, alterum instituit haeredem. filio domi redeunte, huius institutionis vis est nulla.[1]

---

[1] *De oratore*, Cicero

(A father, believing his son to be dead, appoints another heir. Upon the return of the son, the force of this appointment is null.)

This was taken to imply that a parent could not disinherit a legitimate child by overlooking him or her. The birth of a legitimate child therefore acts to revoke a previous will.

Lugg v Lugg

This matter was also contemplated in Common Law, based on those same principles.

The case of *Lugg v Lugg*, from 1696, boils this down a bit. This case decided that marriage alone was not sufficient to assume that the deceased's wishes had changed. A wife was not her husband's heir, and would have a settlement or her dowry to rely upon, or could return to her family.[2] But marriage *and* the birth of children would make a man wish to provide for his legitimate children, and even without committing this wish to paper, the presumption is that his previous wishes, as recorded in an old will, no longer stand. The previous will, therefore, is deemed to have been revoked.

Treby, Chief justice, wrote,

there being... circumstances so different at the time of [the testator's] death from what they were when he made the will, here was room and presumptive evidence to believe a revocation, and that the testator continued not of the same mind.[3]

---

[2] *Wellington v. Wellington*, 4 Burr. 2165, 98 Eng. Rep. 129 (1768)
[3] *Lugg v Lugg* (1696) 91 Eng. Rep. at 497

Lancashire v Lancashire

A subsequent case pondered the question of the inheritance rights of a child born after the father's death. This is the nub of Lucy's claims against Robert's estate, for she wishes for her unborn child to inherit the Ferrars' fortune.

In 1792, Lord Kenyon wrote his ruling in the case of *Doe ex dem. Lancashire v Lancashire.*

> ...*a tacit condition annexed to the will itself, at the time of making it, that the party does not intend that it should take effect, if there should be a total change in the situation of the testator's family.* [4]

Thomas Leach summarized the findings in 1793, saying,

> An *infant in* ventre sa mere *is now considered, generally speaking, as born for all purposes for his own benefit...*
> In the case of Doe ex dem. v Lancashire, *Lord Kenyon, after much argument, held that marriage, and the birth of a posthumous child, amounted to an implied revocation of a will of lands made before marriage, and the puisne judges of the Kings Bench were concurrent with him in this judgement.*[5]

In other words, a posthumous child does indeed hold the same status as a living child for the purposes of inheritance, on the condition that the father knew of that expectation.

[4] 101 Eng. Rep. 28; 91 Eng. Rep. at 497; *Doe v Lancashire* 5 T.R. 49 (1792)
[5] *Modern Reports* Vol 12, Thomas Leach, 1796 (G. G. J & J. Robinson)

White v Barford

At the time of this novel, 1814, another case was still under consideration by the courts, this one involving a posthumous child about which the father was unaware. Alexander knew the case was being heard, but it was not adjudicated until April 13th of the following year. The Court of King's Bench decided the case of *White v Barford* as follows.

> *J. B. died leaving his wife enseint, which was unknown to either of them at the time of his death, and afterwards the wife was delivered of a daughter, from whom, as heir at law, the defendants derived title. And the question was, whether this alteration of circumstances was an implied revocation of the will. The learned Judge ruled that it was not, and there was a verdict for the plaintiff.* [6]

In other words, if the father died without knowing about the impending birth of a child, the court would not deem there to have been an alteration of circumstance, and the previous will stands. This speaks to both the father's imputed wishes—he could not be expected to have the intention to change his will for a child he knew nothing about—as well to the question of paternity.

---

[6] *Doe, on the Demise of White, against Barford and another, Doe ex dem White v. Barford,* 4 M. & S. 10 (1815).

London in the Regency

Londonis one of my favourite cities, and I was so excited to set this novel there. I made an effort to have the places I wrote about be as real as possible, and I spent a great amount of time calculating distances between the various locations to check how long it would take to walk from one to another, or find a hackney carriage. The Tube, of course, was not an option in 1814, although it might have made things easier for our characters if it were.

It goes without saying that Regency London differs quite a bit from present-day London. Some of the big landmarks we picture were there, but many were not. Even some streets have changed, as parts of the city were rebuilt after the bombings of World War II. Back in Regency London, there would be no London Eye, of course, and no Shard. But also no Tower Bridge, that marvellous structure by the Tower that we all picture in our heads. It was not completed until 1894! Likewise, there was no Big Ben (the clock on the Elizabeth Tower at Parliament, completed in 1859), no Nelson's Column (1843), and no Marble Arch (1827, moved to its present location in 1851).

But it is still possible to walk in our characters' footsteps and see many of the things they saw. Here are a few locations that have been around since Mary and Alexander wandered those streets over 200 years ago.

Cheapside

In *Pride and Prejudice*, Jane Austen locates the home of the Gardiners on Gracechurch Street, very near Cheapside. The Bingley sisters turn up their noses at this location, but Cheapside has a long and prosperous history. The street itself takes its name from the Anglo-Saxon word "chepe," meaning "market," and it has been a centre of industry and trade for over a thousand years. It is situated well within the walls of the ancient Roman town of Londinium, running roughly from St Paul's Cathedral to the now-buried Walbrook river, where the ancient Temple to Mithras stood (which you can still see in the basement of the Bloomberg headquarters). The first church of St. Mary-le-Bow was built on the street in about the year 1080 by Archbishop Lefranc, and there may have been an older church on the site. In the 12th century, it was probably more like a market than a street, at 62 feet wide, and jousting tournaments were held there, with the roofs of surrounding buildings providing stands for the crowds.

By the early modern period, the area had become a centre for the jewellery trade and most goldsmiths had their shops here, but it was all destroyed in the Great Fire of 1666. St Mary-le-Bow was rebuilt by Sir Christopher Wren in 1680, and its tower uses the ancient Roman roadway as its foundations. By the mid-1700s, the area had recovered from the devastation of the fire, and became prestigious once more. Caroline Bingley might have sniffed at it, but being situated in this part of London marked the Gardiners as being quite well off, even if their wealth came from trade.

As a side note, in 1912 some workmen uncovered a huge collection of early 17th-century jewellery in a cellar, which became known as the Cheapside Hoard. Mary and Alexander might have walked past this building every day and not known a thing about the treasures under their feet.

Holborn

Moving west and a bit north from the old City of London, we arrive at Holborn, which is where Lucy and Anne Steele stayed with their cousins, the Richardsons, while in Town. The name comes from "hole bourne," meaning a stream in a hollow. This area began as a settlement beyond the city walls in the early Middle Ages. The present Holborn Viaduct, which crosses the hollow where the Fleet River used to run, was established and known as Holeburnestreete by 1249.

The area flourished as a Medieval suburb of the City, and was one of the Liberties—an area outside of the rule of the City of London. It grew increasingly prosperous over time, and the Bishop of Ely built his huge townhouse there in the late 1200s, at present-day Ely Place. In October 1546, Ely Place was the site of a mass poisoning that claimed the life of the Earl of Ormond from Ireland, and seventeen of his followers. This poisoning is commonly thought to have been a political assassination over Ormond's dispute with Henry VIII, although there is some evidence that it was accidental. Perhaps, had this happened 250-some years later, Alexander might have solved the mystery.

In Shakespeare's *Richard III*, the Duke of Gloucester says, "

My lord of Ely, when I was last in Holborn
I saw good strawberries in your garden there
I do beseech you send for some of them." [III, 4]

Presumably these berries were not poisoned. Richard had other ways of dealing with his adversaries.

Several colleges for lawyers were established in Holborn during the Middle Ages, some of which developed into barristers colonies. Of these, Gray's Inn and Lincoln's Inn survive.

Covent Garden and St Giles

Alexander, my investigator, has his offices and living space down a narrow lane near Covent Garden. A recent visit to London sent me exploring in search of just such a street, and I did find a few excellent candidates. One even had a bakery at the corner.

This area, to the south-west of Holborn, was settled by the Saxons in the seventh century, and the square might once have been a convent garden, hence the name. Excavations done between 1985 and 2005 revealed a Saxon trading town called Lundenwic, which spread from current Trafalgar Square to Aldwych, with Covent Garden as its centre. In the 1630s, Inigo Jones laid out a set of streets around his church of St Paul and the large market square, and the area become home to the elite, who enjoyed entertainment and places to socialise. But the coffee houses and theatres also attracted the masses, and as the aristocrats moved out, more dubious types moved in.

Immediately to the east of Covent Garden, facing the Royal Opera House, is the site of the Bow Street Magistrates' Court, where the famous Bow Street Runners were founded by Henry Fielding in 1749. The court itself was closed in 2006, but the building now hosts a police museum. It is just steps away from where I picture Alexander's office to be, a rather convenient location that worked out by chance and not by planning on my part.

To the north of the great market square and the glittering theatres were Seven Dials and St Giles. This area was first established in 1101 when a hospital for lepers was founded there by Matilda, wife of Henry I, and until the mid-19th century, it was one of the worst slums in London. Theatregoers could find other sorts of entertainment after the curtains came down, and the well-to-do had to watch their pockets and reticules. St Giles was also conveniently close to the wealthier areas just to the west, a perfect place for my thugs to live before setting upon poor Robert Ferrars.

Seven Dials was originally open land owned by the hospital of St Giles, but was developed by Thomas Neale in the 1690s to its current plan of a series of streets radiating out from a central hub. But instead of attracting the wealthy to its bosom, the area became increasingly less reputable over time, until, by the 19th century, it was one of the most dangerous slums in London, as part of the rookeries of St Giles.

In 1835, Charles Dickens described the area as, "... streets and courts [that] dart in all directions, until they are lost in the unwholesome vapour which hangs over the house-tops and renders the dirty perspective uncertain and confined."

Mayfair and Marylebone

At the time during which this story takes place, Mayfair was, as it is now, one of the most prestigious areas in London. With Hyde Park bordering the neighbourhood to the west, and fashionable Bond Street to the north, it was where the *crème de la crème* of society lived.

The area had been muddy fields and swamps along the River Tyburn, where a fair was held for two weeks in May, 1686. Hence, the area become known as May Fair. In 1710, Grosvenor Square was built by Sir Richard Grosvenor and the Earl of Scarborough, and settlement in the area began. Hanover Square was built nine years later, and by the 1720s, the muddy fields were being developed into luxury residences for the aristocracy, who wanted something newer and nicer than their old, cramped accommodations in Soho and Holborn. Of the original houses, 117 of 227 were owned by the nobility. This is the area where the Ferrars have their townhouse.

Presumably, Darcy's London abode, as well as that of his noble relations, would be in Mayfair as well.

Immediately to the north of Mayfair, on the other side of Bond Street, is Marylebone, where Mrs Jennings has her house on Upper Berkeley Street. This area was first mentioned in the Doomsday Book (1068) as a collection of muddy fields with a population of 50 people. At that time, it was known as Tyburn, for the river that ran through it (*bourne* being the word for river). In the 1400s, a church was built, dedicated to St Mary on the banks of the bourne (the river), which became known as St Mary la Bourne. In time, this was shortened to the form of the name we now use. Henry VIII built a hunting lodge in North Tyburn in 1544, and when he died three years later, the land passed to Sir William Portman, whose lands are now known as the Portman Estate.

In 1715, John Prince began to draw up plans to develop the fields into an area of elegant homes and the neighbourhood slowly became incorporated into urban London. In the late 1750s, a subsequent stage of development started, which saw the construction of a new set of squares and fashionable streets, including Harley Street, where so many medical men had their rooms. By the time Mrs Jennings was there, most of the construction had been completed, but this was still a "new" part of town, chic and fashionable, just on the edge of where the *haute ton* lived.

The Bow Street Runners

In my novel, Alexander works with Mr. Atkins from the Bow Street Runners to catch his killers, and every good investigator needs a friendly policeman to help clean up at the end. There has been a great deal written about the Bow Street Runners, and I will not rehash what others have done better, other than to give a very brief history of the organisation.

Prior to the establishment of the Runners in 1748, policing (such that it was) was a private matter, with "thief takers" being engaged by individuals concerned to find criminals and negotiate for the return of property, often while lining their own pockets. They were answerable to no central authority, and were essentially mercenaries, willing to bargain for the best price from different interested parties.

In 1749, Henry Fielding, magistrate at the Bow Street Magistrates' Court, organised a set of uniformed and professional law enforcement officers, who operated within the scope of the law and who were answerable to the courts. This group, originally six men, became known as the Bow Street Runners, although they never referred to themselves by this name. They operated until 1839, when they were incorporated into the Metropolitan Police.

Gretna Green and Elopements

Elopements to Scotland, and specifically to Gretna Green, often play a key role in Regency and Victorian romance fiction. In the case of *Death in Sensible Circumstances*, it is Lucy Steele and Robert Ferrars who make the journey. In *Pride and Prejudice*, Lydia and Mr. Wickham are thought to be heading there, but are discovered (to everyone's alarm) that they are not. Why Gretna Green? And what is so special about eloping there?

The answer lies in a piece of legislation. In 1754, Parliament passed the *Marriage Act*, proposed by Lord Hardwicke. In an attempt to prevent "irregular marriages," this law had three major elements. The couple both had to be 21 years old if they wished to marry without the consent of a parent or guardian. The marriage had to be performed by an Anglican officiant, the only exceptions being Jewish and Quaker weddings. Even Catholics had to find an Anglican clergyman to perform their marriages. And the marriage had to be a public ceremony in the couple's parish (or that of one of them), after the calling of banns or the procurement of a licence. This meant an Anglican ceremony from the *Book of Common Prayer*, and the impossibility of a secret marriage. The law was strictly enforced, with harsh penalties for any clergyman found breaking it.

So what did a couple do, who were under-age or who did not have societal approbation for their union? They went to Scotland, of course.

The loophole in the *Marriage Act* was that it applied only in England. Scotland never changed its laws regarding marriage, and their laws were much more relaxed. All that was required for a marriage to be legal in Scotland was for the couple to assert a wish to be married in the presence of witnesses. There were some limitations: they had to be of age—it was 16 years there, not 21—and not too closely related or already married to someone else. But there were no banns, no licence, no waiting period, no publication of the marriage if not wanted, and no inconvenient parents preventing true love from taking its course.

Even more conveniently, while non-*Marriage Act* marriages were forbidden in England itself, all foreign marriages were considered legal and binding. So, a quick trip to Scotland was all that was required to get around this law.

And Gretna Green itself? It was one of the furthest-south towns in Scotland, and was easy to get to for English lovers. When a toll road was built through the village in the 1770s, it became even more accessible, and Gretna Green soon became synonymous with elopements to Scotland.

While no rites were necessary for a legal marriage, outside of stating their wishes before at least two witnesses, couples did enjoy some sort of ceremony, and the local blacksmith, often a senior member of the community, stepped into the role of officiant. The ceremony itself, if it can be called that, might be as simple as this:

Are you of marriageable age? *Yes*
Are you free to marry? *Yes*
You are now married.

The blacksmith might then strike the anvil to punctuate the ceremony, but this was for show.

More from Mary and Alexander

You can read about Alexander Lyon's first case with Mr. Darcy in the prequel novella, ***The Mystery of the Missing Heiress***.

And don't miss Alexander and Mary's earlier adventures together.

Miss Mary Investigates 1
Death of a Clergyman: A Pride and Prejudice Mystery

Mary Bennet has always been the quiet sister, the studious and contemplative middle child in a busy family of five. She is not interested in balls and parties, and is only slightly bothered by the arrival of the distant cousin who will one day inherit her father's estate. But then Mr. Collins is found dead, and Mary's beloved sister Elizabeth is accused of his murder. Mary knows she must learn whatever she can to prove Elizabeth innocent of this most horrible crime, or her sister might be hanged as a murderess!

Alexander Lyons has made a pleasant life for himself in London, far from his home village in Scotland. He investigates missing documents and unfaithful wives, and earns an honest living. Then one day Mr. Darcy walks into his office, begging him to investigate the murder of Mr. Collins and to prove Elizabeth innocent of the crime. It seems like a straightforward enough case, but Alexander did not count on meeting a rather annoying young woman who seems to be in his way at every turn: Mary Bennet.

As the case grows more and more complicated, Mary and Alexander cannot stop arguing, and discover that each brings new insight into the case. But as they get close to some answers, will they survive the plans of an evildoer in the midst of quiet Meryton? www.books2read.com/deathofaclergyman

Miss Mary Investigates 2
Death in Highbury: An Emma Mystery

A Jane Austen-inspired mystery, set in the world of Pride and Prejudice and Emma.

When political chaos in London forces Mary Bennet to take refuge in the picturesque town of Highbury, Surrey, she quickly finds herself safe among friends. Emma Woodhouse welcomes her as a guest at Hartfield, Jane Fairfax is delighted by her love of music, and Frank Churchill can't stop flirting with her. But it is not long before Mary starts to suspect that beneath the charming surface, Highbury hides some dark secrets.

Alexander Lyons is sent to Surrey on an investigation, and at his friend Darcy's request, heads to Highbury to make certain Mary is comfortable and safe. But no sooner does he arrive than one local man dies, and then another!

Soon Alexander and Mary are thrust into the middle of a baffling series of deaths. Are they accidents? Or is there a very clever murderer hiding in their midst? And can they put their personal differences aside in time to prevent yet another death in Highbury? http://books2read.com/deathinhighbury

Miss Mary Investigates 3
Death of a Dandy: A Mansfield Park Mystery

The worlds of *Pride and Prejudice* and *Mansfield Park* meet when Mary Bennet lands in the middle of her third adventure with handsome investigator Alexander Lyons.

The two friends are travelling back to Mary's home after a visit to the Darcy family at Pemberley when their journey is interrupted by the news that Tom Bertram, the heir to Mansfield Park, has disappeared. Alexander is asked to take the case, and he and Mary find themselves as guests at the estate. The house is abuzz with activity as plans go ahead for a fox hunt and the performance of a play, and Mary sees intrigue in every interaction between the beautiful residents of Mansfield Park and their sophisticated guests.

When the hunt ends in tragedy with the discovery of a body, Alexander's involvement grows even deeper, but every clue leads to even more questions. The more Alexander digs, the more it seems this death might involve people much higher up than he can reach. And the biggest question of all is who, exactly, was the intended victim of what is surely murder most foul?

Mary and Alexander find themselves hard at work to unravel a web of secrets and dark goings-on that enshroud the elegant estate of Mansfield Park. But Alexander is hiding a secret of his own, one which he knows will forever doom any possible future for him and Mary.

Will they solve the mystery before somebody else dies? And will any hearts remain unbroken if they succeed?

http://books2read.com/deathofadandy

Coming soon:

Miss Mary Investigates 5:

Death in Smooth Water:

A Persuasion Mystery

About the Author

Riana Everly was born in South Africa, but has called Canada home since she was eight years old. She has a Master's degree in Medieval Studies and is trained as a classical musician, specialising in Baroque and early Classical music. She first encountered Jane Austen when her father handed her a copy of *Emma* at age 11, and has never looked back.

Riana now lives in Toronto with her family. When she is not writing, she can often be found playing string quartets with friends, biking around the beautiful province of Ontario with her husband, trying to improve her photography, thinking about what to make for dinner, and, of course, reading!

If you enjoyed this novel, please consider posting a review at your favourite bookseller's website.

Riana Everly loves connecting with readers on Facebook at facebook.com/RianaEverly/

Also, be sure to check out her website at rianaeverly.com for sneak peeks at coming works and links to works in progress!

RIANA EVERLY

Also by Riana Everly

Teaching Eliza: Pride and Prejudice Meets Pygmalion

The Assistant: Before Pride and Prejudice

Through a Different Lens: A Pride and Prejudice Variation

The Bennet Affair: A Pride and Prejudice Variation

Much Ado in Meryton: Pride and Prejudice Meets Shakespeare

Preludes: A Modern Persuasion Improvisation

Miss Mary Investigates

The Mystery of the Missing Heiress

Death of a Clergyman: A Pride and Prejudice Mystery

Death in Highbury: An Emma Mystery

Death of a Dandy: A Mansfield Park Mystery

302

Made in United States
North Haven, CT
08 March 2023

33764473R00173